Roisin McAuley

CW01619533

review

Copyright © 2005 Roisin McAuley

The right of Roisin McAuley to be identified as the Author of the Work has been asserted by her in accordance with the Copyright, Designs and Patents Act 1988.

'September Song' (from 'Knickerbocker Holiday'). Words by Maxwell Anderson. Music by Kurt Weill. © 1938 Chappell & Co Inc and Kurt Weill Foundation For Music Inc, USA. Warner/Chappell Music Ltd, London W6 8BS. Lyrics reproduced by permission of IMP Ltd. All Rights Reserved.
'Let's Face The Music and Dance'. Words and Music by Irving Berlin. © 1935, 1936 (renewed) Irving Berlin Music Corp, USA. Warner/Chappell Music Ltd, London W6 8BS. Lyrics reproduced by permission of IMP Ltd. All Rights Reserved.
Extract from 'Meeting Point' by Louis MacNeice, published in *Collected Poems* by Faber and Faber and reproduced by kind permission of the publisher.

First published in 2005
by REVIEW

An imprint of Headline Book Publishing

1

Apart from any use permitted under UK copyright law, this publication may only be reproduced, stored, or transmitted, in any form, or by any means, with prior permission in writing of the publishers or, in the case of reprographic production, in accordance with the terms of licences issued by the Copyright Licensing Agency.

All characters in this publication are fictitious and any resemblance to real persons, living or dead, is purely coincidental.

Cataloguing in Publication Data is available from the British Library

ISBN 0 7553 0855 7 (hardback)
ISBN 0 7553 0856 5 (trade paperback)

Typeset in Giovanni by Avon DataSet Ltd,
Bidford-on-Avon, Warwickshire

Printed and bound in Great Britain by
Mackays of Chatham plc, Chatham, Kent

Headline's policy is to use papers that are natural, renewable and recyclable products and made from wood grown in sustainable forests. The logging and manufacturing processes are expected to conform to the environmental regulations of the country of origin.

HEADLINE BOOK PUBLISHING
A division of Hodder Headline
338 Euston Road
London NW1 3BH

www.reviewbooks.co.uk
www.hodderheadline.com

Meeting Point

Also by Roisin McAuley

Singing Bird

For Richard

Acknowledgements

I would like to thank Inspector Debbie Crawford and Inspector Raymond Ramsey of the Police Service of Northern Ireland (PSNI) for their help. Raymond Ramsey, in particular, answered my questions about police procedures with great patience and checked my mistakes. My thanks also to Major Nigel Bovey, editor of *The War Cry*, for answering my questions about The Salvation Army with equal forbearance.

Chapter 1

My grandparents were runaway lovers. They eloped from Scotland to Northern Ireland in 1937. My great-grandfather considered a butcher's boy from Belfast no match for his daughter.

My grandmother slipped out of the house just before dawn, and ran down the lane to meet my grandfather who was waiting on the road to Stranraer. They ran the mile from the farmhouse to the ferry. My great-grandfather's new Ferguson A tractor could not compete with them. He jumped from it on the quayside and shook his fist in fury at the departing steamer. My grandfather shouted back in triumph, 'She's mine now!'

In 1961, their son – my father – stopped to listen to a Salvation Army band outside Belfast City Hall. He was drawn to the dark curls escaping from the navy blue bonnet worn by a girl playing the cornet. He put a shilling in the collection box and boldly said, 'That's a pretty cornet player. Do you think I could ask her out?'

Dad told me Mum's father looked him up and down. 'Are you God-fearing?'

'I am,' said my father.

'Then you can call at number seven Bavaria Street on Friday evening. She'll be in after six o'clock.'

Dad was so surprised by his own audacity and by the straightforward response, he forgot to ask Mum's name.

As a child, these stories never ceased to charm me.

'Tell me about Granny and Granda,' I would demand. Mum would recite the story again.

'Tell me about meeting Dad.'

'I saw him talking to Daddy, but I couldn't hear what they were saying because of the band. We were in the middle of "Mary's Boy Child".'

I would close my eyes and picture snowflakes drifting from a grey sky, blanketing the formal flower beds outside the city hall, turning the giant Christmas tree into an obelisk of white lace, coating the dome, lying on the tops of the red trolley buses clanking down Royal Avenue, but lasting only moments on the pavement before turning to slush under the feet of the Christmas shoppers.

My mother glances sideways at the tall young man in a Crombie overcoat and tweed cap talking to her father. She has noticed his open appraisal. She finishes a phrase, and lowers the cornet to blow on her hands before raising it to her lips again. A blush warms her cold cheeks.

The story was told so often, detail piled up in my memory like the snow on the city hall. Was it my imagination, or my mother's, that added the snow? It was an exceptionally wet winter. There was no snow. It was probably raining.

'I thought your dad was asking for a favourite carol. People often did that. At least in those days they didn't ask for "Jingle Bells".'

When Mum had recounted the story, I would lean forward, my elbows on the kitchen table, my small fists under my chin, and say, 'Now tell me about Auntie Madge.'

My mother's younger sister found ten half-crowns outside the Crown Bar in Great Victoria Street and handed them into Donegall Pass police station. The coins were unclaimed for a year, after which it was finders keepers. My Uncle Eric, then a young RUC constable, was given the job of returning the coins to Madge.

'You're pretty as well as honest,' Eric said to Madge when she opened the door to him. He asked her out on the spot. They were married six weeks later.

These stories conditioned me to expect romance in equally quirky circumstances. So, last summer, when a red convertible roared round a corner and nearly knocked me down, it was inevitably driven by a tall, dark handsome man.

I had heard the drone of the engine, seen a flash of reflected sunlight on the windscreen as the Mustang took the bends below me on the winding road into the mountains, but the blare of the horn, the slide and crunch of wheels on gravel as they skidded behind me, took me by surprise. I half jumped, half fell into the shallow ditch between the edge of the road and the rocky hillside. Sharp stones scraped skin from my palms and my bare knees. My face hit the back of my hands. My ribs hit hard ground and the breath left my body with a whoosh.

A moment of silence. The whine of the engine stopped. The car door slammed. I sucked hot air and dust into my flattened lungs, and rolled, coughing and spitting, on to my side. The cicadas resumed their chirruping.

A torrent of French accompanied the driver's sprint across the road. He scrambled into the ditch and crouched beside me. I must have shut my eyes against the glare of the sun, for I felt his hand on my shoulder. More urgent French.

My eyes felt gritty. I lifted a stinging hand to shield them and blinked twice to focus on the face about a foot's distance from mine. Tanned, smooth-shaven. A wing of dark hair flopped over the rim of his sunglasses. He swept it away with his free hand. The other was shaking my shoulder.

I was suddenly self-conscious, aware of breathing heavily, my face hot. I leaned on my elbow to bum-shuffle myself into a sitting position, pulled my knees towards me, tucked my bruised hands into my armpits, took a deep breath, and said in my schoolgirl French, '*Je ne parle bien français*.'

'Are you all right? Can you wiggle your toes?' He spoke perfect, exasperated English.

'What?'

'Wiggle your toes. It's a good sign if you can wiggle your toes.'

He lifted his hand from my shoulder and sat back on his heels as I wiggled my toes.

'What about your head? Did you hit your head?'

'No.'

'You might have a cracked rib. Can you take a deep breath?'

I took another deep breath. 'I'm fine. Just bruised.'

'You're a tourist.'

'It's not a capital offence. You nearly killed me. You were on the wrong side of the road.'

'Excuse me?' A dark eyebrow soared above the rim of his sunglasses and his mouth twitched in a smile.

'I was walking on the right hand side . . .' I began, before trailing off, feeling stupid as well as sore.

'We drive on the right here.' He was grinning now. I couldn't see his eyes. I wondered what colour they were. He picked up my white cotton hat and handed it to me while he scrabbled in a dusty shrub to retrieve my sunglasses. 'They're not broken. Maybe a bit scratched.'

'Like your car.'

He stood up and turned his head to look at the gleaming red convertible, askew in the opposite ditch. Sam and David came bounding down the hillside above it, crashing through the scrub. Isabel was about twenty yards behind them, slithering sideways down the chalky track that joined the road just before the bend, one hand held out for balance, the other holding on to her pink straw hat. Sam jumped on to the road, steadied himself, and ran to me.

'I heard the brakes,' he said breathlessly. 'Are you all right, Mum?'

'Playground knees,' I said. 'Sore hands. No bones broken.' I smiled up at him.

Sam blew out a short breath and smiled back. David, a few paces behind him, relaxed as well. I saw him turn his attention to the car.

'Awesome. What year is it?'

'Nineteen seventy-nine. Do you want to ring your dad? You can use my mobile. I think I should take your mum to hospital.'

'She's not my mum,' David said cheerfully, his attention still on the car. 'She's Sam's mum. She's my auntie, sort of.'

Isabel was panting when she reached me. 'Are you OK, Claire?'

'I don't need to go to hospital,' I said. 'Give me a hand to get up.' Sam and Isabel offered a hand each and hauled me to my feet. I stood a little unsteadily at the side of the road. 'Just give me a minute. I'll be fine.'

Isabel whispered in my ear, 'I can see why you were swept off your feet.' The focus of her admiration had crossed the road, got behind the wheel of his car and switched on the engine. It roared into life, heaved itself out of the ditch and rolled smoothly forward to rest on a straight section of road.

'She's twenty-five years old,' Sam said, reverentially.

'You can't walk back with those knees,' Isabel said. 'I'm sure . . . whatsisname . . .'

He was walking towards us, taking off his sunglasses, tucking them into the top pocket of his slightly crumpled cream linen shirt before proffering his hand to me with a smile. 'Welcome to France.' His smile broadened. 'Where they drive on the wrong side of the road.' His eyes were a deep, dark blue. 'My name's Rocky,' he said.

I managed a shaky laugh, and held up dusty, blood-streaked palms. 'I'm Claire.' I inclined my head towards Isabel and the boys. 'My friend, Isabel. My son, Sam. Sam's cousin, David.'

He shook hands with Isabel and the boys, then lightly touched my fingertips. 'Those cuts need seeing to. How far away is your car?'

'We walked from the campsite,' Isabel said. 'Les Arcs.'

'I'll take you to my house. It's nearer. We can all squeeze into the Mustang. I'll drive you back afterwards.'

Without waiting for an answer, he took my elbow, steered me across the road and into the front passenger seat of the red convertible. I leaned back into the cream leather upholstery and felt the heat spread across my back, taking the ache out of my bones. He helped Isabel and the boys clamber into the back, before sliding into the driver's seat, releasing the handbrake and accelerating up the hill towards the village perched on top.

The breeze beat the dust out of my hair and my lungs cleared. I closed my eyes and inhaled the mingled smells of eucalyptus, lavender, rosemary, juniper and thyme.

'Sweet,' Sam shouted in my ear. 'I've never been in a Mustang before. Nice one, Mum.'

What a way to begin a holiday, I thought.

Chapter 2

It had been Isabel's idea, conjured up on a wet night in February. Isabel was lying on the sofa. I was sitting on the floor, my toes stretched towards the fire. We were watching the closing credits of *To Catch a Thief*.

'Filmed entirely on location . . .' rolled off the screen. I crawled across the carpet to the television and switched it off.

'I've never been to the Riviera,' Isabel said.

'Too touristy. Too expensive.'

'Wouldn't you like to see Nice and the Baie des Anges? Drive along the corniche? Picnic overlooking the Mediterranean?'

'Isabel,' I said. 'I don't have a sports car. I have a Renault Clio with a leaking sunroof and a bashed-in bumper that I haven't time to get fixed.'

'We could hire a car.'

'Hire a sports car?' I was incredulous.

'Well, maybe not a sports car. But we could hire something.'

'Too expensive on top of a hotel. What's wrong with Brittany?'

'Rain.'

'It didn't rain much last year.'

'Claire! It rained every other day!'

'That's an exaggeration.'

'You said it was like being in Ireland only a bit warmer.'

'A lot warmer.'

'The Riviera would be warmer still,' Isabel said.

'The hotel in Piriac is reasonable.'

'We could go camping.'

A pause. I tried to absorb the idea of Isabel in a tent. Isabel, always beautifully groomed, lipstick perfectly applied, never seen awake without mascara. I started to laugh.

'Isabel, you'd hate it. Wasps in the jam. Cooking on a camping stove. Clothes damp and creased and all bundled up.' That's clinched it, I thought.

But the idea had captured her. She stretched along the sofa like a cat in the sun. Her eyes closed. Her imagination hovered somewhere between Hyères and Menton.

'The boys would love it,' she said.

'Going pop-eyed looking at topless women on the beach. At least in Brittany they had their clothes on half the time. There's a lot to be said for rain.'

Isabel opened her eyes and regarded me affectionately.

'Sam's lovely,' she said. 'He's always courteous to the girls at school. I notice the boys who aren't. You can't protect him from everything. Short of holidaying with the Taliban. Do you talk to Sam about sex?'

'I've left it to his father,' I said. 'The rat.'

'Maybe you'll meet someone on holiday,' Isabel said. 'There must be some attractive, unattached men left in the universe.'

'Not on a campsite,' I said, 'even in the south of France.'

I had met Isabel on my first day at Reading University. She knocked on the door of my room in the hall of residence as I was unpacking my suitcase. When I opened the door I saw a slightly built blonde wearing tight blue jeans, black suede pixie boots and an anxious smile.

'We seem to be the only people on this corridor just now. I suppose the others haven't arrived yet.' She produced a bottle of Bull's Blood from behind her back. 'Got a corkscrew?' She had a lilting Scottish accent.

I shook my head.

'I wanted to celebrate my first night at university but it's no fun on your own.'

I was stiff with shyness.

'Och, well,' she said, her smile fading as she turned away. 'No bother.'

'We could go to a pub,' I said tentatively. 'Only I don't know where the nearest one is.'

She turned back. A big smile this time. 'We'll find out just now.'

I reached for my navy cardigan. She paused for a moment before saying thoughtfully, 'You're about the same size as me. Taller. You have narrow shoulders. You'd look fantastic in my pink bomber jacket.'

She's been my friend and fashion guru ever since.

I smiled now at the memory. Glancing up at the driver's mirror, I saw that Isabel was smiling too. I flicked my gaze to the hands turning the wheel to the right, steering into a narrow road snaking back down the valley. No wedding ring. But that didn't mean anything. A lot of English men didn't wear wedding rings.

The road was quiet. Modern villas, glimpsed through tall hedges of laurel and myrtle, squatted in the late-afternoon heat. We drove through open gates and parked beside a grass circle in the middle of a wide sweep of tarmac, almost level with the terracotta roof of a rectangular villa built into the hillside. A topiarist had been at work on the shrubs in the grass circle. Box and laurel were trimmed and trained into a guitar, a saxophone, a clarinet and even a piano with a keyboard of white blossom and black twig. A flight of wide stone steps led down to a heavy oak door.

As I fumbled for the handle, Rocky appeared at my side, opened the door and offered his hand to help me out of the car and down the steps to the house.

The front door opened directly on to a landing with a corridor to the left running the length of the house. To the right, an archway opened into a kitchen. Steps descended from the landing to a stone-flagged room with sliding glass doors opening on to a terrace, where a round wrought-iron table, and four chairs painted deep blue, overlooked a rectangular swimming pool as wide as the house.

Rocky slid back the glass doors. 'Make yourselves comfortable. I'll get the first aid box.' He pushed up the pale blue sun umbrella, pulled out a chair each for Isabel and me, and went back inside.

The boys stood gazing into the sapphire depths of the pool. Isabel and I sat at the table and looked around us.

Beyond the pool, the land fell away into a wide valley sweeping up to a village perched on a crag. Below the church tower and the ancient, honey-coloured houses clinging to the hillside, the valley slopes were dotted with similar, terracotta-tiled villas, each with an adorning sapphire, turquoise or emerald pool. The air was still, and filled with the complacent croaking of frogs and the click-click of cicadas. Yellow butterflies flapped languidly along the purple bougainvillaea dividing the flagged area round the pool from the descending scrub.

Rocky reappeared with a blue plastic basin of water, a white cloth, and a green plastic box with a white cross and *'Premier Secours'* in white letters on the lid.

'I'm not sure what's in here. This is the first time I've used it.'

He lifted out a roll of gauze, a small pair of scissors, a tube marked *Antiseptique* and a packet marked *Aspirine*.

I cleaned the dirt and dried blood from my hands and knees. 'Thank you. Professional-looking kit.'

'I bought a couple of them for the bar. I run a music bar in Nice.'

I sensed, rather than saw, two pairs of twelve-year-old ears flare to attention.

'I'll get you a glass of water for the aspirin.'

'I don't need aspirin, thank you.'

'In that case, I recommend a glass of wine.' He disappeared again.

Two heads turned. 'Can me and David have a glass of wine, Mum?'

Isabel smeared cream on two squares of gauze and handed them to me, smiling quizzically. I placed them on my knees.

'You're too young.' I said.

The stinging in my hands had subsided. I held them out for a dab of cream and rubbed it into my palms as clinking glass signalled the arrival of the wine.

A tray appeared on the table before us. A bowl of black olives, a plate of thickly sliced salami, three wine glasses, two tumblers filled with ice, two cans glistening with condensation, a bottle of white wine in an ice bucket.

'I've brought you boys Coca-Cola, in case you'd like a swim in the pool.'

'We've no togs,' David said, his mouth turning down in disappointment.

'You could swim in your underpants. They'd dry quickly in this heat.'

I looked at Sam and David, their faces a mixture of embarrassment and dismay. Twelve is an awkward age. 'We can swim when we get back,' I said.

'Or I could drive the boys to Les Arcs to collect their swimming trunks, and you could stay here and relax. We could get your swim things, too, if you like.'

The boys beamed at the prospect of another ride in the red Mustang.

'We'll swim when we get back,' I repeated firmly.

'Mum's worried in case you're a paedophile,' Sam said in a confiding tone.

I felt my colour rising.

David said, 'My mum says go for their eyes and kick them in the groin.'

Rocky suppressed a smile. He managed to keep his voice steady. 'That would do the trick all right.'

'We've got our mobiles,' Sam said.

Rocky looked at me, one eyebrow raised.

'It's too much trouble,' I said feebly.

He grinned and swung the car keys on his index finger. 'Bring the cans with you. Let's go.'

Chapter 3

The front door banged behind them.

Isabel said, 'Am I dreaming? Or are we being entertained by an attractive man, with his own teeth and house and a red sports car? Pinch me.'

'He's probably attached,' I said. 'He probably has children that age. That's why he's so good with them.'

Isabel stood up. 'I reckon we've got about twenty minutes. Come on.'

'Isabel! We can't go poking around someone's house when they're not there.'

'We can hardly poke around when he is here. Come on. You're the one who used to be a detective. Find the clues.'

'It doesn't feel right.'

'Wouldn't you like to know if the man making eyes at you, the man prepared to drive your son halfway to Nice and back to impress you, is single and free?'

'It's not halfway to Nice,' I said. 'It's no more than five kilometres to the campsite and back.'

'Then we'd better be quick.' Isabel has a slightly crooked

tooth, which adds mischief to her smile.

'Maybe it's you he fancies,' I said.

She closed one big blue eye and tapped the side of her nose. 'Trust me, I'm a psychologist.'

I took off my sunglasses and followed her into the house, up the short flight of stairs, and down a corridor hung with framed photographs. I had an impression of blue skies, white snow, smiling people in sunglasses and red ski suits; blue sea, white sails, waving figures in orange life jackets.

'We can look at those later,' Isabel said. She opened a door. 'Spare bedroom. Nothing here.' Another door. 'Bathroom. Count the toothbrushes.'

'One. Electric. Wall-mounted.' I felt a little swell of optimism, mixed with excitement.

'He's tidy, I'll say that for him,' Isabel said.

I scanned the bathroom shelves. Toothpaste, shaving brush, shaving cream. Razor. Neatly stacked packets of blades. Suntan lotion. Dental floss. Aqua di Parma aftershave. A box of soap.

A copy of *Nice Matin* lay in the bidet.

'Reads in the loo,' I said.

'Doesn't everybody?'

I twisted my head to see the date.

'Yesterday's. Front page photo of a villa and armed policemen. Screaming headline about *Vol* something.'

'*Vol qualifié*? Robbery. Rich pickings in this part of the world, I'd say.'

To the right of the wash-hand basin, a door stood ajar. The room beyond was dark. Isabel took a step towards it.

I tried to dampen my curiosity. 'No. We can't go in there.'

We heard a car draw up outside.

'Try to look as though you're waiting to use the loo,' Isabel hissed, pushing me into the corridor.

The bathroom door shut. The front door opened. My stomach was cold jelly and my cheeks were burning.

Behind me, a female voice said something sharp and interrogative in French. I turned as nonchalantly as I could. A whippet-thin blonde in white cut-off jeans and shirt, sunglasses pushed back over short, sun-bleached hair, was emptying the contents of a black plastic sack on to the floor of the landing. Trousers, shirts, a jacket, underpants and socks tumbled free. She surveyed me coldly as she shook the remaining contents of the sack on to the pile of clothes. A maroon and grey striped washbag; electric razor, flex attached; a clatter of CDs; three paperbacks; a scattering of magazines.

I heard the lavatory flush. Isabel stepped out of the bathroom. The blonde threw up her hands, shook her head wildly, hurled some angry-sounding words in our direction and stalked out of the front door, slamming it behind her. The empty plastic sack fluttered in the draught before subsiding on top of its former contents. I felt equally deflated.

'That explains the tidiness,' Isabel said.

There was the roar of an exhaust, a squeal of tyres, and the vanishing sound of a car being driven smartly away.

We advanced slowly to the heap of belongings. Isabel pushed the empty sack to one side with the toe of her pink espadrille. I sighed.

Isabel looked at me with concern. 'We should sit down. You're still a bit shaken up.'

She put her arm round my waist and guided me past the pile of clothes, down the short flight of stairs and outside again. The ice in the bucket was beginning to melt.

'So he has a girlfriend,' I said.

Isabel poured two generous glasses of wine and sat down. 'You could give her a run for her money,' she said.

Doors banged in the house. Sam and David raced past me, barefooted, in swimming trunks, Sam calling over his shoulder, 'Rocky says he'll take us all for a drive some day.'

Two splashes in quick succession. Two heads burst out of the water. Two voices shouted, 'Wicked!'

My yellow-striped beach bag presented itself at my feet.

'I hope you don't mind,' Rocky said, pulling out a chair to join us. 'The Mustang's a great hit with the boys.'

'It's a boy's car all right,' I said.

'You mean I'm a boy too?' he said, hanging his head, looking at me sideways.

'If the cap fits . . .' I said, a little coolly.

'How are the cuts and bruises? Feeling better?'

'Fine. Thank you.'

He sat down. 'Sam told me you and his dad are divorced. I suppose it's tricky bringing up a son on your own.'

I flushed.

'Claire does it brilliantly,' Isabel said. 'Do you have children yourself?'

'Not that I know of,' he said. 'Sorry. That's a really bad joke.' He flashed an apologetic smile.

There was a pause. He refilled our glasses. 'What part of Scotland are you from, Isabel?'

'Aberdeenshire,' she said. 'A wee place called Banchory.'

'What about you, Claire?'

'I'm Irish.'

He looked surprised. 'You don't sound it. David has a Northern Irish accent, but you and Sam don't.'

'I was born in London. My parents were from Belfast. We went back there when I was ten. I moved back to England a couple of years after Sam was born.'

'What about you, Rocky?' Isabel asked.

'Born in Kenya. Sent to school in England. Hated the climate.'

'Not as cold and wet as Scotland,' Isabel said.

He laughed. 'How do you two know each other?'

'We met at university in Reading,' Isabel said. 'I stayed there after graduating. We met again when Claire moved there.'

'You both live in Reading?'

'Claire lives in Henley,' Isabel said.

He whistled. 'Nice spot.'

'You know it?' I said.

'I've been to the regatta a few times. I know it's had a huge rise in house prices. Or so the English tourists tell me. Sometimes I think house prices are the only things they talk about.'

Isabel laughed. 'I think Claire's house made more money last year than I did.'

I felt embarrassed. 'My great-uncle died and left me a farm in Ayrshire,' I said. 'I swopped it for a house. I'm no farmer.'

'So what do you do, Claire?'

'I'm a solicitor.'

'Then I'd better watch what I say to you.' A smile crinkled the corners of his mouth. He held my gaze.

I felt my colour rise and I looked away. The valley seemed still and silent as a painting. Yet all my senses felt alive. I could feel the sun on my skin, smell the wine, the oily saltiness of the salami, the antiseptic cream on my fingertips. I took a gulp of wine. A mouthful of sweetness, followed by the dryness of a green apple and an impression of lemons.

'I'm going to swim,' Rocky said. 'Are you going to join me? The boys brought your things.'

'I'll pass,' I said. 'I don't want them thinking it's OK to drink and swim.'

I glanced at Isabel. She shook her head.

I waved at Sam, spreadeagled like a pink starfish on the blue sparkle of the water. He raised his arm to wave back, flipped over, and swam to the edge of the pool.

Rocky stood up. 'I'll drive you back afterwards.'

At the edge of the pool he kicked off his loafers, pulled his shirt over his head, and took off his trousers to reveal an even tan north and south of blue striped swimming trunks. He beamed at the boys, splashing around at the opposite end of the pool, cried, 'Geronimo!' and jumped in.

Chapter 4

The black plastic bag and its contents had vanished from the landing when we made our way through the house to the car. I made Isabel sit in the front seat.

'What about a day for a drive?' Rocky slid behind the wheel. 'The boys are keen. Where would you like to go?'

'The Haute Corniche,' Isabel said promptly.

'Good choice,' he said.

Before I could stop myself, I said, 'You had a visitor. We forgot to say.'

'Maxine? Did you talk to her?'

'You could say she spoke to us,' I said drily.

He bent his head and put the key in the ignition. I saw the edge of a smile. 'She was just dropping off a few things,' he said.

Sam, squashed against my elbow in the back seat, bombarded me with questions.

'Can we go to Rocky's music bar? Please?'

'You're not old enough,' I said.

'Pleease. We could go and not stay late.'

'We'll talk about it another time.'

'You and Isabel would like it.'

'You don't know what kind of music it is,' I said.

Sam leaned forward. 'Rocky, what kind of music do you play in your bar?' he shouted.

'Small bands, solo artists. Some jazz, some blues, some folk and country. Anything goes,' he called back, eyes not leaving the road ahead.

'Can young people come to your bar?'

He changed into a lower gear to slow down at a roundabout. The car stopped for a moment. The rush of wind abated. He looked back at me and smiled.

'If it's OK with their mums,' he said, 'it's OK with me.'

He turned his attention back to the road. I heard him say casually to Isabel, 'Drop in some time. We open from four until midnight. Old Nice. Near the Préfecture. It's called Doctor Rock.'

The brakes squealed. Something stirred in my memory, but slithered away before I could capture it. We turned sharp right, sailed under the floral rainbow at the entrance to the campsite and came to a halt in the visitors' car park beside the reception hut.

I pushed down the back of the passenger seat and clambered out. 'Thank you for the first aid, and the hospitality.'

Rocky remained behind the wheel of the Mustang, one arm draped over the back of his seat. 'Saturday for a drive along the corniche? Pick you up here about eleven?'

I looked at Isabel. She made a gesture of deferral to me. I looked at Sam.

'That would be lovely,' I said.

The boys grinned and ran off, whirling their wet swimsuits

above their heads. They're having a good time, I thought, smiling at the memory of Sam's first reaction to our holiday plans.

'Camping? Sounds cool, Mum.'

'Isabel's coming too.'

'Mu-um!' He made it sound like a moan.

'What's wrong? You didn't mind her coming last year. She's not from another planet.'

'Only planet school.'

'She's hardly ever at your school. You don't go to see her.'

'I can't tell my mates I'm going on holiday with the school psychologist.'

'Then don't tell them.'

'Mu-um!'

'You've got David coming. Don't I get to take a friend too? The campsite has two swimming pools, waterslides, footie, tennis, and a disco. What more do you want?'

'Disco is so eighties.' He rolled his eyes.

'Seven nights a week. You can stay up late.'

'Can David and I have our own tent?'

I had foreseen this one, but made a show of considering it.

'I suppose Isabel and I could share the mobile home on our own,' I said slowly. 'We'd have to bring a tent for you. It would be a lot to carry on the plane.'

'They have tents that pack really small, Mum.'

'You'd have to be near us. Where we could keep an eye on you.'

'Please, Mum.'

'Oh, all right,' I said. 'I'll see what I can do.'

I should have been a diplomat, I reflected, as I watched Sam and David slowing to a walk.

Rocky parked his sunglasses on his nose. 'See you on

Saturday,' he called out before reversing smartly under the rainbow arch.

Two cyclists, heads down, spun past the Mustang and braked where the tree-lined avenue narrowed to meander through the campsite.

'They're the two men in the mobile home at the other end of our row,' I said. 'They're not young, but they look fit.'

Isabel's eyes followed them into the stippled shade of the parasol pines. 'It's the Tour de France,' she said. 'Everybody starts cycling. It's the French equivalent of Wimbledon, when we all get out the tennis rackets.'

We turned on to a track between two rows of mobile homes, like a street of metal houses, each in a hedged rectangle of sunburned grass, with a brick barbecue and space for a car alongside. Our blue and silver rectangular box was the last on the right. It had a kitchen, with L-shaped seating at a table, a bedroom at each end and a tiny bathroom.

'Neat,' I had said, when we stepped through the door.

'Bijou,' said Isabel.

I liked the friendliness of the campsite. I had no qualms about letting Sam and David run free within its boundaries. On our first evening, we had got to know our opposite neighbours, Sven and Ingrid, retired teachers from Malmö, in Sweden. They had abundant, pale blond hair and bright blue eyes, and they looked younger than their years. They chatted easily to Sam and David, who didn't try to avoid them, but stood shyly, scuffing their trainers in the white dust.

Sven and Ingrid were keen golfers. They were gone most mornings by the time we had fetched our bread from the camp shop. They returned, sunblushed and weary, before sunset. Now we waved to them as their car bumped past us towards their caravan.

Ingrid called out to us, 'Nice day?'

'A wonderful day,' I called back.

Isabel squeezed my arm. 'What daft body said we wouldn't meet any nice men in the south of France?'

Chapter 5

Sam and David decided to spend the next day at Les Arcs. They had devised a game that combined Sam's curiosity with David's interest in cars. It involved collecting European car numberplates. Sam liked to know where people came from. 'Good for your geography,' I told him. David liked to calculate how long the journey had taken them. 'Good for your maths,' I said.

Sam stored the numbers in his mobile phone – a recent present from his father. It had the ring tone of a Caribbean steel band and it took photographs.

Now, with my mouth full of croissant, I heard the swish and click, and Sam's chortle of delight. 'Gotcha!'

'I'm sure your father doesn't want to see a picture of me with a mouthful of crumbs,' I said. Girls in bikinis, maybe, I muttered under my breath.

'What's that, Mum?'

'I might do some sightseeing with Isabel. Sure you and David don't want to come?'

They waited just long enough for me to give them money for lunch before they raced off.

Isabel and I spent the afternoon viewing sculpture and paintings at the Maeght Foundation near Vence. We stood for a long time in front of a painting so real it might have been a photograph. A dark-haired woman stood in a shaft of yellow sunlight beside a half-open door. Inside, in a dark bar, a man stood at the counter. I felt like reaching out to touch the fabric of the woman's blue, daisy-patterned dress. I could see the downy hairs on her arm, and feel the weight of her silver bracelet, and the warmth of the sun on her skin. The man was a blur of shadows behind her.

'There are finer paintings here,' I said to Isabel, 'but this is the one that will stay in my head.'

'Mine too,' Isabel said.

'Why are we so drawn to it?'

'Because the artist makes us curious about the man in the shadows,' Isabel said.

She didn't need to add anything. I knew we were both thinking about Rocky.

After we got back to Les Arcs, I dragged a sunlounger into the shade of the cypresses. The novel I had been saving to enjoy on holiday lay unopened on the scorched grass beside me. I closed my eyes to rerun the events of the previous afternoon. I was sure the blonde had been returning the belongings of a man who had been living with her. Had Rocky been living with her? Was the relationship over? Did I care? Yes. Maybe. Could I handle a holiday flirtation? I wasn't sure. I sighed, opened my eyes, and saw Rocky looking down at me, holding out my white cotton sun hat.

'You left it in the car,' he said.

I tried to sit up too quickly. The sunbed tilted. A flash of deep blue canvas flew up at the pale blue sky. I tumbled sideways on to the grass.

Rocky hunkered down and held out a hand to help me to my feet.

'I seem to have this effect on you,' he said.

I gabbled something about clumsiness, conscious of a blush spreading from my neck to my cheeks.

'My fault,' he said. 'I startled Sleeping Beauty.'

'Beast,' I said.

He grinned, and tugged on my hand. 'I think that's a different fairy tale. Come on, I'll buy you a coffee.'

We walked through the campsite to the café by the swimming pool.

'Thank you for dropping off my hat,' I said. 'I didn't realise I'd left it behind.'

'A psychologist might say you had a subconscious desire to see me again.'

'Or that you had a large ego,' I said.

He laughed. 'Touché!'

Isabel was sitting at a table near the pool, reading *Nice Matin*. She looked up and waved at us. Rocky went to the bar.

'I left my hat in the car,' I said when I sat down. 'And don't say a word about subconscious desires.'

'Sometimes people just forget things,' Isabel said.

Rocky put three tiny cups of coffee and a plate of golden biscuits, shaped like scallop shells, on the table.

'Madeleines,' he said. 'The biscuit responsible for all those volumes of Proust.'

'I haven't read Proust,' I said.

'He dipped a madeleine into tea,' Isabel said. 'The taste took him back to his childhood. Taste and smell are powerful memory triggers.'

'Isabel's a psychologist,' I said.

Rocky lit a Gauloise. I wondered when I had last inhaled that tarry smell.

'Doctor Rock is a good name for a music bar,' Isabel said.

'It's my real name,' Rocky said.

'Are you a real doctor?'

'I have a PhD in sociology from Witwatersrand. But academic life wasn't for me. Boring.' He laughed. 'I've learned more about society from running a bar than from a dozen dissertations.'

'I imagine you learn a lot about people,' Isabel said.

'Oh, yes,' Rocky said. 'Especially when they've had a few drinks. You'd be amazed what they tell you.' He finished his coffee and stood up. 'Must go, alas. I have an appointment in Nice. I'll see you both on Saturday.'

I lifted my hand in a wave.

'Till Saturday, Dr Rocky Rock,' Isabel called out.

In my brain, a memory hammered to get out.

Rocky called back over his shoulder, 'John, actually. My name's John Rock.'

Rocky. Rock. John Rock. Doctor Rock. The names ran round my brain like an electric train set.

Isabel said, 'Are you all right, Claire? You're as white as this table.'

'I met a Dr John Rock once,' I said.

'And?'

'I thought he'd murdered his wife.'

Isabel's hand paused in the act of raising the cup to her mouth. 'Did he?'

I watched Rocky, fifty yards away, walking to his car. 'We couldn't prove anything. We didn't charge him.'

'You think he's the same person?' Isabel's mouth stayed open in amazement.

'John Rock. Doctor Rock. It's too much of a coincidence.'

'The first eligible man who crosses your path in aeons and you think he's a wife murderer.' Isabel slumped back in her chair.

'I don't know,' I said.

'You don't know he's the same man or you don't know if he murdered his wife?'

'Both,' I said.

'He doesn't have a Northern Irish accent.'

'He was English.'

'Can you remember anything about him? What did he look like?'

'It was ten years ago. I think he had long hair, a beard and a moustache.'

'Rocky has short hair, and he's clean-shaven. What else can you remember?'

I tried to picture the concrete and glass tower at Coleraine university. The rain beating on the window, the man with the beard and moustache. But the scent of lavender and pine filled my nostrils and my ears were assailed by happy cries and splashes from the pool. My imagination could not sustain a wet autumn night in Northern Ireland. I shook my head.

'You're not sure,' Isabel said quietly.

I looked around. The tables were beginning to fill up. 'I can't think here. Let's go.'

Isabel tucked her hand under my arm as we walked down the avenue. A young cyclist whizzed by, blowing kisses at us.

'He's nice,' I said, distractedly.

'The first attractive man we meet might be a wife murderer,' Isabel said gloomily. 'That guy's probably a jewel thief.'

At least she had made me laugh. We reached our mobile home. She disengaged her arm and turned to face me. 'Is this going to ruin your holiday?'

'I can't help wondering.'

'Just ask him when we see him on Saturday.'

'It's not that easy,' I cried. 'What do I say? Excuse me but are you the John Rock who may have murdered his wife ten years ago?'

'You're attracted to him.'

'It's not that,' I said, turning away. 'I don't recognise him. No beard. No moustache.' I walked over to the barbecue and spread more charcoal briquettes under the metal grille. 'It's not that easy to remember faces. I interviewed hundreds of people when I was in the police.'

'So what makes you think he's the same person? Is it just the name?' Isabel began unfolding the white plastic chairs and a table stacked against the wall of the caravan.

'The name. A sort of tremor in my bones,' I said.

'You're different too. Do you think he recognised you?'

'He didn't seem to,' I said. I squirted lighter fuel into the barbecue.

'Was he like that before?'

'Like what?'

'You know, flirtatious.'

'I don't even know if he's the same person,' I said angrily. 'His wife had just died. Whether he killed her or not, he wasn't going to be making eyes at a detective. Especially one who looked like a drowned rat.' I struck a match. 'Besides, he was having an affair.'

Faboom! A blue flame shot from the barbecue. I stepped back from the white smoke spiralling towards the darkening sky and almost collided with Sam.

'Cool. Can I do the barbecue, Mum?'

And that was the end of confidences for a while.

* * *

When we had cleared the table after supper, and Sam and David, despite feigning nonchalance, had gone to the disco, Isabel set a bottle of Mirabelle on the table and lit the gas lamp. It flared red and blue before settling into a fizzing ball of white light, and, as though by prearranged signal, rosettes of light appeared one by one along our metal street.

The air was still, the ranks of pines and cypresses stood black against a purple sky, filling with faint stars. I could hear the muffled thump, thump of the disco from the far side of the campsite.

'They won't be back for a while,' Isabel said. 'Tell me about it.' She sipped the sticky liqueur and waited for me to speak.

'It was the second worst week of my life,' I said.

Chapter 6

I could recall every minute of it.

Joel left the house at eight o'clock on the Monday morning, carrying his navy blazer on a white plastic coat hanger. I stood in the doorway, watching him hook the blazer on the grab rail and ease himself behind the wheel. Sam detached one arm from round my neck, pointed at the red Alfa Romeo, and cried, 'Dada, car.'

Joel turned and smiled at him. 'One of the perks of Daddy's job,' he said.

I kissed Sam's forehead. 'Maybe we should buy him a toy car. If you didn't play golf on Saturday we could go shopping. All three of us. Maybe drive to Belfast. There'd be more choice.'

'Why do you always start a discussion when I'm just about to leave the house?' Joel said.

I could hear the irritation in his voice and tried to keep my response cheerful. 'Because at breakfast you have your head buried in the sports pages, I'm busy feeding Sam, and when I'm not working late you're working late.'

'I can't talk about this now.'

'When?' I said.

'Not tonight. You're working late, aren't you?' He pulled the door shut. I followed the car to the gate, Sam still in my arms. 'Say bye bye to Daddy,' I said, raising my hand in a wave. Sam copied me. As Joel slowed down to turn on to the main road at the end of the avenue, I thought I saw an answering salute.

'Could you keep this wee man some night next week?' I said to my cousin Helen when I dropped Sam off just before going to work that afternoon. 'Joel and I need a bit of time on our own.'

She held out her arms for him. 'Any time,' she said. 'Sure two's as easy as one. He's company for David.'

She hoisted Sam over the rail of the playpen in her bright, roomy kitchen, and set him down beside his cousin. The two babbled contentedly to each other. 'They get on great, don't they? Sam's no bother.' She put her head on one side and surveyed me with her calm brown eyes. 'Is everything all right?'

'Fine,' I said, handing her Sam's bottle and red security blanket.

Her eyes continued searching my face. I sighed. 'We don't get much time to talk. When I'm not on late shift, I'm busy with Sam. But fundamentally we're fine. We've been thinking about having another baby.'

Helen hugged me. 'Malcolm and me too,' she said. 'More than thinking.' She stepped back, her face shining with delight, and put her forefinger to her lips. 'Say nothing. It's early days yet.'

I beamed back at her, almost as pleased for her as I would be for myself.

'Malcolm's parents are here until Saturday,' she said. 'They're going to babysit for us on Friday night. They can keep Sam as well. Why don't you and Joel come with us to that new restaurant in Portrush?'

She had cheered me up. When I walked into the CID office in

Ballymoney just before two o'clock and saw George McCracken sitting at my desk, drinking tea from my mug, I was in good spirits.

'Hello,' he said, raising the mug in greeting. 'How did I know this was yours?'

'Because it says Claire in bloody great blue letters and you're a bloody great detective,' I said, taking off my coat and hanging it on the hook behind the door.

'I bet you didn't swear like that when you were in The Salvation Army.'

'You taught me to swear, George,' I said, perching on the edge of the desk. 'Along with a few other things. What brings you here?'

'I got a lift over here to collect Maggie's car. It's been in for a service. It's a nice day for a drive,' he said, pointing at the sun-splashed, yellowing leaves on the chestnut trees outside the window, the bright blue sky beyond. *'The autumn weather turns the leaves to flame.'*

'Poetic,' I said.

'Just a line from a song. It's that kind of day.'

'More than the weather has put that smile on your face, Sergeant McCracken.'

He set down the mug. His smile broadened. 'Inspector McCracken, as of this morning.'

'George! Congratulations. I couldn't be more pleased.'

'I just wanted to drop in and tell you in person.'

We sat smiling at each other.

'I bet Maggie is thrilled,' I said.

'She's in Glasgow with Judith. Interview at the ballet school. Judith's got a good chance of a place.'

'Fantastic,' I said.

'It won't be cheap. Promotion's come at the right time. We've a big mortgage on the new house.'

'Even better news then,' I said.

'I haven't told them yet. You're the first to know.'

I was touched, honoured even, that he'd brought his good news to me. His handsome, big-boned face was less than an arm's length away. I was surprised by a sudden urge to kiss my finger and lay it on his cheek. But I was still too much in awe of him. I held out my hand instead.

'The best of luck, George.'

'Thanks, Claire,' he said, shaking my hand.

I had met George on my first day as a detective. Chief Inspector Jordan ushered me into the CID office in Coleraine with the hesitant air of a man introducing a goose to a group of swans.

'New addition to the team. Woman Detective Constable Claire Watson. I'm sure you'll all delight in showing her the ropes.' He pointed at a vacant desk beside the window overlooking the yard, and hurried out of the room.

The wolf whistles began as the door closed behind him. I focused on the map of North Region on the back wall.

'I'd be glad to show you my rope!'

The four men in the room were out of focus. I couldn't tell which of them had spoken. I felt the heat spreading from my neck up to my ears.

Then another, more authoritative voice on my right said, 'Shut up, Robbie. Leave the wee girl alone.'

I turned my head and saw a tall, blond man getting to his feet. He looked about ten years older than me. I squared my shoulders and looked him straight in the eye.

'I'm not a wee girl. Unless you put on high heels.'

That got a laugh. The blond man grinned and held out his hand. 'George McCracken. Sergeant. Welcome to the team.'

From that moment, he was my mentor, protector and friend. 'You're the swan. We're the geese,' he told me. A father figure, Helen said. But I saw him more as a big brother. He wasn't old enough to be my father. Besides, nobody could replace my dad.

George taught me to be a detective. 'Be nosy, Claire. Listen, observe. Don't be afraid to think the worst of people. The world is more full of secrets than you think.'

Six months later, when I was transferred to Ballymoney CID, George began dropping in to see me, sometimes at the station, sometimes at home. 'I was just passing,' he would say, or, 'Just doing a wee job round here,' or, 'Sure you're only ten miles down the road.'

Now he said, 'What are you working on?'

'A stolen car,' I said. 'Woman selling a red Toyota Corolla, one year old. Advertises in the *Coleraine Times*. Man rings up and says he's interested in buying. He has no car. Can she bring the car to his home? Address in the town here. She says no problem. He's waiting outside the house. Charmer. Pays her a couple of compliments. Asks if he can take the car for a test drive.'

'Don't tell me,' said George. 'Half an hour later the vendor rings the doorbell and says she's worried he's had an accident in her car. The people in the house don't know a thing about it. Or him.'

'Dead on,' I said.

'See if Mickey Greer is out of prison,' he said. 'That used to be a favourite scam of his. There's a row of Housing Executive semis on the Ballycastle side of Armoy. He lives in the one at the end.'

I laughed. 'Is there anything you don't know, George?'

'More than you think,' he said.

'Will you be transferred?'

'No. I'll still be able to drop in and see you. If you have any problems, any at all, just come and see me. You have my numbers. All right?'

'Yes, inspector,' I said.

By five thirty, I had established that Mickey Greer was out of prison but not at home. His thin, furious-faced wife stood on the doorstep, arms folded, her gaze darting up and down the row of houses, avoiding my eyes.

'Up to his old tricks in more ways than one,' she said. 'He's got another woman. More fool her. I don't know her name and I don't care.'

'How did you get that cut lip?' I said.

'How do you think?' she said. 'I never want to see another policeman on my doorstep again. Or woman,' she amended, with a jerk of her head in my direction. 'Good riddance to him.'

I felt sorry for her. Before I could offer advice, or a consoling platitude, she had stepped back into the house and slammed the door.

I was pulling away from the kerb when I realised I was less than a mile from North County Motors, where Joel worked. The showroom didn't close until half-past six. I was just in time to drop in and tell him about Helen's invitation for Friday night.

'A whole night to ourselves,' I'd say. 'Breakfast in bed on Saturday morning.'

There were only two cars on the forecourt. Joel's fire-engine red Alfa and a sleek silver Lancia with a personalised number-plate, K1 LUV.

Gary looked up from the reception desk as I pushed open the wide glass doors.

'Joel's not here,' he called out, getting to his feet. 'He's taken a customer for a test drive.'

'A rich customer, by the looks of it,' I said, jabbing my finger back over my shoulder at the Lancia as I weaved through the crouching cars towards Joel's office at the back of the showroom. 'I'll just leave a wee note for him.'

Gary skidded towards me on the polished floor. 'He's not coming back in again.'

I looked at him in surprise. 'His car's here. He has to come back.'

Gary was in front of me now, hands up, blocking my route. 'He asked me to lock up. He doesn't need to come into the office again. He was going to drive straight home.'

'In the test drive car?'

Joel's office had a window to the showroom. The venetian blinds were drawn. But I could see a strip of light along the bottom of the office door.

'He's left the light on,' I said. 'Why are you shouting, Gary? What's going on? Who's in there?'

He moistened his lips with his tongue and tried to speak. His Adam's apple bobbed up and down behind the collar of his white shirt. A pimple blazed in his forehead like a third eye.

A cry, somewhere between a shout and a moan, came from the office.

I pulled my gun from the shoulder holster under my jacket, motioned Gary behind the nearest car, slowly depressed the handle of the office door and pushed it wide open.

When I saw Joel's trousers hanging over the chair in front of his desk, my first, horrified thought was that he'd been made to strip before being tied up. Then Joel rose unsteadily from the carpet, attempting to shield his naked body with a wastepaper basket, his dark hair dishevelled.

A woman's voice said, 'Shit.'

Behind me, I heard Gary whimper.

I turned and ran, blindly, bumping into shining bonnets, bile rising in my throat. Outside, I vomited copiously over the alloy wheels of the silver Lancia.

Chapter 7

I didn't care where I was going when I swung away from the showroom. I just wanted to be as far away as possible. When I saw a red telephone kiosk, I stopped the car and jumped out.

A black shape hurtled past, an inch from my nose. There was a rush of air, an angry blast of the horn, then a sustained screech as the monster that had nearly killed me braked to a stop. Two white-faced figures sprang out and stared at me. A man in a dark jacket and jeans. A woman in a pale pink suit. I stared back at them, breathing heavily. My legs felt like straw. I waited for my heart to stop racing before looking right and left and crossing the road to the kiosk.

It smelled of urine and greasy chips and I felt like vomiting again. I wedged myself into the doorway to gulp fresher air, and watched the driver and passenger change places. The woman reversed the big black car into a gateway and pointed it back the way it had come. I listened, panting, for the pip pip pip and pressed coins into the metal slot as the car purred past me, returning to its lair.

Helen's mother-in-law said, 'She's just popped out. She'll be back at six thirty. I'm keeping an eye on the wee ones. Can I take a message?'

I looked at my watch. It was ten past six.

'No message, thank you,' I said, replacing the receiver before the sob could rise further in my throat.

George was standing in front of his garage door, a bunch of keys in his hand, his face startled in the security lights that came on as I swung jerkily into his driveway and braked a few feet from him. I switched off the engine and sat trembling for a few moments before he yanked open the car door.

'My God, Claire. What's happened?'

I eased my straw legs on to the tarmac and thought about standing up. George, one hand on the car door, stared, uncomprehending, as he held out his other hand to me.

I took a breath to steady my voice. 'I found Joel with somebody else,' I said. 'They were having sex. In his office.' I leaned my head against the doorjamb and began to cry.

George enveloped me in a great hug. I buried my head in his waxed jacket. It smelled of heather and the sea. He uncoupled one arm to shut the car door before turning me gently towards the house.

'Hold on a minute.' He fished the keys from his pocket and opened the front door, directing me down the dark hallway towards the kitchen. 'Go on through. I'll hang up my coat.' I heard him moving fishing rods about.

The light was fading. The white appliances glowed in the dusk. The fridge hummed. Red and green electric dots glimmered on the cooker and the dishwasher. The digital clock on the microwave winked the hours and minutes. The room felt like a spaceship moving through time.

'Don't switch on the light,' I said quickly as George entered the kitchen behind me. 'It makes things too real.'

He'd taken off his boots. I sat at the square pine table by the window and watched him pad around the kitchen in the half-light, filling a kettle, taking the tea caddy from the cupboard, mugs from the dishwasher. He stirred two spoonfuls of sugar into each mug. 'Hot sweet tea,' he said. 'Good for shock.'

'I'm sorry,' I said. 'I didn't know where else to go.'

George took the chair opposite. 'It's all right.' He gulped down a mouthful of tea. 'Drink up. It'll do you good.'

'I can't stay too long. I'm on duty, George.'

'Have you got your pager?'

I nodded.

'That's all right then.'

I took a long swallow of soothing sweetness. 'I don't know what to do about Sam,' I said distractedly. 'Joel's supposed to collect him about now and put him to bed.'

'Have you any reason to think he won't?'

'I just don't want him near Sam.' The tears started again. I gripped the mug so tightly I felt it might crack.

George stretched his hand across the table and touched my arm. 'Easy,' he said softly. 'Don't go down that road. Leave Sam out of it. He's better off in his usual routine. While you two sort this out.'

'I don't know if I can bear to speak to him. See him, even. I heard them. I thought he was being robbed. Or worse. I had my gun out. I could have shot him,' I cried.

'But you didn't,' he said. 'Calm down.'

'Why did he do it, George?'

George sighed. 'Do you mind if I smoke?'

I shook my head and dug a paper handkerchief from my pocket. 'Go ahead if you want to kill yourself,' I said, blowing my nose. 'I thought you were giving them up.'

'I've cut down,' he said, taking a packet of cigarettes and an ashtray from the window ledge, searching in his trouser pockets, pulling out a lighter. 'This is only my third today.'

For a moment I wished I smoked. I envied him the steadying ritual as he lit the cigarette, inhaled and leaned back to blow invisible smoke at the ceiling.

'Do you love Joel?' he said.

'Yes. I don't know.' I shook my head. 'I thought I did. I thought we were a happy family. Now I don't know what I think. He's my husband, George.'

The tip of his cigarette was a bud of flame in the dark. I could barely see his face.

'When I was about twelve or thirteen,' he began slowly, 'my father took me to Barry's Amusements one Saturday in the summer holidays. It must have been about nineteen sixty-six. The place was full of girls. All bare legs and stiletto heels and miniskirts, or pleated skirts that flew up and showed their knickers when they were on the swings and the helter-skelter. My eyes were on stalks. My father was walking along beside me. He didn't look at me. He just said, "Son, beware the oul tomcat." I had a sort of idea what he meant, but I said anyway, "What do you mean, Dad?"

'He said, "There's a bit of the tomcat in every man. But the sort of girl you want to marry, a nice girl, like your mother, doesn't want a tomcat. She wants a tiger or a lion. To look after her, and defend her. When you find the right girl, son, don't play away from home. Watch out for the oul tomcat. He mightn't growl for long. But he can cause an awful lot of trouble." '

I had stopped crying. I sniffed. Took a sip of tea. 'Are you trying to excuse Joel?'

'I'm just saying there's a bit of the tomcat in every man. We're the weaker sex. This woman is probably not important. Don't make her more important than she is.'

'I was always sorry my parents never met Joel. Now I'm glad they didn't,' I said.

'What advice would they give you? If they were here,' George said.

'I'm sure neither of them looked at anyone else in the whole of their married life,' I said.

'But they met and talked to people who did. And what did they tell them?'

'They told them Jesus saves sinners,' I said.

'Is that what you believe?'

'I've haven't known what I believe for a long time,' I said. 'I gave up on God when Mum and Dad died. I believe they were the best in the world. Their whole lives were about giving no-hopers the chance to redeem themselves. Dad thought everyone deserved a second chance.' I felt a sudden surge of mingled hope and gratitude. 'Thank you, George. Maggie is a lucky woman, married to a wise old tiger.'

He made a sound, somewhere between a laugh and a sigh. 'I think Maggie just wants a pussy cat,' he said. The glow of his cigarette died in the ashtray. 'And less of the old, if you please.' His chair scraped the floor as he stood up. 'Will I make more tea?'

'It's all right,' I said. 'I feel better for being able to talk about it. Thanks, George.' I glanced at the luminous clock on the microwave. It was after eight o'clock. 'I need to call into the office before I go home.' Before I faced Joel. 'What will I say to him, George?' I looked up at his dark, dependable bulk.

'Just listen to your heart.'

'I can't hear what it's saying to me.'

'When the message is important enough, you'll hear it. You'll know what to say.'

I reached out and gave his hand a grateful squeeze. 'You can switch on the light. I think I can face it now.'

Chapter 8

I thought about Mum and Dad as I drove home. They had programmed me for optimism, as well as romance. Assured me there was good in everybody. The teacher had scolded me for no reason? Poor Miss Dawson spent all her spare time looking after her elderly parents. Ellie Boyd stole the fountain pen I got for my birthday? Ellie's father had a drink problem and they never had enough money for food, never mind fountain pens. 'Tell her you know she took it by mistake and you'd like it back. Offer her your old pen.' My parents had a solution for every problem.

Just before I went to university, I had told them I had difficulty believing in God. 'It's not logical. It doesn't make sense.'

'We all struggle with faith,' Dad said. 'You have to give yourself up to it. It's like being in love.' He smiled at Mum. 'Falling in love is not logical either. You just know it. You have to work at it, too. Not give up.'

When I stopped Joel for speeding on the Knock dual carriageway and he said, 'I didn't realise I was over the speed limit. I'm sorry'; and then, with barely a pause for breath, continued, 'Actually I'm not sorry because if I hadn't broken the law I wouldn't have met you,' I had just known he was the man for me. When we married, six months later, I thought our love would last for ever.

What would Mum and Dad have advised me to do now? Not give up?

I noticed Joel's car was parked on the road outside as I approached our house. I turned into the driveway. A slash of light split the curtains in the sitting room window. I let myself into the house and stood for a few moments in the dark hallway before easing off my shoes to climb the moonlit stairs. I slipped through the half-open door to Sam's bedroom. The teddy bear nightlight glowed palely yellow on the white chest of drawers beside his cot. Sam was curled up, bottle on his pillow, one hand still gripping his red security blanket.

I resisted the impulse to lean over and stroke his silky cheek. I thought about forgiveness. I took three slow, deep breaths to stop my knees trembling. Be strong, I said to myself. Be dignified. Be calm.

Joel was sitting on the sofa, staring into the empty fireplace, a glass of whiskey in his hand.

'You bastard,' I said.

He indicated the bottle and glass on the mantelpiece. 'Help yourself.'

'You know I don't drink spirits.' I moved to stand in front of him. His gaze slid past me to the wall. He had the mutinous expression of a man who has drunk too much. 'Who is she?'

'A client.' His mouth closed tightly on the word.

'Shouldn't that be the other way round?'

He flushed.

'How long have you been seeing her?'

He swallowed a mouthful of whiskey. 'Not long.'

'How long?' I shouted.

'Keep your voice down, you'll wake Sam,' he muttered.

I tried to keep my voice low. 'You sanctimonious shit.'

'You're the sanctimonious one,' he said. 'Sitting over the same drink all evening. Disapproving if my friends have more than a couple of pints. You can't loosen up. You're all the fun of a damp dishcloth.'

This wasn't the way the conversation was supposed to go.

'You never said that before. We used to have fun, Joel. Didn't we? We can have fun again. We were talking about having another baby.'

'No. You were talking about it,' he said.

It was like a punch in the stomach.

Joel swirled the whiskey round in the glass. 'I just need a bit of space.'

'You can have all the space you want in the spare room.'

'Actually,' he said, still not looking at me, 'I'm going to stay with Gary for a while. Till I sort myself out. I feel suffocated.'

'How can I suffocate you when I hardly ever see you?' I couldn't stop my voice rising.

'I feel trapped. I need to work out where I'm going with my life. I married too young.'

'You were twenty-five, Joel. Lots of men are married younger than that. Your father got married when he was twenty-three.'

'Yeah. Same house, same job, same routine, same boring life for thirty years.'

'I'm boring? Is that it? You fancied a bit of excitement? So why not humiliate your wife?'

'I didn't plan on you walking in,' he said.

I locked my fists to my sides. I wanted to hit him.

A cry crackled through the baby alarm above the door. Joel jumped up from the sofa. 'See. You've wakened Sam.'

I slapped him. The marks of my fingers glowed red then white on his cheek. He put a hand to his face. Edged sideways to set his glass down on the mantelpiece. 'I'll pick Sam up as usual tomorrow,' he said slowly.

'I don't want that bitch near him,' I shouted. 'Don't you dare let her near him.'

He backed towards the door, one hand still holding his cheek. 'I'll be on my own. OK? I'll bring him straight here. I'll put him to bed. There won't be anybody else around.'

'Get out.'

'I just want some space,' he said.

I put my hands over my ears. Closed my eyes. When I opened them again, he had gone. I took my hands away from my ears and heard the front door click shut, Joel's footsteps receding to the gate, the soft cough of the car before it growled away into the night.

I thought about having him stopped and breathalysed. Sweet, petty revenge. But he needed the car to collect Sam. I picked up his whiskey glass and hurled it at the wall. A second wail came from the alarm. I stepped over the shards of glass on the carpet and stumbled upstairs.

Sam was standing in his cot. I lifted him up over the bars and hugged him to me, fighting tears. I kissed his forehead. Put him back into the cot. Gave him his bottle.

I went next door and switched on the light. Pairs of socks lay like larvae on the carpet. The doors of the built-in wardrobe were slid back, revealing gaps in the rail where Joel had filleted a row of shirts. He had skimmed the top layer of freshly ironed vests and underpants on the shelf below.

The edge of his dark blue pyjama jacket was just visible under the edge of the white pillow. I walked to the other side of the bed, picked up my pillow, looked at the black, satin nightdress coiled underneath. Sickness rose in my throat again. I tucked the pillow under my arm, trailed the duvet into Sam's room, laid it on the floor beside his cot, and, without bothering to undress, lay down in the snowy heap.

Sam turned over on his side and lay looking at me, sucking on his bottle. I pulled the duvet round me, closed my eyes and hoped for sleep.

Chapter 9

Work was a welcome distraction. 'I'll be all right,' I whispered to a shocked Helen, during a hurried conversation on her doorstep the next morning. 'Joel's coming to pick up Sam as usual. It's easier if we do that. Don't say anything to him, or to anyone else,' I pleaded, waving with pretend cheerfulness at Helen's mother-in-law, hovering in the hallway, making clucking noises at Sam in Helen's arms. I drove the five miles to Ballymoney, hoping something would happen to keep me busy.

The duty sergeant telephoned as I was hanging my coat behind the office door. 'Ballycastle have been on to us about a suspicious death. They want CID to take a look. It's a body at the bottom of the cliffs at Fair Head.'

'I'm the only one here,' I said. 'They're all in court.'

'Then you'll have to go on your own,' he said cheerfully. 'Boots and a waterproof. Sounds like you'll have a bit of a hike. Army's been and gone. Route cleared. Constable McAllister will be waiting for you at Murlough Bay. He'll take you round from there.'

I put down the phone. God forgive me, I thought. Some poor

soul is dead, and I'm glad. As I drove across the Antrim plateau to the coast, every nerve in my body was on alert, every sense heightened. Misery and rage were temporarily stowed behind my heart, manifest only in a dull ache.

At Ballycastle I dropped down to the harbour and saw, to my right, beyond the beach, the unmistakable outline of Fair Head, shaped like a giant anvil above a sea shining like steel. I took the road towards it, following the curve of the coast, losing sight of it as the road climbed to the plateau again.

At the signpost for Murlough Bay, I turned left on to a narrow ribbon of road, lined with twisted, blackened trees, bowing in obedience to the prevailing wind like a procession of witches snaking down to the sea.

Where the land began to fall more steeply to the shore, I pulled in behind a blue and white squad car and a police Land Rover parked on the right hand side of the road. On the left, where a platform of rock made a natural car park, white tape encircled a red Fiat Uno.

I got out and looked around me. White clouds floated above the headland. The boomerang shape of Rathlin Island was diamond sharp; chalk cliffs shining like a row of teeth. White dots of houses on the Mull of Kintyre glinted in the low-angled, lemony rays of the sun. The island of Sanda lay like an upturned spoon on the surface of the water. It looked close enough to touch.

Joel and I got married on an autumn day like this, I thought, remembering his two hands round my waist; the tingle of my skin as he lifted me, effortlessly, on to a bench outside the Causeway hotel; his flushed, happy face, dark eyes shining; my veil floating sideways in the breeze; the click of cameras as I flung my bouquet of pink roses into the laughing crowd.

'The nearer the island the nearer the rain,' said a white-faced James McAllister, jolting me into the present, as he lifted the tape for me to duck under. He pointed to a line of black clouds massing on the horizon. 'Let's hope it stays dry for a bit. The body's on the rocks below the headland. It'll take a while to move.'

'Man or woman?'

'A woman. Mid-twenties, I'd say.' He was only about twenty himself.

'Is this her car?'

'We haven't looked in it yet. We were waiting for you.'

He pointed to three uniformed constables unrolling white tape through the tawny fern and heather that carpeted the headland between the car park and the edge of the cliffs in the distance. He wrote my name and arrival time in his notebook.

'We think she walked from here to the cliffs. There's a path down to the sea from the top. We went down it to get to the body. But we're taping it all off, just in case. We'll go along the bottom instead.'

We drove down the steep, twisting road dropping from sunlight into the shadow of the plateau behind us.

'Who found her?'

'Climbers. From Queen's University. They scrambled up the path to the top and ran to a farmer's house. Dan McKay. He dialled 999 and came back to wait for us.'

'Where is he?'

'We let him go home. He had sheep to get in. He's only a mile up the road.'

'Where are the climbers?'

'They left before we got here. We've got a contact number.'

'Who's we?'

'Me and Sergeant Campbell. Sergeant Campbell taped off the scene and sent for you. Was it all right to let the farmer go?' he asked anxiously.

'I don't suppose he'll run away,' I said. 'But the sheep might.'

We turned left and bumped along a grassy track on a narrow shelf of land above the shore. On our right, black boulders tumbled towards the water's edge. On our left, ferny slopes gave way to bare, grey columns of rock rising sheer from a rubble of scree. James McAllister pulled up where the track ended and a field of boulders began sloping from the cliff face to the sea.

About twenty feet away, in a mossy patch among the boulders, lay a fallen puppet, legs and arms at impossible angles. I stared for a moment through the windscreen before getting out of the Land Rover.

'Six hundred feet.' James McAllister answered my un-spoken question. 'Millions of years old. Makes you think, doesn't it?'

The sea lapped the shore with the regularity of a pulse. I was lost, for a moment, in the immensity of my surroundings. The cliffs mocked me and my concerns. What will it matter in a million years? I clambered across the debris of millennia.

'No chance falling from that height,' Sergeant Campbell said when I reached him. 'God help her.'

She lay beside a giant boulder, one arm trapped beneath her back, her head twisted to one side, frizzy dark brown hair lifting in the wind, a purple bruise on her temple, a jagged gash, black with congealed blood, across her cheek. Her pale blue wind-cheater had been shredded by the rocks. A bone protruded through a gash in her jeans. It looked thin and fibrous, like a stick of white celery.

'Her neck broke when she landed,' Willie Campbell said. 'She must have bounced and rolled down to here.'

His broad, ruddy face looked puzzled and sad. 'Married, too.' He pointed to the gold band on the left hand below the elastic cuff. 'Maybe she had children.' He shook his head with a great sigh.

'I hope not,' I said. We were all silent for a moment.

'It's a sad business either way,' he said.

'And you don't think she jumped?' I said.

'Look at her boots. They still have the wee plastic loop where the label was attached. They're scuffed from the fall, but they're new boots. Why would you put on a pair of new boots to jump off a cliff?'

'You'd need boots to get up there from where she parked,' James McAllister said. 'The ground's terrible boggy.'

We raised our eyes to the ominous height of the cliffs. A gust of damp wind lifted the hem of my raincoat. The fabric fluttered behind me like a sail, tugging me backwards.

'If the wind was from the other direction, it could blow you off the top,' Willie Campbell said. 'Do you think she could have been blown off?'

I braced myself against another blast of wind from the sea. It stung my cheeks. I tasted salt. 'Maybe. We can ask the Met Office. When we know the time of death.'

'I suppose she could have fallen,' Sergeant Campbell said. 'It's a wild place to go walking on your own.'

'Maybe she had a row with her husband and came out here to get her head straight,' I said.

'She's cold as the grave,' James McAllister said. 'She could have been here since the weekend.'

'Somebody would have seen her on Sunday,' said Willie

Campbell. 'There's always walkers around on Sunday.'

'Dan McKay thought he saw two red cars parked up there yesterday.'

'I'll call in the scene of crime officers,' I said.

Sergeant Campbell was right about the boots. She had bought them the previous day. Kenny McKittrick from SOCO found the box and receipt on the back seat of the red hatchback, along with her discarded, black high-heeled shoes, and a black leather handbag. He extracted her driving licence.

'Dolores Margaret Rock,' he said, looming over me like the abominable snowman in his white protective suit. 'Portstewart address. Attractive.' He studied the licence again before holding it out for me to see. 'She looks like you.'

She had a pale, oval face and a cloud of dark hair. Date of birth, July 1965.

'She's the same age as me,' I said, feeling a prickle on my spine. 'There's only a few months between us.'

'Never easy to bring news of a death,' Kenny said.

A memory jumped into my mind. Walking back from the Students' Union with Isabel. Laughing. The nervous young policeman leaping to his feet as I pushed open the lobby doors of the hall of residence. 'Miss Watson?'

'That's me,' I said. Surprise stopped the laughter in my throat.

'Mr and Mrs Watson,' he began.

'Major and Captain Watson,' I corrected, before I noticed the pity in his face.

'Sorry, Major and Captain, your parents. I'm afraid I have some bad news. An accident.' He stumbled now.

'How bad?' I asked, crushing Isabel's hand.

'Bad,' he said.

'Both dead?' Not believing it.

Isabel said quietly, 'What happened?'

'Joyriders,' he said. 'The car mounted the pavement and hit them. The police in Belfast said to tell you it was quick. They were killed instantly. They wouldn't have . . .' he trailed off.

'Did they catch them?' I said, still not taking it in.

'I don't know,' he said. 'I'm sorry. Will you be all right with your friend? Do you want to talk to anybody?'

'Only to them,' I said.

After that it was a bit of a blur. I only dimly recall the coach to Heathrow, the flight to Aldergrove. Madge and Eric and Helen waiting for me, red-eyed. The four of us bent with grief. The worst week of my life.

Kenny McKittrick said, 'Are you OK? Claire? Are you feeling sick? Is this your first jumper?'

'Yeah,' I said. 'No. I'm all right.'

He dropped the driving licence into a clear plastic bag.

'There's this as well.' He held up a pale blue card in a plastic wallet. 'British Actors Equity Association. Miss Dolores Dargan.' He pursed his lips. 'Name rings a bell. I think my wife brought me to a play she was in.'

The light was falling. Two white-suited figures moved slowly, heads down, across the headland to the cliffs. 'I'll leave you lot to get on with it,' I said. 'Detective Sergeant Dunbar is setting up an incident room in Ballycastle. We'll go and break the bad news to her husband. See you tomorrow.' I waved goodbye and got into my car.

Chapter 10

'Did she fall or was she pushed?' Robbie Dunbar said, when I picked him up at Ballycastle police station. 'A good, old-fashioned murder, eh? Makes a change. Married, you said?'

'But uses her maiden name. Dolores Dargan. She's an actress.'

'I suppose the husband's got to be in the frame.' The steel security gates closed behind us. I accelerated up the hill, out of the town. 'What notorious murderer lived at number ten Rillington Place in London?'

'I don't know, Robbie,' I said. 'I hear you got through to the semi-finals. Congratulations.'

'John Reginald Christie,' he said. 'That was one of the questions. The Electricity Board didn't know and we got the bonus point.'

'Well done,' I said mechanically. Wondering how a man is supposed to react when you tell him his wife is dead.

'What's the capital of Mongolia?'

'What?'

'That was another one. Ulan Bator.'

Robbie kept this up for the next half-hour, falling silent only when we reached the Strand Road in Portstewart and began looking for the address on the driving licence.

The yellow street lights had the misty glow that betrays moisture in the air. The semi-detached, brick and pebble-dashed house, high above the road, looking out to sea, was in darkness. There was no reply when we rang the doorbell and no cars were parked in the steep driveway. We were about to walk back down the flight of stone steps to the road when a dapper, elderly man in a beige raincoat, with a dachshund on a lead, began ascending the steps to the house next door.

'There's nobody in,' he called to us. He loped across a terrace in the tiered lawn to face us across the low wall that separated the gardens. 'She's probably up in Belfast. And he doesn't get home until after nine on a Tuesday.'

'Do you know where he works?' I asked.

'Who are you?'

'He'll know all about it soon enough,' Robbie muttered to me. 'Police,' he said loudly, proffering his ID. 'And you are?'

'Larry Lyons.' He peered at us through the descending gloom. 'I'm at home most of the time. Except when I take Felix for a walk. There's been nobody next door since yesterday morning.'

'Do they have children?' I said.

'No,' he said. 'I'm not surprised. They're hardly ever there at the same time. She's an actress, you know.'

'Where does Mr Rock work?' I asked.

He corrected me. 'Dr Rock. He's got a PhD. He teaches at the university. Can I ask what this is about?'

'We can't say anything at this stage,' Robbie said. 'We need to talk to Dr Rock.'

'He's in Social Sciences. Research into community relations. It seems to involve sitting around in pubs talking a lot of the time.'

He gave an inaudible sniff. 'Waste of money if you ask me. I was in the finance department until I retired. It's the first big building on the left when you drive into the main campus.'

'The finance department?'

'No,' he tutted. 'Social Sciences.' The dachshund gave a little yelp. 'Is there something wrong? Do you want me to take a message in case you miss him?'

'If we miss him we'll call back,' I said.

'If I can be of any help, just let me know.' He tugged the lead. 'Dinner time, Felix.' The dog scampered beside him up the steps and into the house.

The wind was shearing the young trees dotted over the flat campus, plastering yellow and brown leaves to the pavements and the lamp posts, as we drove up to the security barrier in the almost dark. Robbie wound down his window and presented his ID to the guard.

'Social Sciences?'

'Turn left at the roundabout. Follow the signs for the Riverside Theatre. It's just before you come to it. You can park opposite the theatre.' He looked up before stepping back into the shelter of his wooden hut. 'There's a lot of rain in thon sky.'

The wipers slapped back and forward like a metronome, sweeping a shroud of moisture from the windscreen. I imagined the broken body below the cliffs, the stretcher being manoeuvred across the slippery rocks, yellow oilskins glowing in the wet gloom. It was now raining steadily. Shivering, I got out of the car and followed Robbie across the car park. A red Toyota Corolla was parked near the entrance.

'Hang on a minute,' I said, stopping beside it, ignoring the rain now trickling down the back of my neck.

'I didn't know you were keen on cars, Claire.'

'Joel's the one who's keen on cars.' My stomach contracted as I said his name. 'I'm only interested in this Toyota. There was a red Corolla stolen in a scam at the weekend. I just wanted to check the number. But it's not it.'

We pushed open the double glass doors of the two-storey glass and concrete building and shook the rain from our coats like spaniels. 'Maybe the bad news should come from you,' Robbie said. 'Woman and all that.'

The security guard lowered the *Coleraine Chronicle* and looked at us over his reading glasses. 'Dr Rock? Room ten. Ground floor.' He reached for the telephone on his desk. 'Is he expecting you?'

Robbie produced his ID. 'Don't call.'

The guard replaced the receiver and came out from behind the desk, his pale eyes greedy with curiosity. 'Has something happened? I'll take you to his office.'

'No need,' I said, outflanking him. The rooms were signposted.

'It's the one at the end. I don't know if he's in,' he called after me. I was already halfway down the dimly lit corridor, Robbie a few steps behind me.

The door to 10G was hemmed with light. I rapped on the door. No reply. I heard low voices, laughter. I knocked again. A female voice exclaimed, '*Merde!*'

I pushed down the door handle and stepped into the room. A woman was stooping to pick up a book from the floor. A curtain of blonde hair obscured her face.

The man behind the desk was leaning back in his chair. I could see only a brown beard above a black roll-neck sweater. A wisp of blue smoke carried the acrid tang of a French cigarette.

The door swung shut behind us. The man in the chair bounced upright. He brushed his shoulder-length hair back from his forehead with both hands and stared at us. A blank, interrogative stare. A luxurious brown moustache. A beard that followed the line of his chin. He looked like a buccaneer. I guessed he was about thirty.

He stubbed out his cigarette in the ashtray on the desk and stood up. I thought I saw a glint of alarm in his eyes. 'Hello?'

Robbie glanced at me.

I stepped forward. 'I'm Detective Constable Watson. This is Detective Sergeant Dunbar,' I said. 'We need to speak to Dr Rock.'

'I'm John Rock,' he said.

The blonde got to her feet and set the book down on the desk. They both stood waiting for me to continue.

'I'm afraid we have some bad news, Dr Rock.'

The woman made as if to move, but he reached across the desk and touched her arm. 'It's all right, Jacqueline.' He pronounced her name the French way. 'Madame Duchêne is a friend.' He hesitated. 'Is it one of my students?' He had an English accent with a faint, public school drawl.

'No.' I paused. 'Is your wife Dolores Margaret Rock?'

He sat down, gripped the armrests of his chair. 'My God.' He took a deep breath. 'Has there been an accident?'

'The body of a woman was found at the bottom of the cliffs at Fair Head this afternoon. We found a handbag in a red Fiat Uno. With her driving licence and Equity card.'

Jacqueline moved round the desk to stand beside him. 'An accident? When?'

'We don't know yet,' I said. 'There'll have to be a post-mortem.'

'We need you to formally identify the body,' Robbie said.

'Where is she?' John Rock's face was pale now, above the moustache.

'The mortuary in Coleraine hospital. We can arrange transport if you like.'

He shook his head. 'I'll drive myself.'

Robbie handed him a leaflet with printed directions to the mortuary. John Rock stared at it for a moment before setting it down on the desk. He closed his eyes. Bowed his head.

Robbie said, 'We'll wait there for you.' He glanced around the office, nodded towards the electric kettle and mugs on a tin tray by the window, and addressed Jacqueline. 'Hot sweet tea,' he said. 'Good for shock.'

He turned to John Rock. 'Could you bring a photograph of your wife, sir? To show people when we're trying to piece together her last movements.' He paused. 'With regard to that, sir, when was the last time you saw her?'

Jacqueline paused en route to the tea tray. John Rock lifted his head, opened his eyes, stared blankly at the door behind us. Eventually he said, 'Sunday afternoon. She was going to Belfast for a rehearsal.'

'She didn't come home on Sunday night?' I didn't hide my surprise.

'I don't know,' he said. 'I wasn't there.'

He glanced at Jacqueline, but she was head down, hunting in a red handbag on the window sill. 'I was a guest of Madame Duchêne's.'

'An overnight guest?' I was conscious of the edge in my voice.

'Dolores sometimes stayed with a friend in Belfast during rehearsals. I sometimes stayed in Cushendun.'

'What about last night?' Robbie asked.

'I don't know. I wasn't at home last night either.' He dropped his head into his hands.

Jacqueline withdrew a fat black fountain pen and small white card from her bag. 'I have a weekend cottage in the Glens of Antrim,' she said, scribbling on the back of the card.

'I was there most of yesterday. I stayed there last night,' John Rock said, not lifting his head. 'I came straight here this morning.'

The kettle blasted into life. Jacqueline dropped a tea bag into a mug.

'Most of yesterday?' Robbie said.

'Alone?' I asked.

'I drove to the Jordanstown campus for a nine o'clock meeting. Then I drove back to Cushendun.'

'Why didn't you go home to Portstewart?' I asked.

He raised his head. 'I was going to talk to a community group in Cushendun on Monday night,' he said in a tired voice. 'It's only an hour or so up the coast from Jordanstown. It was simpler to go straight back there. I took some essays to mark.'

Jacqueline tapped him gently on the arm and set a mug of tea on the desk in front of him. She said, 'Please. He is upset. Must you ask questions at this time?'

I looked at Robbie. He said, 'I'm sorry, but we have to ask questions when there is a suspicious death.'

'Suspicious?' The mug trembled in his hand.

'Was your wife depressed? Is there any reason to think she might have taken her own life?'

'I spoke to her yesterday morning. She telephoned the office just after the meeting. Said the afternoon rehearsal had been cancelled and she was going shopping. I assumed she was phoning from Belfast,' he cried.

'Maybe she was,' I said. 'What time did you get back to Cushendun?'

'About half past twelve, one o'clock. I don't know.' He looked around him wildly. 'Can't this wait?'

Jacqueline handed the card to Robbie. He read it, raised an eyebrow, handed the card to me.

Mme Jacqueline Duchêne
Consul de France
Belfast
Tel: 00 44 232 459000/1/2
Facsimile: 00 44 232 459100

I turned it over. On the back she had written the address in Cushendun.

John Rock set the mug down on the desk and stood up. The muscles in his cheek tightened. 'I need time to take this in. I haven't even identified her yet.' He walked over to the door. 'I'd like to be left alone for a while. Please. I have your directions. I'll be there in half an hour.' He opened the door.

Robbie gave an almost imperceptible shrug. 'Fine, sir. We can have this conversation another time.' John Rock stood stiffly, holding the door open, until I followed Robbie out of the room.

'Cushendun. Not that far from Fair Head,' I said, as we walked to the car.

'You know what I think?'

'I can imagine.'

'Gives a new twist to the phrase diplomatic relations,' he said, with a foxy smile. 'How's Joel?'

A lump of misery slid from behind my heart and settled in my stomach. My ribs hurt. 'Busy,' I said.

'Did you notice their body language? The way he kept touching her arm? A sure sign he fancies her. Do you think they're having an affair?'

'Yes,' I said. 'I feel it in my bones.'

Chapter 11

A white-coated mortuary assistant, carrying a bucket and mop, met us at the hearse entrance to Coleraine hospital.

'She's in the fridge,' he said. A faint smell, like bleach mingled with raw meat, hung around him. 'We're all cleared up for the night. You can go on in.'

The sound hit us when we pushed through the heavy, rubber-skirted doors. Bright notes from a trumpet, bouncing off the white walls, echoing in the cold space.

Alan McCrea was beating four four time with a scalpel. It sparkled like a magic wand in the blue fluorescent light.

'Terrific, don't you think?' Alan called out. 'Bach. Played by Wynton Marsalis. He's better known as a jazz musician.'

The cassette player shared a trolley with a stainless steel bowl, an array of medical instruments and a sheaf of A4 notes attached to a clipboard. Alan dropped the scalpel on the trolley and began divesting himself of his green surgical gown, moving with a sort of hop and skip, in time to the music. He timed himself perfectly, dropping the gown into a red plastic sack, on the last, sustained note.

A dark rattle of timpani and a blast of trumpets signalled the beginning of another track on the cassette.

'Music makes me perform better,' Alan announced.

'Sinatra works for me,' Robbie said, with a half-leer. 'This is a bit full on.'

Alan looked at him over the top of his half-moon spectacles. 'You jest. I'm serious. You can measure the effect of music on the limbic system.'

'Limbic system?' Robbie pounced like a squirrel on a nut. He loved to collect and store new information.

'The most primitive part of the brain. Cockpit of our emotions,' Alan said. 'Bigger in the female. Which is why you, Claire,' pointing at me, as though directing a section of orchestra, 'are more in touch with your emotions than Robbie.' A nod in Robbie's direction. 'Who finds it easier to joke. Yes? You find it difficult to dissociate emotion from sex, Claire. Yes?'

A reply was redundant.

'When the limbic system is inflamed, we're depressed,' he continued in the bright tones of a lecturer addressing students. 'We don't know if inflammation causes the depression, or if depression causes the inflammation. But music seems to reduce it.'

The tune spiralled to its triumphant conclusion. Alan said, with a brilliant smile, 'A counterblast to death, trumpets. Don't you think?'

The sound of trickling water filled the silence. I stared at the slanting, steel table, the row of steel sinks, the square, steel refrigerator doors lining the walls.

'Yes,' I said.

Robbie said, 'Are you all right, Claire? You look like death warmed up. Go on home to Joel. I'll wait for yer man.'

My shoulder hurt. The result of sleeping on the floor, I thought. I felt nauseous. 'Thanks, Robbie. I'll take you up on that,' I said. 'Goodnight, you two.'

It was after ten o'clock when I got home. I didn't recognise myself in the hall mirror. Robbie was right. My face was green. My hair was lank. My eyes looked hollowed out.

There was a suitcase at the bottom of the stairs. The kitchen door was ajar. Joel's voice drifted in monosyllables into the hallway. When I walked into the kitchen, he hung up the telephone.

'You took your time,' he said, looking at his watch. 'I've been here since seven o'clock.'

'And I've been telling a man his wife's dead at the bottom of a cliff.'

There was a time when Joel would have expressed interest, sympathy, horror. Taken me in his arms. Now he merely muttered something that could have been commiseration.

'Sam's asleep. I'll pick him up at the same time tomorrow.'

'Who was on the phone?'

'Don't interrogate me,' he said, sweeping his car keys from the table.

'We have to talk, Joel,' I cried. But he was already brushing past me on his way out.

He had taken more of his clothes from the wardrobe. Discarded coat hangers lay scattered on the bed. I yanked his pyjamas from under the pillow, carried them downstairs and pushed them into the bin underneath the kitchen sink.

When I came back upstairs, Sam was standing up in his cot, one hand clutching his red blanket, the other holding on to the rail. I hoisted him into my arms and hugged him, rocking back and forwards. He gurgled with pleasure. When I put him back into his cot, he refused to lie down. He sat looking up at me. Wide awake. Not crying. I dragged his blue baby chair to the landing, switched on the light, and stood on the chair to open the trap door in the ceiling. I groped around the entrance to the roof space until my hand settled on the handle of a hard-edged, rectangular black case. I swung it down and knelt on the landing to open it.

The silver cornet caught the light and sent bright flashes flaring to the ceiling as I eased it from its moulded bed of blue velvet and weighed it in my hand. It felt surprisingly light. Sam's eyes shone with wonder. I pushed the cup mute into the horn and put my lips to the mouthpiece. I pointed the horn at the carpet to deaden the sound still further as, still kneeling, I pressed my fingers on the shining keys and softly blew the first bar of Brahms's lullaby.

My mouth was stiff and unresponsive at first, my tongue unsure. The melody trembled in the air. I closed my eyes to better hear my father's voice instructing my ten-year-old self. 'Take in enough breath. You can't drive a car without petrol. Easy, Claire. It's not the end of the world if you split a note.'

By the time I blew the last, consoling cadence, Sam had gone back to sleep. I put the cornet into its case, got to my feet and stood looking down at him for a few moments before picking up the duvet and pillow and trailing them into the spare room.

There was no hot water when I ran the shower the next morning. I shivered in the flesh-tingling spray for half a minute before springing out of the bath to feel the radiator. Cold. I pulled on a towelling robe and hurried to the kitchen to check the boiler. No oil. I could feel panic rising as I wedged the telephone between my ear and my shoulder, hunted through a drawer to find the oil-supplier's card with one hand, dialled Helen's number with the other.

'Can you give Sam a bath at your place? I've no hot water.'

'Is there a problem with your boiler? Do you want Malcolm to look at it?'

'No bloody oil,' I said, and burst into tears. It's the little things that tip you over the edge.

George telephoned as I was about to leave the house. 'How's things?'

'Joel's moved out.' My jaw ached. It was an effort to speak. 'He says he wants space.'

Silence.

'What do you think he means, George?'

'He might just want space.'

'And what else?' I cried.

'I don't know, Claire.' He sounded tired.

'He says he got married too young.'

'Wild oats,' George said. 'Maybe he didn't sow enough. Are you still chasing stolen cars?'

'On the back burner. Suspicious death at Fair Head. I thought maybe you'd be in charge.'

He cleared his throat. 'I'm tied up with this counterfeit cigarette stuff.'

'That's a pity. It would be good working on a murder with you.'

There was a pause before George said, 'First lesson, Claire. Don't jump to conclusions.'

Chapter 12

The incident room – a spare office overlooking the yard of the police station in Ballycastle – was a fug of cigarette smoke and coffee by the time I arrived for the morning briefing.

'Good call, Claire,' said Chief Inspector Jordan, nodding approval as I came in. He was pacing up and down, hands behind his back. With his big hooked nose and black hair and sharp eyes, he looked like an intelligent crow. He perched on the edge of a desk, and asked Robbie to sum up. I took a chair near the window, beside Kenny McKittrick, and tried to concentrate as Robbie recounted our conversations of the previous evening.

My mind was dull with misery and lack of sleep. I made myself focus on the blown-up photographs sellotaped to a whiteboard on the back wall. A studio portrait of Dolores, bare shoulders swathed in chiffon, hair swept into a knot, lips glossy and slightly parted, eyes smiling at the camera. Beside it, a police photograph. A broken china doll with one sightless, violet eye above a pale pink cheek. The other eye was buried in a puffy mass of livid bone and tissue.

'Alan McCrea says the injuries look consistent with a fall from the cliff top. No obvious sign of previous injury. He thinks she died about four o'clock on Monday afternoon. We'll get the full report tonight.'

'Thanks, Robbie,' the chief inspector said. 'What did you find at the scene, Kenny?'

Kenny McKittrick unfolded his great height from the desk and indicated the map, roughly drawn with black and blue marker pens, beside the photographs.

'We covered the ground between the car park and the cliffs.' He traced his forefinger along a straggly black line on the map. 'It takes about forty minutes if we assume she stayed on this route. It's pretty boggy if you stray off it.' He shrugged his wide shoulders. 'Didn't find much. Walkers seem to be a tidy lot. No crisp packets. No empty beer cans. Only significant find, four cigarette butts. French tobacco. Tipped. Two were within five yards of each other, about halfway to the cliffs. One with lipstick, one without. Two were beside a rock, near where she must have gone over. Again, one had lipstick. One didn't. Packet of twenty Gauloises minus four, found in her pocket. Forensic to confirm lipstick match. Boots brand new.'

'Well spotted by Willie Campbell,' said Chief Inspector Jordan. Willie's face reddened at the compliment.

'Boot prints on the path from the cliff top to the shore,' Kenny went on. 'Going up and coming down. Too big to be hers. Waiting for forensic on them too. But I'd say the ones going up were the climbers. The ones coming down looked like steel-tipped, standard RUC issue. Sergeant Campbell and Constable McAllister, I assume. Any questions? Any answers?'

'I checked with the Met Office,' I said. 'A light westerly wind.

No big gusts recorded. Not enough to blow a sweetie paper off the top.'

'The shop remembered her,' James McAllister said. 'She was on her own when she bought the boots. Monday morning. Not many customers. The young lad who served her said she seemed cheerful enough. Not depressed or overexcited.'

Willie Campbell said, 'Dan McKay, you know, the farmer who phoned in. I had a wee word with him. He was putting out lick for the sheep. Monday afternoon. About three o'clock. He thought there was two red cars went down the road.'

'Lick?' said Robbie.

'Concentrated feed for sheep. They lick it.'

'Together?'

Willie looked at him in astonishment.

'The cars. Were they together?'

'No. About five or ten minutes apart.'

'What make?'

'One was a wee hatchback. The other was one of those Japanese saloons. Toyota, Nissan, something like that.'

'Did he see anybody walking towards the cliffs?'

Willie shook his head. 'He drove into Ballycastle after putting out the lick. Saw a few cars on the main road on the way there and back. Didn't take particular notice of any of them, he says.'

'Contents of her handbag?' I asked.

Kenny McKittrick consulted his clipboard. 'Driving licence, Equity card, tissues, comb, lipstick, lip gloss, black leather wallet with two ten pound notes, two pounds fifty in change, and the usual credit cards. Biro, two tampons in a plastic case, a tube of make-up.'

'Anything else in her pocket?'

'A tissue. Car keys.'

'No lighter? Matches?'

Kenny shook his head.

'So who lit her cigarettes?'

There was a pause. 'Ping!' Robbie said. 'Our starter for ten.'

'We're still out there,' Kenny said. 'The rain hasn't helped.'

'Her husband smokes,' I said.

Robbie said, 'He arrived at the mortuary last night in a red Toyota Corolla.'

Chief Inspector Jordan caught up with Robbie and me in the yard, as we were about to get into the car. He was slightly out of breath.

'About this French consul business. I've had a word with the Secretary of State's office. We have to jump through a lot of hoops before we can talk to her. Diplomatic immunity.'

'We're not accusing her of anything.'

'Still applies.'

'We just want to check he was at her house on Monday afternoon.'

'Not admissible without a waiver of immunity.'

We stared at him in dismay.

'We have to put in a written request to the Foreign Office to contact the French Embassy. She can't waive her own immunity.'

'How long will that take?'

'About two weeks.'

Robbie banged his fist on the car.

'We've got no good reason to suspect him,' the chief inspector said.

'He smokes Gauloises. He drives a red car. We think somebody was with her,' I said. 'You always say look close to home.'

'Kenny and his boys are still out there. We can afford to wait.'

'What about speaking to the husband again, sir?' Robbie said.

'You haven't spoken to her family yet. Or her friends in the theatre. Follow the suicide angle first.' He banged lightly on the roof of the car, 'All right?' before walking briskly back into the building.

'You look lovely when you're cross, Claire,' Robbie said, putting his hands up, shrinking in mock fear from imaginary blows.

I glared at him.

'Come on. Makes sense,' he said, sliding behind the wheel. 'He didn't say don't speak to him. He just wants us to talk to a few other people first. We can start with her family.'

'Fine,' I said, buckling my seat belt.

'I was only paying you a compliment.'

'Save them for your girlfriend.'

Robbie put the car into gear. 'I'm not seeing anybody at the moment,' he said.

I glanced at him in surprise. He was looking straight ahead at the security gates. A flush was rising from his collar to his cheek. 'I envy people like you and George. You've someone to come home to,' he said.

The gates parted. The car nosed towards the widening gap.

My throat tightened. I tried to sound light. 'Those who are in want out, and those who are out want in. Isn't that always the way?'

We tramped along the rough path across the headland to the cliffs. The land was bathed in buttery morning light. A blustery, southwest wind chased high white clouds towards the Scottish coast. A few hundred yards to our left, a small lake glinted in the bog.

'Lough na Crannog,' I said. 'Willie Campbell says you can fish there. Brown trout. There's another route from the cliffs that goes past it and through a farm, back to the main road. Nobody came that way on Monday, according to the farmer.'

On the far side of a stile, white tape marked off an area where two of the cigarette butts had been found.

'They probably lit them in the car park and finished smoking them about here,' I said. 'No dead matches found in the car park or along the path. Whoever was with her had a lighter.'

SOCO had taped off another patch of ground in front of a rock near the top of the cliffs.

'So they stopped here for a smoke,' Robbie said, looking around.

The grass had been cropped short by sheep. There were a few pebble-hard sheep droppings, but no sign of footprints, or a struggle.

'They were lucky to pick up those butts before the rain started,' he said.

Two lines of white tape sloped gently upwards for about ten yards from the rock to the edge of the cliffs. We dropped to our hands and knees a few feet short of the brink, and crawled forward. White tape fluttered in the black rocks below us. Robbie patted his hand along the fringe of marram grass. 'No sign of crumbling underneath.' He sat back on his haunches. 'If she fell, or jumped, why didn't whoever was with her run for help?'

'You think she was pushed?'

He shrugged. 'I'd like to know who smoked those cigarettes.'

'Suppose the owner of the red saloon came out here after she fell. Didn't know there was a body at the bottom of the cliffs. Smoked a couple of cigarettes.'

'And the butts landed, both times, just where Dolores had dropped hers?'

We inched back from the edge and stood up.

'We're assuming two people came out here, right?'

'A man and a woman,' I said.

'You're not wearing lipstick, Claire.'

'I didn't know you cared.' I mentally kicked myself. Of course, Dolores could have been with a woman.

Chapter 13

Dargan's pub was a low, whitewashed building, attached to a two-storey pebble-dashed house set back from the road on the northwestern outskirts of Belfast. There was space for half a dozen cars in front of the pub. The house had a fenced-in front garden with glossy-leafed evergreen shrubs and a monkey puzzle. Blinds were drawn in both buildings.

As we crunched to a halt outside the pub, a tall brunette with a ponytail was pinning a black-edged card to the door. She came towards us as we got out of the car. We introduced ourselves.

'John said you'd probably call. I'm Dolores's sister, Bernadette.'

She had a thinner face, but the same long neck and pink and cream complexion as her sister. Her narrow shoulders were slightly hunched in a mute appeal for consolation. Her dark grey eyes were red-rimmed.

'My mother's not up to it. You can talk to me.' She ushered us through the garden and into the house. There was a pile of coats on a chair at the bottom of the stairs. 'Just a minute.' She put her head round a door at the end of the hallway. I heard low voices, the clink of teacups, a cough. She closed the door.

'People have been calling at the house all morning. It's like a wake without a body.'

She led us along a short corridor off the hallway, through a tiny, windowless storeroom lit by a single neon strip, into the murky space behind the bar. It smelled of cigarette smoke and stale beer, overlaid with bleach. I felt a familiar prickle of discomfort.

I had been brought up to regard pubs as places to hurry past on the way home from band practice, wherever we were living. Sometimes, through a swinging door, I would glimpse red faces in smoky light, hear laughter, bursts of raucous singing, shouts in half-aggressive, jokey tones. 'Mind my drink!' 'Fuck you, Donnelly.'

One pub in Belfast seemed smaller and less threatening than the rest. On winter evenings, sweet tunes on the fiddle and banjo escaped into the street and made me want to skip. Once, on a frosty January night, I stopped and listened to a tenor alternately singing and lilting 'My Lagan Love'. I knew the tune, and could play it on the cornet.

'Where Lagan stream sings lullaby,
There blows a lily fair.
The twilight's gleam is in her eyes,
The night is on her hair.
And like a lovesick lenanshee,
She holds my heart in thrall.
No life I own, nor liberty,
For love is lord of all.'

The wind swept his words up and over the black edges of the roofs and into the starry sky.

It was a young man's voice and his was a siren song, calling me into the warmth. For a moment I thought maybe pubs weren't such bad places after all. Then a door opened further up the street. A man and woman lurched across the pavement to steady themselves against a lamp post. Their faces were slack and sallow in the blue light. The woman mumbled, 'Piss off. I'm going to be sick.' I crossed to the other side of the street and hurried home, head down, in the shadow of the eaves.

Even when I broke my pledge not to drink alcohol, I rarely went into a pub. At university, I started drinking wine, mostly to keep Isabel company. Now, when I went into a pub, it was usually to make an arrest or, as on this occasion, interview a witness.

Bernadette helped herself to a packet of cigarettes and a book of matches from behind the bar before lifting the flap of the polished mahogany counter and motioning us into the lounge. The room was half in darkness, half in daylight.

'We only drew the blinds at the front. Go on through to the back. Would you like some tea? The kettle's on the go all the time.'

We refused her offer and made our way through the shadows to where the pale October sunlight streamed through the wide back window and glimmered in the glass ashtrays on the round oak tables. A faux-leather banquette ran along the wall, under the window. I slid behind a table and sat down. Robbie pulled out a chair for Bernadette before settling himself beside me on the banquette. She tapped a cigarette from the packet with practised ease.

'Smoke?'

I shook my head. Robbie said, 'I'll have one of my own if you don't mind.' He lifted the book of matches from the table and lit

Bernadette's cigarette before attaching the flame to his own. 'Was your sister depressed?'

She drew on the cigarette and exhaled with a shuddering sigh. 'Not depressed. Discontented maybe.'

'Could she have taken her own life?' Robbie said.

Bernadette slowly shook her head. 'She wasn't that discontented.'

We waited for her to speak again. After a few moments she said, as though to herself, 'She wanted more excitement in her life. She didn't want to live in Portstewart. She wanted to live in London. She dreamed of Hollywood.'

She intercepted the glance between Robbie and me.

'It wasn't a lunatic dream,' she cried. 'Dolores had real talent. She was beautiful.'

'You're very alike,' Robbie said.

She stared at him.

'I mean like her photograph,' he said, embarrassed.

'Why do you think she went to Fair Head on a Monday afternoon?' I asked.

'I've been trying to think of a reason,' she said. 'Maybe she wanted space to think about something. We used to picnic at Murlough Bay when we were children. We'd walk across the headland to the cliffs. Daddy loved it. We loved it too. It's where John proposed to Dolores.'

'How did they meet?' I said.

'I introduced them. I met John at university in Canterbury. He was one of my lecturers. I brought him home a couple of times. He was doing research into community relations. He liked talking to customers in the pub and listening to the music. We had folk music here on a Friday and Saturday night. Still do.'

'What kind of crowd do you get?'

Bernadette made no pretence of misunderstanding him. 'We have Catholics and Protestants both drinking in this pub. They leave their politics at the door.'

'Tough. Losing your boyfriend to your sister,' Robbie said.

Bernadette shrugged. 'I wasn't that keen. I didn't blame him.' She attempted a smile. 'He'd no chance once Dolores decided he was the man for her.'

'You didn't mind?' I said.

'He wasn't right for me.'

'Was he right for Dolores?' I asked.

'She thought he was.'

'What kind of marriage did they have?'

'Who knows what goes on in any marriage?'

'Were they happy?' I persisted.

There was a pause. Bernadette focused on the tip of her cigarette.

'Was your brother-in-law having an affair?'

The cigarette trembled in her hand. Robbie kicked my ankle under the table. After a moment Bernadette said, 'I think they were both having affairs.'

'What makes you say that?' Robbie said quietly.

'About two months ago I saw Dolores in a car with a man. Not John. He was blond and he didn't have a beard. They were parked in Botanic Avenue, near the theatre. The next time we were on the phone I asked her who he was. He's sauce for the goose, she said.'

'What kind of car was it?' I asked.

'Why does that matter?' Her hand was still shaking. I thought she was going to cry.

'Maybe we'll have that wee cup of tea after all,' Robbie said.

'I thought you were going at it a bit hard,' he said, when

she had left the room. 'Not every man is playing away from home.'

'Is that why you kicked me on the ankle?'

'I was afraid she'd clam up. But you got away with it.'

He reached across the table and tapped the blue and white packet of cigarettes.

'Gauloises. And she used to go out with him.'

'I thought you were rather taken with her, Robbie,' I said with surprise.

'In this job you have to think the unthinkable. I can still see her as a suspect,' he said. 'And the converse is true as well. I thought you took against the husband on sight. But that doesn't mean he pushed his wife over a cliff.'

The bar counter dropped with a crash.

'I've brought a few sandwiches as well,' Bernadette said.

She sat watching as we ate.

'Lovely ham,' Robbie said.

She looked sharply at him. 'Do I know you from somewhere?'

'I don't think so.'

'I've seen you somewhere before.'

'Do you watch television?' I said.

'That's it!' Her face brightened at this distraction from her grief. '*Professional Challenge*. I saw you on TV.'

Robbie came as near to a blush as I've seen.

'I'm surprised you didn't know who directed *Double Indemnity*,' she said.

'It was on the tip of my tongue.'

'Billy Wilder.'

'I know.'

'Still. You got through. Congratulations.'

'Thanks for the sandwiches,' he said. 'You never know when you'll get time to eat on this job.'

I added my thanks. There was an awkward pause.

Robbie said, in a casual tone, 'Where were you yesterday afternoon, about half past three, four o'clock?'

Bernadette swallowed. 'Was that . . .'

Robbie nodded. Waited for her answer.

'I was teaching French to a group of sixth formers until half past three,' she said. 'It takes me a while to clear up. I was probably still in the staffroom at four o'clock.'

'That car,' I said, 'the one you saw your sister in. Can you remember the make?'

'Do you think the man in the car had something to do with her death?'

'We're noting everything at this stage,' Robbie said.

'I want it to be an accident,' she cried. 'I can't bear to think anybody would hurt Dolores. I don't want to think she committed suicide. She wouldn't commit suicide. She was too . . .' she shook her head as though trying to dislodge the words, 'too full of life.' She jumped up, pushing the chair away to stand rigid, hands by her sides, eyes damp and unfocused.

'I'm not very good on makes,' she said, despair in her voice. 'An ordinary sort of red car. Nissan, Toyota, something like that.'

There was the sound of brakes on gravel, car doors thudding shut, footsteps, the distant trill of a doorbell.

'More visitors,' Bernadette said.

Robbie took a card from his inside pocket and slid it across the table. She looked down at it, as though weighing the effort required to pick it up.

'In case you remember anything else,' Robbie said. He touched her lightly on the arm. 'If it's any consolation, the pathologist said she died instantly.'

She blinked to focus on him. Attempted a wan smile. 'Thank you for that.'

The music started up as we made our way back to the hallway. A slow air in a minor key, played on a fiddle. The keening notes rose gravely above the murmur of condolences drifting through the half-open door of the kitchen.

Chapter 14

Robbie and I didn't talk much on the way into the city. I was thinking how half the world seemed to be having affairs. I wanted to rehearse the conversation I intended to have with Joel, and so I was relieved when Robbie pushed a cassette into the car stereo and began tapping his hand on the wheel, yodelling to country music.

> *'When I was feeling so lonesome,*
> *Guarding my heart from more pain,*
> *Spending my time in drinking and gambling,*
> *You made me happy again.'*

'Do you like this? I could play something else. Or nothing at all if you'd prefer.'

'It's fine,' I shouted back. I was wondering how long Joel's affair had been going on, raking my mind for clues. The sales conference in August when I had bumped into Gary in the supermarket. 'Did you enjoy the conference?' Gary's gormless grin. I remembered the golf competition in September. 'We're staying overnight. Not worth driving to Donegal and back two days in a row.' Joel leaving his putter behind. Telling me on his return, in the mysterious language of golf, 'We won four and two.' My question: 'It didn't matter that you forgot your putter?' His pat answer: 'I borrowed my partner's.'

'Robbie?'

Robbie paused in the act of changing cassettes.

'Joel went off to play a competition without his putter. Could he manage without it?'

'He could borrow one from the pro, or buy a new one,' Robbie said.

'Or use his partner's?'

'He can't do that.' Robbie was horrified. 'Not in a competition. He'd be disqualified. Why was it not in his bag?'

'He takes it out to practise on the carpet,' I said.

We parked in a street near Botanic Avenue and walked to the theatre. Robbie tapped the glass-fronted display case at the entrance to the foyer. Inside was a poster advertising *Don't Dress for Dinner* by Marc Camoletti. A sash of white paper had been pasted across the names and faces of the cast. Only eight legs were visible beneath the title. Four in striped pyjamas, four in fishnet tights. A smaller, typewritten notice, sellotaped to the inside of the glass, said the role of Jacqueline would now played by Amy O'Keefe.

'Terrible business,' said the manager, bustling into the foyer to greet us. The swing doors of the auditorium flapped to a close behind him, muffling high-pitched voices and the tap of footsteps on wooden boards. 'Martin Donaghy.'

He reached for our hands, gave them a quick squeeze. 'Poor Dolores. Four days before we open. Amy will be very good but who wants to take over a part in these circumstances? Flu is one thing. Even a broken leg. But this.' His large head quivered. He hunched his shoulders, clasped his hands. 'But . . .' He straightened up and pointed to the poster.

'The show must go on?' Robbie suggested.

'I wasn't going to use that old cliché,' he said, with a hint of annoyance, 'but clearly you know what I mean. I've put you in the green room with a pot of coffee.'

He swept us along a red-carpeted corridor, through double doors marked 'Backstage', and into a room with a faded chintz sofa and armchairs squashed round a low table. It smelled of greasepaint and cigarettes. Grey light fought its way through grubby windows above a row of shelves at head height.

'I've asked Dolores's friends in the cast to pop in and see you.' He paused in the open doorway, hand on the doorknob, ear cocked. 'They've finished rehearsing.'

Robbie said, 'Did you notice any change in her behaviour? Anything to make you think she was depressed?'

'You're not thinking Dolores killed herself?'

'What's that about Dolores?' said a quick, musical voice from the corridor.

'Do you think she was depressed, Amy?' Martin Donaghy flattened himself against the door. A petite redhead with a glowing, pink face and eyes the colour of chestnuts slipped past him into the room and perched, panting slightly, on the arm of the sofa.

'Amy knew her better than any of us,' Martin Donaghy said. 'I'll leave you to it.'

Amy mopped her face with a tissue. 'The last act goes at the speed of light,' she said, tucking the tissue into the pocket of her oversized purple shirt.

'What's the play about?' Robbie asked.

'Typical French farce,' she said, smiling up at him. 'Husband hoping for dirty weekend with mistress. Cook and mistress both called Suzy. Usual mix-up. Very funny.'

'Excruciating,' I said.

'Do you know it?' Glancing from Robbie to me.

'I know the kind of thing,' I said, attempting lightness. 'You took over the part Dolores was playing?'

'The wife. Jacqueline.' She bit her lip. 'Poor Dolores. We're all devastated.' Her glance fell on the cafetière on the table. 'I could murder a cup of coffee.' She jumped up and gathered three mugs from the shelf under the window. 'Sit down.'

Robbie and I took an armchair each. Amy sniffed a carton of milk.

'Sugar?' She swapped a full ashtray for a bowl of brown sugar lumps. The pungent smell of coffee freshened the room as she filled the mugs.

'When did you last see Dolores?' Robbie asked.

'Sunday afternoon. We had a rehearsal here.'

'Do you know where she stayed on Sunday night?'

Amy paused, the coffee pot still in her hand. 'Was she not at home?'

'She stayed up in Belfast sometimes. With a friend,' Robbie said.

Amy settled herself into the sofa. 'That's me. She stayed with me sometimes.'

'But not on Sunday night?'

'Monday's rehearsal was cancelled. There was no point in staying up. She said she was driving home.'

She looked at Robbie over the rim of the mug. Her brown eyes filled with tears. 'Dolores and I were at school together.' She set the mug down on the table, pulled the tissue from her pocket and blew her nose. 'I can't believe she's dead.'

'Did she have any problems?' Robbie said.

'Hasn't everybody?' She sniffed, gave a half-smile and stuffed the tissue back into her pocket. 'Dolores wouldn't commit suicide, if that's what you're saying. It must have been an accident.'

'Did you know her husband?' I asked.

'Che Guevara?' She picked up the mug, swallowed a mouthful of coffee, watching my reaction. 'You think he looks like him too,' she said in a gratified tone. 'Dead sexy, isn't he? Dolores was nuts about him when they first met.'

'You mean she wasn't still nuts about him?' Robbie said.

'I didn't say that.' Amy glared at him. Indignant.

'So how would you describe their marriage?'

'I think the passion had worn off a bit,' Amy said. 'But it does. Doesn't it?'

'I wouldn't know,' Robbie said. 'I'm not married.'

'Neither am I. But it's what people say.'

Robbie waited. After a pause, Amy said, 'Dolores thought John was her ticket out of here. Assumed he'd get a job in London. She was mad keen to leave. He took a job at Queen's instead. He was writing some thesis about divided communities. I think he liked it here. He loved going to bars and clubs and talking to people. Dolores wanted to get out of Northern Ireland. She wanted to get away from all that.' She leaned forward, lowered her voice slightly. 'His uncle was supposed to leave them money. They were going to buy a flat in London. But he left the money to his housekeeper' – she winked – 'instead. Big disappointment. Then John was offered a job at Coleraine University. They bought a house in

Portstewart. Dolores thought it was the back of beyond. She had to commute to Belfast for rehearsals.'

'And the passion had worn off,' I said.

Amy took the prompt. 'Seven year itch.'

'Was she having an affair?' I asked.

'Dolores would flirt with a lamp post,' Amy said. 'But I don't know if she took it any further.'

'Who did she flirt with?'

Amy set her mug down on the table. 'Any decent-looking man,' she said, looking sideways at Robbie. 'It was just a reflex.'

'Do all actresses have it?' he said.

'If we find a man attractive,' she said, toying with her mug. 'You know she stole John from her sister?'

'Stole?' I said.

'Well, maybe not stole, exactly. He fell for Dolores as soon as he saw her. Poor Bernadette. Men don't like brainy women.'

'Do you think so?' Robbie said.

'Did she dump anybody for him?' I said.

Amy's timing was impeccable. She paused. 'Just her fiancé,' she said. 'He's in the cast. Playing the husband. Isn't that the quare joke?'

'Ha bloody ha,' said a voice behind me.

I turned and saw a square-set man with damp, tousled blond hair and a towel round his neck framed in the doorway. 'It's not funny, Amy,' he said. 'It wasn't funny last week, and it's not funny now.'

Amy crumpled. As though the air went out of her. 'I'm sorry, Jimmy. It's just if you didn't laugh, you'd cry.' She pulled the tissue from her pocket and blew her nose vigorously.

Jimmy squeezed past the table to shake hands with us. 'Jimmy Johnson. Martin thought you'd want to speak to me.' He sat down beside Amy, put his arm round her and patted her shoulder. 'It's all right, Amy. We've all had a shock.'

'Dolores and I patched things up long ago,' he said, addressing Robbie and me. 'We were friends. There were no hard feelings.'

'We have to ask you all the same,' Robbie said. 'About your movements on Monday.'

Jimmy withdrew his arm from Amy's shoulders, placed his hands on his knees and sat still. 'What was I doing? Let me think.' He took a deep breath and blew it out slowly. 'Breakfast at home. Then I went running on the Embankment. I live near Stranmillis Lock. Home to change. Went shopping on the Stranmillis Road. Lunch at Roscoff.' He looked from me to Robbie and back. 'If you haven't eaten there, you should. It's in Shaftesbury Square. What did I do after that?' He frowned.

'We'd no rehearsal on Monday afternoon,' Amy said. 'It was cancelled. Remember?'

'That's right,' Jimmy said. He pulled a packet of cigarettes and a lighter from his trouser pocket, waved the packet vaguely in the direction of Robbie and me. 'I went for a walk down Donegall Pass.' He flicked the lighter and focused on the flame for a second before lighting his cigarette. 'Browsed in the antique shops. Looked at cast-iron fireplaces in Alexander the Grate.'

'That's why we didn't miss Dolores,' Amy said. 'We didn't know anything about it until she didn't turn up yesterday.' Her eyes grew moist. 'I can't believe she's dead.'

'What time did you leave the restaurant?' Robbie asked. I could tell he was calculating the time needed to eat lunch and drive to Fair Head; was considering the jilted fiancé as a suspect.

'The table was booked for one o'clock.'

I did the sum myself. Dolores died about four o'clock. An hour in the restaurant. Two o'clock. An hour and a half to drive to Fair Head. He could have got there by half past three. Could just do it, I thought. If his car was nearby.

'How did you manage to find a parking space?' Robbie asked.

Jimmy looked startled. He paused. 'I walked,' he said.

'What time did you leave the restaurant?'

Amy's eyes widened. 'My God, you guys don't think it was an accident, do you?'

'We don't know,' I said. 'We're just making inquiries.'

'As a matter of interest,' Robbie addressed Jimmy, 'what kind of car do you drive?'

'A three-year-old Nissan Sunny.'

'Colour?' I asked.

Jimmy looked agitated. 'Red.' He jumped up. 'You can't seriously think I would do anything, anything at all, to harm Dolores?'

'We're just making inquiries,' I repeated.

'I'm going,' he said. His face was tight with anger. 'You know where to find me.'

I swung my knees to one side to let him pass. The door banged behind him.

'Jimmy was keen on Dolores,' Amy said. 'He thought maybe they would get back together. He told me there was great chemistry between them on stage.'

'And was there?' I asked.

'Dolores was a good actress,' she said.

'But she was seeing somebody?' I suggested.

Amy tilted her head, considering her reply.

'There might have been someone,' she said slowly. 'A few months back, when she was playing Desdemona. I was Bianca. Dolores was all excited one night because she recognised someone in the audience. She wouldn't say who it was. Then, a few nights later, I saw her with a man in the York hotel. They were coming out of the bar as I was going in. She didn't introduce me. She was all edgy and excited. But that could have been because of the court case.'

'Court case?' Robbie and I said in unison, looking blankly at each other.

'Her car was stolen by a con man. She gave evidence against him. It was very dramatic, the way Dolores told it. He swore at her in court. Called her all the names of the day, she said.' She folded her arms. 'You didn't know?'

'We're only beginning our inquiries,' Robbie said.

'Well here,' Amy said. 'I'll tell you what Dolores told me.' She leaned forward and laid her hands flat on the table. 'Dolores decided to sell her car,' she began. 'She put a wee ad in the *Coleraine Chronicle*. This man rang up. A real charmer. All apologies. He'd written off his car. No way of getting over to Portstewart. Could she bring her car to his house?'

I watched her tell the story, animated, gesturing, adopting a man's voice. Robbie enjoying the performance.

Amy finished and sat back with a nod and a smile.

'Mickey Greer,' I said.

I completely forgot to ask for a description of the man she'd seen with Dolores in the York hotel.

Chapter 15

Roscoff was only a short walk from the theatre. It was the quiet period between the end of lunch and the beginning of dinner. A young barman with a deep tan and a blond ponytail was polishing glasses with neat, methodical movements.

'G' day, mate. We're closed.'

Robbie produced his ID and asked to look at Monday's lunch bookings. The barman whistled his surprise and produced a well-thumbed ledger from a shelf behind the bar. Robbie pointed to Jimmy Johnson's name. 'Know him?'

'He's a regular. Table for two.'

'Who was he with?'

'He was stood up,' the barman said cheerfully. 'Not a happy bunny.'

'Had he been here with a woman before?'

'I'd say.'

'Can you describe her?' I asked.

'The blonde or the brunette?'

'The brunette,' I said.

'Top sort. Curly hair. Looks a bit like you.'

Robbie produced a photograph of Dolores.

'That's the one.'

'What time did he leave on Monday?'

The barman put the ledger back on the shelf. 'Couldn't say, mate. I was busier than a brickie in Beirut.'

'Time paid might be on the receipt,' I said.

'You'll need to speak to the manager for that,' he said. 'I'll get him to give you a tinkle when he comes in.' He frowned. 'I remember one thing.'

Robbie had his hand on the door. He stopped.

'He had a gin and tonic when he came in, and a quick snifter at the bar before he left,' the barman said.

'Probably too pissed to drive anywhere,' Robbie said, as we dodged the traffic in Shaftesbury Square on our way to the car.

'Mickey Greer got out of prison three weeks ago,' I said. 'I called at his house on Monday night. His wife said she didn't know where he was. I believed her. She had a cut lip. I think he beats her up. I put a call out for the stolen car.'

'Probably being driven round Dublin with a respray and a false numberplate,' Robbie said. 'Put a call out for Mickey Greer as well. Tell the press office we want to talk to him about a suspicious death. We need to check he was the con man who stole Dolores's car and if he really threatened her in court.'

He settled himself behind the wheel. 'I hate trawling through records.' He drummed his fingers on the dashboard. 'It's going to take ages to get back in this traffic. There's a lot to do.'

'The traffic will clear soon. We'll be fine when we get on to the motorway.'

I wondered if the oil had been delivered. If there was anything to eat in the house apart from cornflakes and baby food. If I would be back in time to shop. I wondered what Joel meant by space. I thought of our angry exchange in the morning.

'You didn't order the oil.'

'I'm with a customer.'

'We have no heat and no hot water.'

'I'll get on to them now.'

'I've already done it.'

'Then why did you bother to call me?'

Because you're my husband. The father of my son. The man I promised to love and honour till death us do part. Because I want us to talk. I had put the phone down, even though I knew we would have to talk some time.

The street lights flared yellow against the darkening sky. I blinked.

'Attractive,' Robbie was saying.

'What?'

'She's attractive. Don't you think?'

'She had eyes for you, anyway,' I said.

'Do you think I could ask her out? It wouldn't be too soon after the death and all that?'

I thought Robbie was being overly sensitive. But actresses were volatile. 'Better to be on the safe side, Robbie. Wait a while. A few weeks, maybe.'

He turned the key in the ignition. 'George will be sorry he missed all these good-looking women.'

'George was going to work on this case?'

'He told Dick Jordan he was too tied up with this joint operation he's doing with Customs.'

I felt hurt. My lip trembled. 'I didn't know he'd been asked to take this case on.'

Robbie glanced at me. 'You all right, Claire?'

'Why do you ask?'

'You seem a bit preoccupied. What's bothering you?'

'We'd no oil for the central heating this morning. I'm just wondering if it's been delivered. We've no coal either. Joel forgot to order it.'

'That's very slack of him,' Robbie said. 'If I forgot something like that when I was living with Sally, she'd be off games for a week.' He spun the wheel. The car splashed through a puddle and joined the queue of traffic waiting to leave the city.

It was dark and raining when I got home. My left shoulder ached. I dreaded a confrontation with Joel. But there was no sign of the Alfa. Helen's Ford Escort was parked in the driveway. I found her sitting at the breakfast bar, reading the *Coleraine Chronicle*, a mug of tea at her elbow.

'Damn Joel.'

'He had to work late,' Helen said soothingly. 'It was no problem to bring Sam over and put him to bed.'

'I'm sorry, Helen.' I moved to feel the radiator under the window. It was warm. I sagged with relief. 'What would I do without you?'

'Do you want to talk?'

The car keys were still in my hand. I hesitated. 'Can you stay a bit longer? It's late night shopping. I want to pop over to Wellworths.'

'And?' Her gaze was direct, questioning.

'And I want to see if Joel is really staying with Gary. It won't take me long,' I pleaded.

Helen smiled and held up her mug. 'You're out of milk,' she said.

Hurrying to the car, I reflected how lucky I was to have Helen living near me. She was a constant in my life. Salvation Army officers stayed in each post for only one or two years. When I was growing up, we moved from Belfast to Manchester, then to Enniskillen, Coleraine, Glasgow and back to Belfast. But every summer we spent two weeks with Aunt Madge, Uncle Eric and Helen in Portstewart. And when Mum and Dad were asked to go to Glasgow and I was doing my O levels, I stayed with Madge and Eric and shared a bedroom with Helen. We tasted forbidden alcohol for the first time together at a barbecue on Portstewart strand.

I remembered being squashed against Helen in the back seat of a Mini, hurtling along the Strand Road to the sound of the radio blaring 'Don't Stand So Close to Me'. Pink, midsummer light rippled along the edge of the dunes and the waves boomed on the black sea. We went into the dunes with two boys. I was more apprehensive about tasting alcohol than I was about being kissed. Being more than kissed by the boy who pressed the can of Carlsberg into my hand. Tugged my other hand where I didn't want it to go. My fingers gripped the cool metal of the can. Lager foamed over my hand. I wanted to take my cue from Helen but I couldn't see the expression on her face.

'Helen?'

'Cheers.' She was nervous too. She tilted her head back to swallow. I did the same. The lager tasted yeasty and metallic. Is this what all the fuss is about? I thought to myself. I felt the same about subsequent thrustings and slobbery kisses in the dunes.

I didn't get what all the fuss was about until I met Joel. Now the thought of him with someone else choked me with sickness and anger.

I turned off the ring road into the supermarket car park, found the nearest space, and sat for a few moments, waiting for my heartburn to subside.

There was a tap on the driver's window. I turned to see George with a trolley full of groceries. I rolled the window down. His face looked sallow in the artificial light.

'Where's Maggie?' I said.

'I dropped her off at the gym. She's taken it up in a big way.' He hesitated. 'Have you much shopping to do?'

'Milk, bread, essentials,' I said. 'For one less person.' I couldn't keep the bitterness out of my voice.

'Have you time for a drink? I could put these things away and wait for you.' He nodded towards a red Toyota. 'I'm in Maggie's car.'

'Robbie told me you'd turned down the case we're working on.'

'Too busy,' George said. He looked uncomfortable.

'I'll pass on the drink, inspector.' I said. 'Good luck with your cigarette smugglers.'

George stretched out his hand as though to pat me on the shoulder, but I rolled up the window and busied myself with my handbag on the passenger's seat. When I looked around again, he had gone. I laid my head on the steering wheel and sobbed myself to a husk.

Joel's car was at the back of the block of flats where Gary lived. Blue light from the stairwell spilled through the rear window and washed over the pale grey leather seats. I could see his blazer hanging from the grab rail. I angled my head to scan the rows of bright-rimmed, curtained windows. No way of knowing which was Gary's flat. But at least I knew Joel's car was here. I circled the block. No sign of the silver Lancia.

* * *

Helen pushed a mug of tea towards me. 'Feeling better?'

'At least he's not with her.'

'Supposing he hadn't been there? What were you going to do?'

'I don't know. Find out where she lives. Slash his tyres. Slash her tyres. I feel so angry, Helen.'

'I know,' Helen said.

'No you don't.'

'Yes, I do,' Helen said. There was an odd note in her voice. I stared at her. The colour in her cheeks was heightened, but she held my gaze.

'When Malcolm came back from that conference in Wales last year I knew something had happened. I didn't know what. I just knew there was something. Someone. He was making excuses to leave the house. I knew he was going to the telephone kiosk at the bottom of the road.' She paused. 'He left me a letter on the kitchen table a week after he got back.'

I opened my mouth to speak.

Helen said quickly, 'I pretended I never saw it. I put a pile of newspapers on top of it. When Malcolm came in, I lifted the pile and put it in the bin. Malcolm said, "Did you see a letter on the table?" I said, "No. What letter? Was it important? I've just put a pile of papers in the bin. Will I look in the bin?" '

She stopped, put her hand to her throat and swallowed. 'Those were the longest three seconds of my life. Malcolm said, "No. It was just the new rota. I'll pick another one up in the office." '

'How did you know . . .'

'I just knew,' she said. 'I didn't tell you. I didn't tell anybody. I was too hurt and ashamed. I'm telling you now because I want you to know that I know how you feel.'

I reached across and squeezed her hand. 'I had no idea.'

'He stopped going out to the telephone kiosk. The phone rang a few times in the evenings after that. He just said, "Wrong number," and put the receiver down.' There was a grim triumph in her smile. 'I like to think there was some fucking bitch in Wales crying her eyes out.'

I had never heard Helen use language like that before. 'We've never talked about it,' she continued. 'Maybe we never will. But I know I saved my marriage when I threw that letter in the bin.' Now she looked defiant. 'Why would I throw away ten good years for one mistake?' She scooped up her handbag and got down from the stool.

I followed her to the front door, thanking her disjointedly, dazed by her disclosure. At the door, she turned and said in a fierce whisper, 'If you love him, fight for him. Don't make it easy for the bitch.'

As I lay in the spare room, waiting for sleep, her words rattled around my brain. I was shocked by their anger and their pain. After a restless hour, I switched on the bedside light and salvaged the cornet from under my lonely bed. When I put my lips to the muted mouthpiece, the first tune that came to mind was number 265 in the Salvation Army Tune Book. 'Tell me the Old, Old Story'.

Chapter 16

It took about ten minutes next morning for the Vehicle Licensing office in Coleraine to trace the name and address of the owner of K1 LUV. By half past eight, I had delivered Sam to Helen. 'Thanks for taking him early. There's something I want to do before I go to work.'

She was longing to ask questions, but Doreen, her mother-in-law, was crouching on the stairs, calling 'Cooee' and waggling her fingers through the banisters at Sam, who was running up and down the hallway like a tiny, drunken sailor, flapping his arms and giggling.

By half past nine, I was standing beside the silver Lancia parked outside Miss K Fashions in a narrow street off the Diamond. The plaster mannequin pouted behind the plate glass window and gestured languidly at me. She wore a bum-freezing green silk shift, slashed to the waist, and thigh-high black suede boots. A black quilted jacket, embroidered with gold dragons, was draped casually on the cream chaise longue behind her. A rope of pearls lay coiled at her feet.

I pushed open the heavy glass door and stepped into the

shop. A petite blonde was unpacking wool jumpers from a cardboard box on the glass counter and sliding them into the open drawers of the display cabinet that took up almost half the available space. A bell tinkled as the door swung closed behind me.

'Are you Miss K?'

She looked up with a toothy, lipsticked smile. 'K for Keeley. Daddy called the boutique after me. Can I help you?'

'Just looking,' I said, taking in the tight white angora jumper, the blonde ponytail.

'Special occasion?'

'In a manner of speaking,' I said. 'How much is the outfit in the window?'

She mentioned a figure a few hundred pounds more than my monthly salary. 'With your figure and colouring you'd look great in it. The green will bring out the colour of your eyes' – she smiled ingratiatingly – 'and the hint of copper in your hair.' She advanced from behind the counter and riffled through the dress rail that ran along the opposite wall. 'I think size twelve is about right for you.' She proffered a flash of emerald silk on a hanger and gestured towards the curtained alcove in the back wall. 'Try it on.'

'No thanks,' I said, looking straight into her baby blue eyes. 'It's more than a detective makes in a month. Only a thief could afford it. And it's a bit tarty for me. More your thing, I'd say.'

A look of alarm crossed her face. She backed into the rail, bunching the clothes, making the hangers swing and jangle against each other.

'I'm not going to let you wreck my life and my son's life,' I said. 'Get out of my marriage.'

She found her voice. 'Get out of my shop.'

'Don't worry. I'm going,' I said. 'The atmosphere in here is a bit rich.'

With a surge of excitement, I grasped the handle of the door and pulled it open. The door tinkled satisfyingly as I marched out into the street, my head held high, grief and anger temporarily assuaged.

'You look pleased with yourself,' Robbie said, surprise briefly replacing the bored expression on his face when I took the seat beside him in the incident room. He was tapping the desk impatiently with one hand. The other was holding the telephone to his ear. 'I've been waiting ten minutes for some time-server in records to confirm Mickey Greer stole the victim's car.'

'Rather you than me,' I said.

Chief Inspector Jordan bustled in and clapped his hands to gain our attention. 'OK, team. What's new? Robbie?'

'I've been asking around about any iffy connections she might have had,' Robbie said, telephone still clamped to the side of his head. 'She was at primary school with at least one known member of the IRA.'

'Like half of West Belfast,' I said.

Robbie winked at me. 'However, it seems she had no interest in politics. I asked a few people about the family pub. Mixed clientele. No obvious bad boys drinking there.'

Dick Jordan gave a brisk nod. 'OK. Fill us in on forensics and the final results of the post-mortem, Kenny.'

Kenny McKittrick held up a typewritten report. 'Multiple injuries as a result of a fall. No sign of struggle or previous injury. Not pregnant. Not drunk. No indication of anything that could have caused dizziness. Time of death, three forty-five Monday afternoon, give or take a few minutes. She had a prawn sandwich for lunch. And she hadn't had sex in the previous twenty-four hours.'

'Definitely suicide then,' said Robbie.

I groaned. Kenny grinned. Dick Jordan said, 'We'll discuss the possibility of suicide in a moment. What else, Kenny?'

'Lipstick on the cigarette butts matches the lipstick on her mouth and in her handbag,' Kenny said. 'Boot prints match RUC steel-tipped size eleven. Big feet.' James McAllister and Willie Campbell raised their hands, a mixture of pride and sheepishness on their faces.

'What about the other cigarette butts? The ones without lipstick?' I asked.

'Could be anybody's,' Kenny said.

'But it's the same brand. You didn't find matches or a lighter?'

He shook his head.

'The only pointers to suicide in a case like this are circumstantial,' Dick Jordan said. 'Like taking a taxi to the spot from a psychiatric hospital. A previous attempt. A visit to a GP about depression.'

'I checked with her doctor. She'd never been treated for depression,' I said.

'A suicide note. Leaving possessions on the cliff top.'

'There was no note at the scene,' I said.

'Notes can blow away. She could have left it somewhere else,' the chief inspector said. 'What did the family say?'

'Her sister and her friend say she wasn't depressed.' I paused. 'They think she'd been having an affair.'

'An unhappy affair?'

'Don't know, sir. They saw her with a tall, fair-haired man and put two and two together. That's all. The sister saw them in a red car.'

'This case is coming down with red cars,' said the chief inspector. 'That farmer mentioned two red cars. You took a few calls on the information line, Willie.'

Willie Campbell read from his notebook. 'Man walking greyhounds says two red cars passed him near the turn-off for Murlough Bay about a quarter past two on Monday afternoon. Near enough five minutes apart. Not sure about the make. Here's a thing.' He paused for effect. 'Two hours later, a fourteen-year-old boy getting off the school bus on the Torr Road saw a red car. Flew past him like the devil, he said. Going towards Cushendun. Male driver. Toyota Corolla. These young fellas know their cars.'

'Just as well,' I said.

'The school bus driver saw the car too. He wasn't sure of the make. Just the colour and the speed.'

It was the cue for me to bring up Mickey Greer. I recounted Amy's story, and added that the same scam had been pulled on a woman selling a red Toyota Corolla the weekend before Dolores died. A quiver of excitement ran around the room. Dick Jordan beamed. 'Well done, Claire.'

Robbie held the receiver up so we could all hear the faint, insistent ringing tone. 'Records. Not answering. We still haven't confirmed he stole the victim's car. Or threatened her,' he said.

'The husband would know if it was Mickey Greer in the court case. He might have kept a newspaper cutting,' I said.

'Fine,' said the chief inspector. 'Get on with it.'

Robbie's face brightened. He replaced the receiver and retrieved his jacket from the back of his chair. Within five minutes we were driving through the security gates.

'Thanks, Claire,' Robbie said as he steered up the steep, curling hill. 'The phone was doing my head in. Did you know the first ever phone call was made from Rathlin Island to Ballycastle?'

'I learned that at school, Robbie. We did a school trip here to see Marconi's cottage.'

In the side mirror I could see the outline of Fair Head, butting into the sea like the prow of a giant ship. It sank out of sight as we sailed over the hill to meet a grey curtain of rain sweeping across the Antrim plateau from the west.

'Dick Jordan's dead chuffed you put two and two together and got Mickey Greer,' Robbie said.

'Why would a petty car thief risk being done for murder?' I said.

'You still think the husband's a possibility?'

'Drives a red Toyota, smokes, is having an affair.'

'Jeez, Claire, that's half the men in Northern Ireland.' Robbie slowed at a crossroads, waited for a yellow oil tanker approaching from the right. 'Just because—' The rest of his sentence was lost as the tanker roared past through a deep puddle. A wave of filthy water engulfed the car. Muddy rivulets trickled down the windscreen, to be slapped aside by the wipers.

'Because what?'

Robbie raised two fingers to the vanishing yellow hulk.

'Because you have a low opinion of men,' he said. 'What a gobshite.'

'Yes,' I said, watching brown water gather in the corners of the windscreen, 'but not worth getting bothered about.'

Robbie glanced quickly at me, an odd expression on his face. I leaned back against the headrest, closed my eyes, and pretended to sleep. I didn't want a conversation about my low opinion of men. I wanted to savour my earlier moment of triumph and the sweet and sour taste of revenge.

Chapter 17

It had stopped raining by the time we squelched to a stop outside the house on Strand Road. The curtains were drawn. There was no car in the driveway. Larry Lyons was planting bulbs along the top terrace of his garden. He stood up as we climbed the steps and drew level with him.

'You're out of luck again. If luck's the right word.' He lowered his voice. 'Terrible business. Poor Dolores.'

The lawn sparkled with raindrops. Felix truffled in the moist brown earth turned over by the trowel. I tried not to think about graves.

A black-edged card was sellotaped to the glass door of the porch and a death notice, cut from a newspaper, was stapled to the card.

Rock: Dolores Margaret née Dargan. October 11th. As a result of an accident. Deeply regretted by her husband, John, mother Rita, sister Bernadette, and the wider family circle. Removal of the remains to St Patrick's, Ardglackin, at 7 p.m. Thursday 14th October. Interment following 10 a.m. mass Friday.

'You don't want to be buried where you don't know anybody,' said Larry. He stepped over the low dividing wall between the gardens, trowel in one green-gloved hand. 'They've only been living here a couple of years,' he confided. 'The wake's in Ardglackin. She's going to be buried with her relations.'

The phrase startled a memory; up and racing away like a hare. I am six, maybe seven years old. Hanging back from a convergence of neighbours at a country wedding. A man chortles, 'Would you like to be buried with my people? How's that for a proposal!' Indulgent laughter greets the familiar joke. I interrogate my parents when we get home.

'If somebody marries twice, like Mr Mullins, do both his wives get buried with him?'

'I suppose so,' says my surprised father.

'Which one is he married to in heaven?'

Dad hesitates.

'Can he have two wives in heaven?'

'These things don't matter in heaven,' Mum says briskly. 'We'll all be spirits.'

I am not satisfied with this answer. I have no concept of death and decomposition at that age. It matters who will share my grave.

'If I don't get married, can I be buried with you?'

The memory unsettled me and blasted a thought into my head. Did I want to be buried with Joel?

My heart lurched. The memory hare was off again, and bounding away. Mum's coffin is lowered on top of Dad's. I throw a handful of sandy soil. It lands on the coffin with a thud. I wonder if there is room in the grave for me. Mourners murmur condolences. Aunt Madge takes my elbow.

'When are you going back, Claire?'

'I'm not going back. I'm leaving university. I'm going to join the RUC.'

'If you want narcissi in the spring you have to plant in the autumn.'

I was jolted into the present by Larry Lyons.

'Narcissi make a great show. I usually do this garden as well,' he was saying. 'But I don't suppose he'll want me digging up the lawn at the moment. Poor Dolores. Her poor husband.'

Robbie nudged me towards the steps.

'I suppose poor isn't the right word,' Larry continued. 'He'll be a rich man now. But you know what I mean.'

We stopped. Turned.

'Rich?' Robbie beat me to the question.

'They had a first death insurance policy.'

On the other side of the wall, Felix barked excitedly and began scrabbling at the soil. 'He's found a bone,' Larry said fondly.

'First death?' I said.

'Joint life insurance payable on the first death.' Larry rattled it off like a mantra. 'Benefits of the policy are . . .'

Robbie interrupted him. 'How do you know this?'

'I have a wee part-time job as a financial adviser,' Larry said. 'I'll give you my card.'

'I meant how do you know they had one of those policies?'

'Sure didn't I sell it to them,' he said.

A car door banged. Larry had his head cocked to one side, a knowing grin on his face. Robbie and I were as still as statues. Robbie said, quietly, 'How much?'

Larry licked his lips. 'Two hundred and fifty thousand pounds.'

I watched Robbie calling Dick Jordan from a telephone box on the promenade, feeling both excited and detached. One half of my brain was processing what Larry Lyons had just told us, the other half was turning over the question: did I want to be buried with Joel?

I was only half aware of Robbie returning to the car. 'Chief says we'll ask him to make a formal statement after the funeral.' He settled himself into the seat. 'You're miles away.'

'Sorry.'

Robbie took a deep breath. 'He's an arsehole.'

'He's just being careful because of this diplomatic stuff.'

Robbie looked left and right before pulling away from the kerb. 'I meant Joel.' His eyes were fixed on the road. 'You didn't mean it when you said you weren't bothered, did you?'

I flushed with shock.

'I'm dead sorry, Claire. He doesn't deserve you.'

'Who told you?'

'The stupid fucker told me himself. I saw him in the golf club last night. He must be off his head.'

I couldn't stop myself. 'What did he say?'

'You and him had split up.'

'Did he say why?' The words seemed to come from someone else.

'No need. She was all over him like a rash.'

I rolled down the window. 'I need some air.'

Robbie said, 'You'll feel better when you've had something to be sick on. Let's get a bite of lunch.'

We sat side by side on a bench near the harbour, eating fish and chips. The sun sulked behind a bank of grey cloud. The fish tasted like sawdust. Robbie said, 'You kept it quiet, Claire. I didn't realise.'

'It was only three nights ago.'

He turned and stared at me. Puzzled.

My heart began to pound. 'What did Joel say, Robbie?'

Robbie said slowly, 'He said he left you a fortnight ago.'

Three soggy chips lay like fat white grubs on the vinegar-stained paper at my side. I wrapped the paper over them. My hands closed like fists round the greasy parcel. I stood up and flung it into the bin.

'I knew he played away,' Robbie said. 'I didn't think he'd be that stupid.'

I kept the tremor out of my voice. 'Does everybody know?'

'Naw, just a few of the lads at the golf club guessed. We saw her pick him up after a game. Surprised he could get his clubs into that boot.'

On the way back to Ballycastle, I asked Robbie to stop the car near a lane that wound into a forestry plantation. I managed to stumble a few yards into the forgiving darkness of the fir trees before vomiting.

When I got back into the car, Robbie said, 'I'm going to drive you home. No arguments.'

He drove slowly, taking the bends with obvious care, glancing at me from time to time. I lay back, my head turned to one side, like a baby in a pram, as the world slid past the window. When I inhaled, I could taste vomit at the back of my throat.

Robbie mused out loud. 'If she gives him an alibi he pockets two hundred and fifty grand. Or they both pocket it, if they plotted something together. Maybe they're not having an affair. Maybe it was an accident. Suicide even. Maybe she had terrible pre-menstrual tension. Sally used to go half crazy.'

A fluttering began in my ribcage, as though a trapped bird was trying to escape. I pulled myself upright in the seat.

'Are you all right, Claire?' Robbie said nervously.

'Just doing some arithmetic.' My heart was hammering.

'I'm working on the timing. He needed at least three hours to get to Fair Head, do the business, and get back.'

Seven weeks, I thought to myself. It can't be. I can't be. I gripped the dashboard.

'Hang on. You're nearly there,' Robbie said, turning into the avenue.

The trees reared above me. I stumbled through my thanks to Robbie. 'I just need to get into the house and lie down. I'll be fine.'

I closed the door on his anxious face and lurched into the kitchen. My skin felt clammy. As I fumbled for my diary in the kitchen drawer, a bolt of pain ripped through my body. The room swirled around me and went black.

Chapter 18

White ceiling, white walls. Alan McCrea's face looming over me. I thought I was dead and on the mortuary slab.

Alan must have seen the alarm in my eyes for he gave me a big smile. 'It's all right, Claire. You're in the land of the living. In a room in Coleraine hospital.'

My throat was raw, my body heavy as lead, my head full of cotton wool. I tried to moisten my lips with my tongue. It was an effort to speak. 'What happened?'

'The Fallopian tube ruptured,' Alan said. 'It was a close-run thing. Ectopic pregnancy. You didn't have any symptoms?'

'I was sick a lot. I thought it was stress.'

'You looked a bit queasy when I saw you on Tuesday night. I thought that was just being in the mortuary. It does that to some people.'

'I had a sore shoulder.'

'Referred pain,' Alan said. 'Classic symptom.'

I blinked. Now Helen's face was smiling at me. 'I popped in earlier but you were asleep.' She pulled her chair closer to the bed. 'You gave us an awful fright. It's a miracle you were found in time. If Joel hadn't called to pick up the post . . .' She shuddered. 'It doesn't bear thinking about.'

I closed my eyes. When I opened them again, a young woman with a narrow, concerned face was looking down at me. She was holding a clipboard.

'I'm Aileen McNulty. I operated on you. How are you feeling?'

'A bit woozy. Sore throat. Thirsty.' Weepy too, though I didn't say it.

'That's the anaesthetic. That will wear off.'

'They tell me I'm lucky to be alive,' I said hoarsely.

She pulled over a chair and sat down beside my bed. 'That's a good context for explaining what I had to do,' she said in careful tones. 'You were bleeding internally from the rupture of the Fallopian tube. I had to remove it. There's damage to the other tube as well.'

'What does that mean?' But I already knew.

'It means you have less chance of getting pregnant again.'

'How much less?'

'Hard to say.'

'How much less?' I repeated.

She looked down at the clipboard. 'You're twenty-eight. You have a good many fertile years ahead. There are many techniques now to assist pregnancy.'

'Please look at me,' I said.

Her brown eyes were full of sympathy. 'You have roughly a ten per cent chance of getting pregnant again.'

Joel came to see me, carrying Sam.

'Thank you for saving my life,' I said.

He held Sam out for me to kiss him.

'Put him beside me,' I said.

Sam put his thumb in his mouth and snuggled up to me. I

kissed the top of his head and felt like crying.

Joel retreated to a chair near the door. 'I thought you'd taken an overdose.' His voice was tight, his expression a mixture of anger and relief.

'I'm sorry you got a fright,' I said.

'You shouldn't have got pregnant.'

'I didn't intend to.'

'You were talking about it.'

'Talk's cheap.'

Joel shifted in the chair. 'I'm sorry about what's happened.'

'Which particular bit are you sorry about?'

He gazed at the grey sky through the window. 'I'm sorry you found out about Keeley the way you did. I'm sorry about your operation.'

I thought about my failed pregnancy, my failed marriage, my infertility. 'I'm glad about one thing,' I said.

Joel turned his head in surprise.

'You know the last thought in my mind when I keeled over? When the pain was so bad I thought I was dying?' Now I had his attention. 'I wondered if I wanted to be buried with you.'

When I left the hospital four days later, Helen announced, 'I'm staying with you till you're strong enough to lift Sam.' I didn't argue. I was glad of her company.

Joel came most evenings and helped me put Sam to bed. We handed each other bottles and nappies and talcum powder. We knelt beside the bath and took turns to pilot Sam's yellow rubber duck through the foamy bubbles. We didn't talk about our marriage or his affair until Sam was in his cot and Helen said, in a bright voice, 'I'll just pop out for half an hour and check everything's all right at home.' Then Joel and I would have low, angry conversations that went round in circles and ended when we heard Helen's car pull up outside.

I felt numb, most of the time. But sometimes, in the middle of the night, I would waken, taste salt on my lips, and realise I had been crying in my sleep.

Three days before I went back to work, Joel told me he had left Keeley's flat and was staying in a bed and breakfast in Portstewart. He looked and sounded miserable. The following evening, when Helen had made her usual tactful exit, he asked if he could move back home.

'I'll think about it,' I said.

The afternoon before I went back to work, Helen and I sat chatting in the kitchen.

'Are you going to take him back?'

'Probably. We have to talk about it. But we haven't had a sensible conversation since . . .' I took a deep breath, steadied my voice, 'since I caught them.' My breath escaped in a whoosh. It was a relief to say it out loud. I found myself adding, 'He looked ridiculous, standing there, buck naked, hiding his balls with a wastepaper basket.'

'Was he wearing his socks?' Helen said. There was just the glimmer of a smile on her lips.

I started to laugh; weakly at first, then hysterically, holding on to the breakfast counter, tears running down my cheeks.

Helen slid off her stool and came to put her arms round me. 'Remember that night in the dunes?'

'You said they looked stupid in their socks and no jeans.'

'We had to eat two packets of Polo mints to hide the smell of beer on our breath.'

'Mum and Dad knew anyway and said nothing.' I hugged Helen. 'Tell me it's going to be all right,' I said.

'It's going to be all right, Claire,' she said.

The next morning I carried the cornet down to the kitchen and played 'Morning has Broken'. It was eight o'clock. I decided the neighbours were awake, so I didn't deaden the sound with the mute. Sam sat in his high chair, beating time with a plastic spoon.

When I put down the cornet I picked up the telephone, called Joel and told him we had to go to counselling. He agreed. In the afternoon, I went back to work.

Not much had happened in the four weeks I had been away. There was still no trace of Mickey Greer. John Rock had come into Ballycastle police station two days after his wife's funeral. Robbie and Dick Jordan had interviewed him.

'Brought a solicitor. Described his relationship with Jacqueline Duchêne as a romantic friendship.' Robbie snorted. 'That's a new word for it. He said his wife had enjoyed a number of romantic friendships too. Otherwise no surprises. He said he hadn't been to Fair Head for months. Signed a statement about his movements on the day.' Robbie handed it to me. 'I thought he was lying.'

I cleared a space on the desk and sat down to read John Rock's statement.

Dolores had left the house on Strand Road, Portstewart, to drive to Belfast for a rehearsal on the Sunday afternoon. John Rock went to Jacqueline Duchêne's house in Cushendun. On Monday morning he went to a meeting in Jordanstown. Jacqueline Duchêne went to the consulate in Belfast. John Rock drove back to Cushendun, arriving about one o'clock.

'He says Jacqueline Duchêne got back about four o'clock,' I said.

'We don't have to take his word for it, Claire,' Robbie said. He had a big grin on his face. 'We got word from the Foreign Office last week. We can talk to her. Put your coat back on.'

Chapter 19

Jacqueline Duchêne's 'weekend cottage' was one of a scattering of houses on the hillside above a pale crescent of beach in the curve of Cushendun Bay. The lane leading to it ran steeply from the coast road and was hedged with ferns and fuchsia and brambles.

At the top, the lane widened into a sweep of concrete on which stood a two-storey, whitewashed farmhouse with a blue door, a roof of black slate and neat windows painted pillar-box red. An open shed, with a corrugated metal roof, leaned against the nearside gable wall and sheltered a turf stack.

We rattled over a cattle grid. Robbie gave a whistle of appreciation. 'You don't see many of those,' he said as we slid to a halt in front of a black car with a long bonnet, a fat chrome radiator, and a curved, chrome fender. 'What car did Inspector Maigret drive in the BBC television series of the same name?'

'Pass,' I said.

'A Citroën Traction. Must be forty years old. Still beautiful.'

The blue door opened, and Jacqueline Duchêne stepped out to greet us. 'I am returned just this minute,' she exclaimed. I looked at my watch. It was half past five.

She was wearing a pale pink tweed suit with navy braid and gold buttons. Her high heels raised her to my height. She looked me calmly in the eye as we shook hands.

'I come down here whenever I can. You can see why.' Her gesture encompassed the patchwork of neat, sheep-dotted fields rolling down to the shore, white ruffles on the wind-whipped sea, the squat black shape of a cargo boat like a cardboard cut-out on the horizon. High white clouds drifted overhead. The tang of peat smoke flavoured the air.

She ushered us into a small white-painted room at the front of the house.

'Please sit down. I'll fetch some tea.'

A turf fire burned in the hearth. A bentwood rocking chair, an armchair, a small sofa and a low, glass coffee table occupied the space between the fireplace and a desk in front of the window. A miniature cassette recorder sat on the coffee table.

Robbie peered at a stringed instrument, like a banjo with a long neck and a high bridge separating two sets of strings, mounted on the wall beside the fireplace. The gourd-shaped case was painted with straw huts and spotted leopards. I tried to imagine how it might sound.

A clink and tinkle announced the return of Jacqueline with a tea tray. 'That's a kora. It's from Senegal. My first diplomatic posting was to Dakar. Please sit down.' She lowered the tray on to the table and began pouring tea from a stout brown teapot into pale blue pottery mugs.

Robbie and I squashed into the creamy depths of the sofa.

'Please help yourself to milk and sugar.' She switched on the cassette recorder before easing herself gracefully into the armchair. 'You don't mind if I record our conversation?'

'We are not taking a formal statement,' Robbie said. 'We just want to ask a few questions.'

'Go ahead.' Her tone was composed.

Robbie cleared his throat. 'How long have you known Dr Rock?'

'About six months, I suppose. I came to a lecture he gave about post-colonial identity problems. He mentioned a field study he'd done in Senegal. We discovered a common interest.'

'Did you know Mrs Rock?'

A shadow passed over her face. 'What a terrible thing to happen!' She shivered. 'I can't believe it.' She reached for her mug of tea.

'You knew her?' I asked.

'We met once or twice.'

'Once or twice?'

'She came to a reception at the consulate. I went to a reception at the theatre.'

'But she didn't come here?'

'She was invited.'

'But she didn't come?'

'She was rehearsing.'

'How often did Dr Rock visit?'

She shifted in irritation. 'Are these questions relevant?'

'Dr Rock said you got back from Belfast about four o'clock on the day his wife died,' Robbie said. 'Can you verify that?'

'I had a business lunch in Belfast at one o'clock.' She spoke slowly, gazing into the middle distance, as though trying her best to remember. 'At Roscoff. That finished about two o'clock, I suppose. I stopped at the consulate to pick up some documents. It's en route. On the Antrim Road. It takes about twenty minutes to get there from the restaurant. It usually takes me about an hour and a half from the consulate to here.'

I did the sums in my head. Robbie continued his questions.

'How long did you spend in the office?'

An apologetic smile. 'I really don't remember. It is hard to estimate. Perhaps ten or fifteen minutes?'

'Was there anyone else in the office?'

She shook her head.

'Did you notice the time you left Belfast?'

'I don't watch the clock when I finish work,' she said with a light smile, 'but it must have been before three o'clock.'

'Dr Rock got back to Cushendun about one o'clock. He could have gone out again for a drive,' Robbie said.

'Oh no,' she said, with a little laugh. 'I don't think so. He prefers to drive my car.'

'More fun,' Robbie said drily. 'You don't see too many cars like yours.'

'My father worked for Citroën,' she said. 'That was his favourite car.' She paused. Her eyes looked misty for a moment. 'I told John I would be back in time to go for a drive before dark.'

'So did you go for a drive?' I asked, already knowing how long it would have taken the black beast lurking at the side of the house to roar up the glen to the main Ballymoney to Ballycastle road.

'We went for a short drive,' she said.

'Did you leave straight away? As soon as you got back from Belfast, I mean?'

I sensed Robbie looking sideways at me, wondering where this was leading.

'I am not sure,' she said.

'Do you change when you get back from work?'

She looked affronted. 'Why do you ask me?'

'It would help us to fix the time,' I said.

She thought for a moment. 'I think we went out immediately.'

'This was between four and four thirty?'

'Yes.' She was more definite now.

Robbie drank his tea in two swallows. He began to extricate himself from the sofa. 'That seems clear enough,' he announced as he got to his feet. 'Just one more thing.' He paused. 'Were you having an affair with Dr Rock?'

Her face tightened. 'We are just good friends,' she said. She switched off the cassette recorder and stood up in a way that made it clear our interview was at an end. We followed her to the front door.

'We are going to close the consulate in Northern Ireland. It is more peaceful. There is not so much work for me. Fortunately for you. Unfortunately for me.' Her smile of regret seemed genuine. 'I am going home to the mountains, but I will miss the sea.'

'Where's home?' Robbie asked.

'Chamonix. In the Alps.'

'Where did you go in the car that evening?' I asked in a casual tone as we shook hands.

She was relaxed now. 'My favourite drive. Up Glendun and down Glenshesk to Ballycastle. Back here across the mountain.'

'Uneventful?'

She thought for a moment before frowning. 'No. Some stupid woman got out of a car right in front of us.' She flashed her hand across her face. 'Whoof. We missed her by a millimetre.' She shivered. 'In fact,' she said slowly, 'John was so upset, we came straight back here.' She looked stricken for a moment. 'All that time poor Dolores was lying dead, and he didn't know. He should have been upset for her,' she cried. 'Not for some silly woman who didn't pay attention.'

Chapter 20

Robbie nearly drove into the ditch at the side of the lane when I confessed I was the silly woman who hadn't paid attention. 'Holy shit, Claire! Why didn't you tell me?'

'I only realised it was them when I saw the car outside the house. Her pink suit.'

'You could have been killed.'

'I know. And it would have been my fault. I wasn't looking.'

Robbie stopped the Mondeo at the bottom of the lane. 'That confirms his alibi.'

'No it doesn't,' I said. 'It was after six o'clock when I saw them. It can't take more than thirty minutes to drive from here to there. If they left as soon as she got back, she's wrong about the time. It must have been nearer five thirty.'

'They might have stopped somewhere.'

'It doesn't take long to look at the view.'

'Have you never had a quickie in the car, Claire?'

I flushed, but held my ground. 'Not in a Chanel suit. And they were going to be in the house all evening.'

Robbie edged the car out on to the road. 'Let's see how long it would take him to get to the car park in Murlough Bay and back.'

'He was only driving a Toyota, Robbie.'

'A two litre Toyota. Fasten your seat belt. It's going to be a bumpy ride.'

The coast road north from Cushendun rises and plunges as it follows the shore. I had an impression of hedges, gates and fences flying past, white faces staring at us as we overtook a bus, the electric glow of sheep in the dusk, and the dark blue blur of the sea.

'Twenty-two minutes,' Robbie said, as we half skidded to a stop in the car park above Murlough Bay. 'Call it twenty-five. Fifty minutes here and back.'

'Add forty-five minutes from here to the cliffs,' I said. 'Plus enough time to smoke a cigarette.'

'He might have gone down to check she was dead. Whether he pushed her or not,' Robbie said. 'Twenty minutes down the path, according to Kenny. Thirty coming back up.'

'If he went down, he would have come along the shore and back up the road to here,' I said.

We retraced the route I had driven with James McAllister, dropping down to near sea level, bumping along the grassy track above the shore, headlights raking through the rubble of rocks below the cliffs.

'Half a mile from the car park,' Robbie said, as we lurched to a stop. 'Walking or running it would still take at least twenty-five minutes.'

We did our separate sums in silence. The headlights swung out over the black water as Robbie reversed the car and pointed us back up the track towards the road. 'If you're right, and she didn't get back until after five o'clock . . .'

'He could have done it,' I said.

Our elation lasted until the following morning.

Chief Inspector Jordan pushed the buff folder back across the desk towards us. 'There isn't enough to go on. A couple of sightings of a red car, a few cigarette butts, a disputed alibi.'

'A big fat insurance policy,' Robbie said.

'We need evidence that'll stand up in court. Red Toyota? Sure half the country drives a red Toyota.'

'Somebody was out on the cliffs with her,' I said stubbornly.

'It could have been Mickey Greer. We've no way of knowing.'

'Can we get DNA from the cigarette butts?'

'Not a chance. You're clutching at straws, Claire.'

'The technique's improving all the time, Kenny says.'

'Well it's not improved enough for a prosecution,' said Dick Jordan. 'This business with the alibi won't stand up.' He pulled the folder back towards him and leafed through it until he found my statement. 'Why did you get out of your car without looking?' Before I could find an answer he barked, 'Your mind was on something else, wasn't it? If you weren't paying attention, how do you know it was after six o'clock?'

'Because I'd just come from the showroom and it closes at six thirty.'

'So it was closed?'

'No.'

'So how do you know it was after six o'clock?'

'I think I looked at my watch.'

'You think?' He glared at me, exasperated. 'Why did you go to the showroom?'

'To speak to my husband.' I tried not to sound agitated.

'Joel Watson?'

I swallowed, 'Yes.'

'Joel Watson who's bonking the owner of a dress shop in Coleraine?'

My face blazed. I felt as though he'd slapped me. I looked accusingly at Robbie, who shook his head and mouthed, 'Not me.'

'Common knowledge,' said Dick Jordan. 'It's all over Coleraine.' He slumped back in his seat and sighed. 'I'm sorry, Claire. The defence would make mincemeat of you.'

I was mincemeat already.

He stood up, walked round the desk and patted me awkwardly on the shoulder. 'Good try.'

'What next, sir?' Robbie said.

'Keep looking for Mickey Greer. We've no case until we rule him in or out. The defence would make a big thing of that too. Put out an official statement. We're still looking for him, blah, blah. But unofficially, I'm winding up this investigation.'

The hissing of the gas lamp suddenly seemed louder. I realised the thump thump of the disco had stopped.

'Case closed,' I said to Isabel. 'I should say, case shelved. No investigation is ever completely closed. There's always the possibility that something new will turn up later. But that's not likely in this case.'

I imagined the file, in a box somewhere, gathering dust. 'It was my first and last murder investigation,' I said.

'But you don't know it was murder.'

'A twenty-eight-year-old woman, found at the bottom of a cliff. No reason to kill herself. Life insured for quarter of a million pounds. What would you think?'

'I'd think it was suspicious,' Isabel conceded.

'I had a gut feeling about it.'

'Gut feelings aren't reliable. They're caused by all kinds of things. The week you caught Joel with Keeley?' she prompted.

'I know what you're going to say,' I cried. 'You think I was identifying this man with Joel. Identifying myself with Dolores.'

'Maybe.'

'Robbie had a gut feeling too.'

'His gut feelings are no more reliable than yours. I've read some studies. They show people who rely on intuition aren't good at detecting lies.'

I sighed. 'So how can you tell when someone is lying to you?'

'Body language. People who lie often won't make eye contact, or they'll look away. But liars know this. So sometimes they'll hold eye contact for a bit too long,' Isabel said. 'Liars are vague about detail. But some liars will pile on the detail because they know this too.'

'Not much help,' I said.

'And they need good memories. To remember all the wee details.' She looked at her watch. 'I'm away to my bed,' she said. 'But I've been thinking. There must have been an inquest.'

'Nearly a year later. I'd moved to England by then. Robbie presented the evidence. The jury returned an open verdict. The coroner criticised our failure to find Mickey Greer. End of story.'

'Not quite,' said Isabel.

Chapter 21

I sat for a while, remembering how a chapter in my life had closed with the investigation.

I had gone back to the CID office in Ballymoney, to a backlog of break-ins and car theft. From time to time, I checked with Mickey Greer's wife in case he had come back home, or had been in contact. The answer was always no.

Helen held my hand when she told me she was definitely pregnant. She looked uncomfortable.

'Don't feel guilty,' I said. 'I'm happy for you. It wasn't the right time for me.'

Once a week, Joel and I went to counselling. We were living apart, but at least we were talking to each other. When I was on late duty, Joel picked up Sam from Helen's house and put him to bed, as usual. Sometimes he would take him for a walk while I went shopping, or did the housework. I knew I should give him a second chance. It was the right thing to do. I just didn't want to make it easy for him.

I bought a book on cornet and trumpet technique. On dry Sunday afternoons, I put Sam's buggy and my cornet in the car and drove to the strand in Portstewart. I pushed the buggy for over a mile along the hardened sand, near the sea's edge, till I reached the spit of black rocks at the far end. There was never anybody there. I liked to imagine that the notes I played followed the course of the river Bann, swirled into the sea and floated up into the air and out over the waves. I summoned up all my muddled thoughts, and sent them skywards in a stream of silver notes. What came back was a kind of clarity and ease. In this way, I suppose I satisfied the vague spiritual longings that had replaced my faith in God, and Joel.

I still went to Sunday worship sometimes. I liked the feeling that all over the world, communities of decent people were gathering to do pretty much the same thing at the same time. Trying to be good in the world. I liked the consoling sense that whatever and however the world is, we're all in it together. I think 'Do as you would be done by' makes a lot of sense.

George telephoned me from Glasgow a day or two after I went back to work. He had been seconded to a special unit working with Customs on the cigarette smuggling.

'It's a big racket,' he said. 'The IRA makes a lot of money out of it.' Pause. 'I heard you'd been in hospital. I'm sorry. I didn't know. I was getting ready to come over here. If I'd known, I would have come to see you. At least sent a card. I'll be here for ages. I'll come and see you first thing when I get back.'

In the final of *Professional Challenge*, Belfast Education and Library Board beat the RUC team, captained by Robbie. He was disappointed but not despondent. 'We only lost by a point. We'll win the next time.' He got a transfer from Ballymoney to Belfast CID. The office didn't seem as bright without him.

At the beginning of December, Joel told me he had been offered a job in England. 'United Kingdom Head of Sales.'

He finished buttoning Sam's coat and stood up. 'What do you think?'

'Why are you asking me?'

'Because of Sam.'

'Is whatsername going with you?' I still couldn't use her name.

He didn't correct me this time. 'That's over.' He paused. 'Is it too late for us?'

I didn't say anything.

'I'm sorry, Claire.'

I wanted him to grovel, to beg forgiveness.

'I've hurt you.' There were tears in his eyes. 'Please. I'm begging you. Forgive me.'

'Where's the job?'

'Between Slough and Heathrow. I could come back most weekends.'

'Expensive,' I said.

'Worth it.' He scooped Sam up into his arms.

I stood at the gate, watching the bobble on Sam's woolly red hat dwindle to a dot as the car reached the end of the avenue. As it turned on to the main road, I gave a tentative wave, and got a definite wave from Joel in reply.

The following day I applied for a job with Thames Valley Police.

'Sam needs you,' I said to Joel when I told him.

'But you don't? Is that what you're saying?'

'I'm saying I'll try to make it work. You have to do the same.'

'I promise.'

'There are no third chances,' I said.

George telephoned, as he had promised. 'I'm back. I have a week's leave.' His tone altered. He sounded hesitant. 'Are you free for a bite at lunchtime? There's something I want to tell you.'

'I have to check a break-in near the Causeway,' I said. 'I could meet you at the Visitor Centre. They do a great bowl of soup in the coffee shop. One o'clock?'

'I'll treat you,' he said.

I was sitting at a table near the window watching a grey mist roll over the grey sea when George arrived, carrying a bunch of brilliant yellow chrysanthemums.

'You should have had these in hospital,' he said, handing them to me. 'Better late than never.'

I smiled up at him. 'Thank you, George.' They had a green, earthy smell. The stiff cellophane wrapping crackled as I set the bouquet on the seat beside me. 'I have something to tell you too.'

He pulled a chair out to sit down opposite me and began taking off his raincoat.

'Joel's going to England. He's got a job near Heathrow.'

'Oh?' His face was bright with interest.

'I'm going as well, George. I've put in for a job with the Thames Valley Police.'

The sleeve of his jacket seemed to have got caught up in the raincoat.

'We're going to try and make a go of it. For Sam's sake,' I said, watching George fight the raincoat for a few moments before wrenching his cuff free.

'Damned coat.' He gave himself a shake and sat down. 'Sorry, Claire.' He took a deep breath. 'When did you decide this?'

'A couple of days ago. Do you think I'm doing the right thing?'

'Do you think it's the right thing?' he said.

'Yes,' I said.

'I'm sorry to lose you,' he said.

'I haven't been on your team for a while,' I said, trying not to sound miffed. It wasn't the right moment to ask why he'd turned down the Dolores Rock investigation. 'I shouldn't have gone first with my news,' I added in a cheerful voice. 'What's your news? Good, I hope?'

'It's my birthday. I'm thirty-nine today.' His tone was embarrassed and offhand.

On an impulse, I plucked a chrysanthemum from the bouquet and presented it to him. 'Happy birthday, George.'

He snapped the stem and carefully threaded it through the buttonhole of his tweed jacket. 'There.' He looked up with a smile.

As we ate our soup and wheaten bread, he told me he had been offered a new job liaising with Customs. 'A lot of travel and surveillance. A lot of waiting for something to happen.' He gave a wry grimace. 'I'm used to that.'

It was raining determinedly as we made our way out. We ran, heads down, hopping over puddles to reach my car. I had both arms wrapped round my bouquet. Rain was running down my face. Before I could offer George my hand, he leaned across and kissed my wet cheek.

'Keep in touch, wee girl,' he said.

I watched him stride away from me across the car park. My best friend in the force. He didn't look back.

Some people stand out like islands in the ocean of our memory. We don't visit them, but we know they are there. Solid, enduring features of our world. We hear about them from visitors to their shores. A postcard arrives, like a message in a bottle. We realise we haven't seen them, spoken to them, for months, years even. We know when we meet again, with cries of surprise and apology, that we will fall easily into our old intimacy, just as Isabel and I did when we met again in Reading.

So it was with George and Robbie when I left Northern Ireland. We exchanged nuggets of information. Short sentences on Christmas cards and summer holiday postcards that got more and more infrequent.

Happy Christmas from George, Maggie and Judith. PS Hope you are well and happy in new house and job. George xxx

Heard your good news, Robbie. Congratulations, Inspector Dunbar! Claire xxx

Escaping Belfast winter. Hello from Florida. Best, Robbie.

Greetings from Palafrugell! Belated congrats to Maggie. Heard she finished fifth in Belfast marathon. Have new job – legal executive! Claire xxx

When Robbie got email, he hit the forward button from time to time and copied me in on announcements: *The Chief Constable today congratulated the winning RUC team in Professional Challenge . . .* and the kind of jokes that circulate in cyberspace: *Knock, knock. Who's there? The RUC. RUC who? We ask the questions round here! Ha ha. Don't you miss it? Best wishes, Robbie.*

Heard it on the grapevine. Congratulations, Chief Inspector McCracken! Claire xxx

Happy Christmas. All the best for the 21st century! George xxx PS Heard Robbie Dunbar got engaged. Nabbed at last!

I intended to get an address for Robbie, to send him my congratulations, but my mind was on other things. Principally on a lipstick I had found in Joel's car. When he told me he was in love with someone else, I wasn't surprised. He had become preoccupied with his health and appearance. He went to the gym at least three times a week. He carried his mobile into the bathroom with him.

We had tried to make our marriage work, but something inside me had given up. Deep down I had known for a long time that

I didn't want to be buried with Joel. The divorce went through in six months.

When I became a solicitor, George sent a card – *Bumped into Helen. Heard your news. Gamekeeper turned poacher! Congratulations. George xxx* – I realised I hadn't seen him for ten years. It felt like ten months.

'Why does time go faster as we grow older?' I asked Isabel as we walked along the Thames on a June evening, about a month before our holiday. She's good at that kind of abstract question.

'Time is relative to how long you've lived. When Sam was one, for example, his second year was half his life. Now he's twelve. A month is like a year. Especially if he's waiting for something.'

'Our camping holiday. He keeps talking about it.'

'When you're nearly forty, like us . . .'

'A year is like a month,' I said gloomily.

'Gather ye rosebuds while ye may . . .' Isabel said.

Chapter 22

The month flew by. The week before we left, Helen telephoned. 'David can't wait to get away. The twins are giving him a hard time. They're in a very girly phase. Teasing him. Or making him introduce them to some boy or other. Were we like that when we were ten?'

'I don't think we'd discovered boys when we were ten.'

'The twins certainly have,' Helen said with a laugh. 'Make sure David wears plenty of sun cream. They tease him about his freckles as well.'

She was about to ring off when she said, 'I nearly forgot. When did you last hear from George McCracken?'

'He sent me a card when I qualified at the end of last year. Why do you ask?'

'I've got a bit of news for you.' She paused for effect. 'His wife has left him for a physiotherapist.' Pause. 'A woman.' A noise somewhere between a gasp and a giggle. 'The wife of a Methodist minister.'

'Are you sure?'

'Front page in the *Newsletter*. They met at a PCUP meeting.'

'A pick-up meeting?' I couldn't believe my ears.

'No. PCUP.' Helen spelled out the letters. Protestants and Catholics for Understanding and Peace. It's a women's peace group. Have you access to the Internet? You can read the story online.'

I went straight to my computer, found *www.newsletter.co.uk* and scrolled down the headlines.

Durkan hits out at DUP.

More hotel rooms needed says Tourism chief.

Attack not linked to loyalist feud.

Minister lied about lesbian love affair.

I clicked the mouse.

Methodist minister the Reverend Bill Steele yesterday admitted he lied about his wife and her lesbian lover.

The minister pretended his wife, 45-year-old Heather Steele, was in London nursing a sick relative. In reality, she had run off with 43-year-old Maggie McCracken, wife of a chief inspector in the Police Service of Northern Ireland.

'I wanted to protect them,' Mr Steele told a special meeting in the Methodist church hall at Kilcrum, County Antrim.

Chief Inspector McCracken is a senior member of the Serious and Organised Crime Squad. Last month he led a team of PSNI and Lancashire police, and Customs officers, in a raid on Liverpool docks that uncovered ten million pounds' worth of cocaine bound for Dublin and Belfast. Last night he was unavailable for comment.

The couple's 20-year-old daughter, Judith, is a ballerina at the Royal Ballet School in London. Mr Steele and his wife have no children.

Some telephone numbers are engraved in my memory. The Police Headquarters switchboard in Northern Ireland is one of them. It was seven o'clock. I thought George might still be in his office. I held my breath as the operator dialled his extension.

'George McCracken.'

I let my breath out. 'It's Claire.'

There was a pause. 'It's an ill wind,' George said softly. 'All my old friends are getting in touch.'

'I'm sorry it's been so long.'

'I'm sorry too.'

'How's serious and organised crime?'

'Organised and serious. How's soliciting?'

'The hours are better,' I said. 'Otherwise it's not that different. I still see people when they're in trouble. Petty criminals, mostly pathetic. Personal injury claims. The usual sad wrangles over divorce.' I almost bit my tongue.

Even over the telephone George could read my mind. 'It's OK to say the word, Claire. How's Sam?'

'He was twelve in May. Twelve, going on forty. Thinks he knows the answer to the world's problems.' I laughed. 'He's great.'

'Joel?'

'I've no idea,' I said, surprised. 'Sam's old enough to take the bus. I don't see Joel. I gather he's on his third girlfriend. Sam likes her.'

'Whoa. Hold on.' He sounded flabbergasted. 'When did you and Joel split up?'

'Four years ago,' I said. 'A gym instructor. He asked for two other offences to be taken into consideration.'

'I'm sorry, Claire.'

'These things happen.'

'How are you? Is there somebody else?'

'I didn't ring up to talk about me.'

'Maybe you're living with somebody?'

'I'm living with a twelve-year-old,' I said. 'How's Judith taking all this?'

'She tells me she's fine.'

'What about you?'

'Strange to read about myself in the paper,' he said. 'Otherwise I'm fine too. So is Maggie. We just didn't want it to come out this way. Bloody journalists.'

I was horrified. 'Is that how you found out?'

'I've known for ages. So has Billy Steele. It was nobody's business but our own, until some nosy parker in his congregation blabbed to the press. Maggie and Heather have been living together in London for the last two years. Ever since Judith moved to the Royal Ballet School.'

'Two years,' I said faintly. 'You never said.'

'You never asked.' He was silent for a moment. 'It's been too long, Claire.'

'Ten years,' I said.

'Ten years and seven months.'

'There's a lot to catch up on.'

'You can read some of it in tomorrow's tabloids,' he said drily. 'They've picked it up. They're camped outside the house. The Chief Constable's told me to take a week off. Go somewhere till the fuss dies down.' He gave a great sigh. 'Trouble is, I'm in the middle of a court case. I won't get away until the end of next week.'

'Where are you going to go?'

'Dunno. Can't think.'

A thought came into my head. I heard myself saying, 'We're going on holiday to the south of France for two weeks, George.

Sam and David and me and my friend Isabel. Why don't you join us?'

A pause. 'I'll see if I can get a flight,' George said.

'A detective!' Sam said. 'Like Sherlock Holmes! Hercule Poirot!' He rolled his tongue around the consonants. 'Like you used to be, Mum.'

'I was only a detective constable,' I said. 'George is a chief inspector. Much more important.'

'He can stay in our tent,' Sam said.

'He's going to stay in a hotel. But he'll spend time with us.'

Isabel was intrigued. 'Of course I don't mind you asking him. It'll make a change to have a man around.' Her eyes narrowed. 'Is he good-looking? Are you interested?'

'Yes and no,' I said. 'He was a good friend to me.'

'There's always a buzz between friends of the opposite sex,' Isabel said, with a knowing smile. 'Like a computer program. It's not on the desktop but it's running in the background.'

'I thought George might suit you,' I said, in a casual tone.

Isabel raised an imaginary glass. 'Here's to an interesting holiday.'

I worked late that week to make sure all my files were up to date and urgent letters had been sent. I liked to leave everything tidy before I went on holiday. As always, new cases came in the day before I was due to leave. Enid, our receptionist, who'd been with the firm for thirty-five years and knew at least as much law as I did, took a telephone call as I was crossing the front office on my way out.

'You'd like this one, Claire,' she said. 'A real charmer. Not due in court until you get back.'

'What has he done?'

'Not done, he says, but they all do, don't they, dear? It's a twoc with a twist.'

Twoc is professional slang for taking and driving without consent. Most people call it car theft.

I hesitated. Although I was anxious to get home and pack, my curiosity was winning when the telephone rang again.

'It's Sam,' Enid said, with a grandmotherly smile. 'Wondering when you'll be home. I can tell from his voice he's all excited about going on holiday. The lamb.'

'Tell him I'm just leaving,' I said. 'I have to pack. Mr Twoc can wait until I get back from France.'

Chapter 23

The air was filled with the creak of cooling metal and the ripping sound of zips through canvas as the campsite settled down for the night. I turned out the gas lamp and made my way to bed.

'Goodnight, Claire,' Isabel called out. 'Sleep well!'

I thought how much I wanted Isabel to meet someone special. I corrected myself. Someone suitable. There was always a man hovering on the edges of her life. 'I like to have someone to dream about in boring meetings,' she would joke. But I sensed an underlying sadness.

Isabel attracted men with problems. Commitment problems. 'He says he's not ready for a long-term relationship.' Work problems. 'He can only see me midweek.' Wife problems. 'He's only living with her because they can't afford to sell the house.'

'Do you think you unconsciously go for unattainable men?' I asked her once.

'I'm the psychologist round here.'

'Then you should know the answer.'

She made a face.

'Is it because you're the one frightened of commitment?'

'No,' she said, with an unhappy smile. 'I'm the one frightened of failure.'

Which is why she had now fallen for an even more unattainable man, I thought.

She had spent a few days in Paris before flying down to Nice, arriving the day after Sam and David and I had settled into Les Arcs. As soon as I saw her wheeling her trolley towards me at Nice airport on Sunday night, I knew something had happened. She was bouncing with excitement.

'I'm in love,' she announced, throwing her arms round me.

'So who is it this time?'

'I'm serious, Claire. I've had one of those *Brief Encounter* moments. You know? When Trevor Howard takes the speck of soot out of Celia Johnson's eye? Only it wasn't a speck of dust, it was a mistake over my flight.'

Isabel is half Italian. She uses her hands a lot when she's talking. I took control of the trolley.

'I thought my flight was nine fifteen p.m., but it was nineteen fifteen. I was looking at the board and I couldn't see my number. I looked again at my ticket. I felt such a fool. I went to the check-in desk to see if I could still get on the flight. I was so distraught I couldn't think of the words in French and I couldn't get anything in the right order.'

As our car climbed away from the coast, and the lights of Nice dwindled to a faint glow in the rear mirror, she told me the rest of the story.

'He appeared out of nowhere. Said, "Can I help you, mademoiselle?" I told him about my mistake. He spoke to the man on the check-in desk. The check-in man said my flight was boarding. I'd never get to the gate in time. Then André, that's his name, said, "Phone the gate. I have a car." ' She paused for breath.

'He had a suitcase on wheels. He put my bag on top of it, and he picked up my big suitcase and said, "Follow me."

'We went through a door marked private and into a lift down to the outside. There was a car with two men in the front seat and he said, "Get in." '

'Isabel!' I was aghast.

'I know. I thought I was mad too. Whizzing along dark alleyways in the airport. Squashed into the back seat with this stranger. Knees touching.' She shivered with delight. 'He said not to worry, he was a detective. He showed me his pass.'

I laughed. 'What did he look like?'

'Intelligent. Fair hair. A tiny moustache. Not muscular but he lifted my suitcase like a feather.' Her voice was full of wonder. 'He had a video camera in his wee suitcase. He ran the pictures back for me. "That man in the leather jacket is a pickpocket. That woman in glasses steals passports."

'We got to another door marked private. He opened it. We were at the gate for my flight.' Her voice rose in amazement.

'Is he going to contact you? Did he ask for your telephone number?'

'It was all a bit of a rush. He gave me his card. He said I was to call him when I was next in Paris. He said, "I am sincere." Then he kissed me.' She sounded dazed.

'You can dream about him for the next two weeks,' I said lightly.

'Longer than that. I mean it. He was amazing.'

An electric rainbow glowed ahead in the darkness. I slowed down. 'The campsite is pretty quiet after ten o'clock,' I said. 'Completely quiet after eleven when the disco closes. Sweet dreams, Isabel.'

* * *

No sweet dreams for me. I couldn't sleep. I didn't want to blame my restlessness on the man who had nearly knocked me down the previous day. But as my mind manoeuvred to avoid him, darting into side alleys – what would we do tomorrow? Should I hire bicycles for the boys? Would they be safe on the road? – he loomed even larger. Was he involved with the angry blonde girl? I hoped not, for I was uncomfortably aware of a tremor in my bones that had been set in motion by simple physical attraction; had begun with a tingle that ran from my elbow to my spine when his hands had guided me to the car.

How long was it since I had felt the involuntary lift of the heart that came with the knowledge that a man had found me attractive? Too long, I reminded myself.

For a year after the divorce, I had felt as though I was swimming underwater. I moved smoothly, mechanically, but always with effort. I felt tired all the time. My colleagues in the police were sympathetic, but I knew my nickname in the squad was the Ice Maiden.

At home, I tried to be cheerful for Sam. I had agreed a routine with Joel. We wanted to make everything as normal for him as possible.

'It doesn't mean we don't love you,' I said to Sam. 'You are the centre of our universe still. We will always be your mum and dad.'

'But Dad doesn't love you any more. He says he loves somebody else.' Sam began to cry. I put my arms round him.

'That happens sometimes, Sam.'

'Can you make him come back?'

'No, Sam.'

I pulled him closer to me and stroked his hair. 'You know what I think, Sam? I think Nature puts people together, makes them attracted to each other, because she knows they'll make beautiful babies. Wonderful human beings. Like you. Nature doesn't worry about the other things. Like whether they're right for each other in different ways.'

'What kind of ways?' He was still suppressing sobs, but I could tell I had caught his interest.

'If they like the same things. If they look at the world in the same way. If they agree about most things.'

'And you don't agree with Dad?'

'We agree about one thing,' I said, 'that we have the best son in the world.'

Isabel had pulled me out of the water. One Saturday, when I turned down yet another invitation to go out, she arrived on my doorstep. When I opened the door, she said, 'Too pale, too sad.' She took me to London, supervised a new haircut, a new wardrobe. She took me to parties, babysat for me.

I began seeing Matthew, a solicitor I had met in the tea bar at the magistrates' court. He had just become a partner in his firm and asked me to a party to celebrate. It was full of his thirty-something married friends, all of whom seemed to have young children.

One couple, Ben and Gilly, invited Matthew and me and Sam to Sunday lunch a few times. They had a son the same age as Sam, with the same dark, curly hair and shy curiosity.

On the third occasion, when we walked to feed the ducks below the bridge over the Thames at Goring, Sam allowed Matthew to take his hand. I was walking behind them, with Gilly.

'We'd so like Matthew to find the right person and settle down,' she said, gripping my arm.

'Sam is beginning to accept him,' I said.

'Matthew is great with children,' Gilly said. She gave me a conspiratorial smile. 'He's told me he wants a big family.'

My stomach lurched.

'I need to tell you something,' I said to Matthew that night.

'You're pregnant.' He sounded almost excited. 'It's a bit soon. But I don't think I mind. Let's face it, you're not getting any younger.' I was thirty-five.

'I'm not pregnant and I'm not likely to become pregnant without IVF.' I told him about my ectopic pregnancy. What the consultant had said.

We met a few times after that, but our relationship petered out, as I knew it would.

Isabel introduced me to a chemistry teacher called Jamie. He had floppy dark hair, eyes like a spaniel, and a way of nuzzling into my neck that made my toes open and shut.

I invited him for dinner one wet Friday night. We drank a bottle of wine. He was leading me by the hand through the hallway when Sam appeared at the top of the stairs in his Batman pyjamas, clutching his red blanket.

'The caped crusader,' muttered Jamie.

'Sam, this is Jamie. He's going to stay in our house tonight,' I said.

'Why?'

Jamie disentangled his fingers from mine. 'I'll get a taxi.' He didn't ring my doorbell when he came to collect his car the next morning. He didn't ask me out again.

I concentrated on studying for my law exams. At least Matthew had pointed me in a new direction. I was grateful for that.

Now Sam was nearly a teenager, he had passed the stage of disliking on sight any man who showed an interest in me. Isabel said it was because he had discovered girls.

'I think he'd like me to meet a man again. Preferably one who'll take him to football matches,' I told her.

'It'll happen.'

'Pigs might fly.'

I turned the pillow over to find a cooler resting place for my cheek. Through the open window of my room, neat and narrow as a ship's cabin, I could see a twinkling of stars. An owl hooted wistfully. A bicycle ticked along the gravel track. I closed my eyes and began counting sheep that metamorphosed into flying pigs. When I opened my eyes, it was morning.

Chapter 24

After breakfast, Isabel wandered off, murmuring something about checking her email and practising her French in the shop.

I sat at the table outside writing postcards, pausing from time to time to summon pictures from ten years earlier. The office in the university. The man behind the desk who looked like Che Guevara. What made me think he was Rocky? The air of confidence, verging on swagger?

John was a common name. So was Rock. There must be hundreds of men called John Rock. Dozens with the nickname Rocky. He had remarked on David's accent. He knew I had lived in Northern Ireland. Yet he hadn't said he had lived there too.

Isabel flopped into the seat beside me and sat, chin on hands, gazing into the middle distance. 'The men over there,' she pointed her chin towards the mobile home at the end of the row opposite, 'have been fiddling with their bikes all morning.'

'It's a boy thing,' I said, following her gaze to where two balding men in shorts, bare backs glistening with oil and sweat, wrestled with a silver bicycle. One held the frame as the other tightened the seat with a spanner. 'They can't resist taking things apart and putting them together again.'

As though suddenly conscious of our interest, the man with the spanner swivelled his head in our direction. Even at a distance of some fifty yards, I felt his eyes flicker over us in assessment. He said something to his companion, who laughed. I looked away, uncomfortable.

'I don't fancy them either,' Isabel said. She stood up. 'We haven't explored Nice properly yet. Let's go.'

We parked in a multi-storey car park a few streets back from the sea and walked to the sea front.

'Where I grew up it was all grey,' Isabel said. 'I could get drunk on this much colour.' She flung out her arms to embrace the sweep of the Baie des Anges, the blue sky, the turquoise sea, the purple bougainvillaea and the palms that marched like giant pineapples down the Promenade des Anglais. Skateboarders and rollerbladers sailed past us on the pavement. Brown bodies lay packed like pencils in boxed-off squares of beach.

At the eastern end of the promenade, we strolled under an archway into the bustle and smell of the Cours Saleya. My senses could scarcely take it in. Rows of stalls piled with pink roses, red carnations, buckets of lavender, crocks of black olives, mountains of tomatoes, pyramids of peaches in the purple shadow of the awnings. Mingled smells of garlic, anchovies, tomatoes, lavender, cigarette smoke and sweat. We captured a table at one of the cafés surrounding the elongated square and ate chickpea pancakes and courgette flowers fried in batter. I had never eaten a flower before.

'It's hot, it's crowded, it's a tourist trap and I love it,' Isabel said happily. 'Now we've had our fun, let's do our homework.'

'Isabel,' I said, in a warning tone, 'I don't think we should look for this music bar.'

'Why not? He told us to drop in.'

'It's a bit . . .' I hesitated, 'obvious.'

'You fancy him,' she said.

'I don't.'

'Then why not drop in, as he said?'

'Do *you* fancy him, Isabel?'

'I'd like to know if he's a wife murderer,' she said.

'Suspected wife murderer.'

'So you *do* fancy him.' She flashed a wicked smile.

We turned into a narrow street of high houses and angular shadows and almost ran into him. He was walking, head down, jingling car keys in his hand. Before he could see us, I pulled Isabel into a shop doorway.

'Look!'

'Where?'

'There.' I pointed through the glass door at a row of pink canvas espadrilles. My heart was thumping and I felt foolish.

'Smart,' Isabel said. She stepped past me and peered into the street. 'He's gone. No excuse now for not dropping in.' She pointed to the black lettering on a yellow sign on the wall opposite. *'Doctor Rock. Bar Musique. 500m à gauche.'*

Doctor Rock occupied the ground floor of a tall building that seemed to lean towards the opposite side of the cobbled street. It was cool and dark and smelled of wine casks and cigarettes. A shaft of sunlight falling through the open doorway made a path across the stone floor to the wooden counter behind which a lanky young man was polishing glasses with a white cloth.

'Hi there. *Bonjour.*' American teeth. His smile was the brightest object in the bar.

'Hello,' Isabel said. 'Are you open?'

'Sure thing. What can I get you?'

We ordered a couple of beers and sat on high stools at the counter. 'Pretty quiet,' I said.

'We're a music bar. Mostly busy at night. We don't get much custom in the afternoons. Just people escaping the heat.' He set two foaming glasses on the bar. 'Enjoy.'

My eyes had grown accustomed to the gloom. Half a dozen round wooden tables and chairs sat between the counter and the door. To the right of the counter, an open space extended into the back. I could just make out the outline of an upright piano and a microphone on a small stage. Standing room for about fifty people, I calculated.

'We have music every night,' the barman said, 'except during the jazz festival. Most folk go up to Cimiez for the big concerts. Including the boss.'

'He's a musician?' Isabel sounded artless.

'More like a fan. Actually, he's a bit of an academic. The Doctor is for real. He has a PhD.'

'Is the Rock for real too?'

He laughed. 'Yeah. Dr John Rock. Neat, isn't it? Doctor Rock. Good name for a music bar.'

'I think we've met him,' Isabel exclaimed. 'Tall, good-looking guy, about forty?'

'Yep. That sounds like him all right.'

'What's he like to work for?'

I had to admire Isabel's effrontery.

'Rocky? Pretty easy-going, for a man who's had a tough time.' He poured himself a beer. 'Doesn't mind me having a beer if we're not too busy and there are a couple of attractive tourists to talk to.'

'Do we look like tourists?'

'I guess.'

Isabel was relentless. 'What kind of a tough time?'

The barman dropped his voice. 'He lost his wife. A terrible accident.' He mopped the counter gently with his cloth. 'I understand she fell about six hundred feet. Broke her neck.' He shuddered. 'Rocky never talks about it. I only know because an old friend from Chamonix called in.'

'Jacqueline.' I said the name automatically as the picture of a woman in a pink suit framed in the doorway of a farmhouse floated into my mind.

He was disconcerted. 'How did you know her name?'

'I think I met her as well,' I said, trying to hide my confusion.

'Small world.' He shook his head in wonder. 'Must be true what they say. Six degrees of separation.'

'What?'

'We're connected to everybody in the world through a chain of no more than six people. That's the theory.'

'I've played that game,' Isabel said. 'It's true. It works.'

I challenged her. 'Che Guevara?'

She laughed. 'Tricky. But I can do it. My cousin works for the *Glasgow Herald*. He knows the Prime Minister. The Prime Minister knows the Foreign Secretary. The Foreign Secretary knows Fidel Castro and Fidel Castro knew Che Guevara.'

A shadow blocked the path of sunlight. 'Uh uh,' the barman said. 'Gotta get something.' He was gone before I could blink.

'Duffy,' said a female voice behind us. 'Where is he? Duffy?'

I turned. The blonde girl we had seen at the villa was advancing on the bar. She ignored Isabel and me and addressed the empty space behind the counter. 'Rocky? Duffy?' Then she burst into tears and ran out.

The barman stood up, dusting the knees of his jeans,

looking shamefaced. 'Sorry about that. Maxine's a bit upset.'

'I take it you're Duffy,' Isabel said.

He put his hands up. 'That's me all right.'

'Who's Maxine?' I said.

He took a deep breath. 'She's a college student. Same as me. Rocky gave her a job. She . . .'

He was interrupted by a tinny blast of the Marseillaise. He pulled a mobile phone from his pocket, smiled ruefully, held the phone to his ear and sighed. 'Do you mind if I take this call?'

I could see from the resigned expression on his face that the conversation would take some time. I slid from the barstool and pointed to my watch. 'We should go, Isabel. The boys will want to be fed.' My curiosity would have to remain unsatisfied.

'Definitely the same man then?' Isabel said, as we made our way back to the car.

'Has to be.'

'I think he was living with Maxine and she threw him out,' Isabel said.

We walked in silence for a while.

'Sounds as if he's still seeing Jacqueline Duchêne as well,' I said, 'the diplomat he stayed with in Cushendun.'

'She's clearly just a friend. An occasional visitor. He's not married to her.'

A curious sensation swelled inside me. Relief, mixed with nervousness.

'Maxine wasn't wearing a ring. But he could be married to someone else, I suppose,' Isabel said.

'He doesn't behave like a married man.'

'A lot of them don't,' Isabel said. 'Remember those two men we met on the train to Glasgow? Three hours flirting outrageously and their wives waiting for them.' She paused for a moment. 'I hope my nice detective isn't married.'

We emerged from the shade and quiet of Old Nice into the heat and noise of the modern city. Cars and lorries, their windscreens winking in the sun, crawled along a wide boulevard. The air was thick with dust and exhaust fumes. As we threaded our way through the shoppers, looking for landmarks that would guide us to the car park, I was brought to a halt by the sound of a brass band, barely audible above the roar of the traffic. It seemed to be coming from a first floor window above my head. I looked up and saw the familiar crimson flag of The Salvation Army with its blue border and yellow star. Beneath swung the sign, *'L'Armée du Salut.'*

My reaction must have been written in my face for Isabel touched me lightly on the arm and said, 'You still think about them, don't you?'

'They ambush me sometimes,' I said. 'I used to think about them every minute, then every hour, then once a week, then once a month. After a time, you don't know when you last thought of them. Then something reminds you.'

I focused on the sound I had always associated with grey skies and light drizzle. The heat and the noise of the traffic seemed to subside. The melody grew bolder. I hummed along. The tune came to a climax in a clash of cymbals before ending in a majestic cadence.

'You're smiling,' Isabel said.

'That's because they're always with me,' I said. The traffic reasserted itself. 'It's a good feeling.' I linked arms with her.

'Don't worry about what to say to Rocky. He'll probably tell us about Dolores when we go for the drive tomorrow,' she said. 'Or we can ask him. Now that Duffy's told us.'

'We'd have to say we've been to Doctor Rock.'

'So?'

'I wouldn't like him to think we were interested in him.'

We arrived at the multi-storey car park.

'He strikes me as a man who assumes all women are interested in him,' Isabel said. Her voice echoed in the concrete space.

We stepped into the lift. I pressed the button. The doors closed. 'Well, he won't be making assumptions about me,' I said.

We found the boys lying outside their tent, elbows supporting their chins, heels in the air. David was playing a game on Sam's mobile phone. Sam was reading *The Complete Sherlock Holmes*.

'This is great, Mum. Listen. Dr Watson says to Holmes,' Sam affected a deep voice, ' "At each instance of your reasoning I am baffled, until you explain your process. And yet I believe that my eyes are as good as yours."

'And Holmes says,' Sam lightened his voice slightly, ' "You see but you do not observe. The distinction is clear. For example, you have frequently seen the steps which lead up from the hall to this room?"

' "Frequently," says Dr Watson.

' "How often?"

' "Well, some hundreds of times."

' "Then how many are there?"

' "How many? I don't know." Sherlock Holmes says, "Quite so! You have not observed. And yet you have seen. That is just my point. Now, I know that there are seventeen steps, because I have both seen and observed." Isn't that marvellous, Mum?'

'Marvellous,' I agreed.

'David and I are going to observe as much as we can.'

'You can start by observing how much help I need to get the supper ready,' I said.

Chapter 25

'Funny how we all fall into a routine.' Isabel dropped a bag of croissants and a baguette on the table the next morning. 'When I go for the bread and the paper in the morning, the men with the white van in the row behind us always pass me. They leave at the same time every morning and come back about twelve hours later.'

'Like Sven and Ingrid. They've gone to Monte Carlo today.' I poured the coffee.

Isabel settled down with *Nice Matin*. 'This is the routine I like.'

'Sam and David have it cracked,' I said. 'Get up late. Swim. Photograph cars. Eat. Go to the disco. Sleep. Get up late.'

Isabel lowered the newspaper. 'What did Cary Grant's character do in *To Catch a Thief*?

'Cat burglar.'

'I thought he was the good guy.'

'A reformed cat burglar. Somebody is copying his methods. Why do you ask?' I bit into the chewy softness of a baguette spread with apricot jam.

'There's a piece here about robberies along the coast. Made

me think about it. Five in the last month. The police can't work out how the thieves get in and out.' She muttered to herself as she translated and summarised the story for me. 'Roadblocks erected . . . dah di dah di dah . . . stopped and searched cars within ten kilometre radius . . . dah di dah di dah . . . number-plates of all cars entering and leaving area . . . di dah . . . That made me think about the movie.'

'The thief is a girl,' I said. 'She's in love with Cary Grant and jealous of Grace Kelly. Don't you remember?'

'All I remember is the scenery and that sports car and thinking I'd like to drive around the Riviera in one of those.'

'You've got your wish,' I said.

'He has a sort of feline grace,' she mused.

'Cary Grant? I know what you mean.'

'I meant Rocky,' she said. 'Maybe he's a cat burglar as well as a wife murderer.'

'Please don't joke about it, Isabel,' I cried.

She put down the newspaper. 'I'm sorry, Claire. I didn't mean to upset you.' She looked at me with concern. 'You seem pale. You're a bit on edge about all this, aren't you?'

'I feel uncomfortable not telling him I know who he is.'

'We're still not one hundred per cent sure. You didn't recognise him.'

'Dr Rock. Wife died in a fall. Friend called Jacqueline from Chamonix. It's him all right.'

She leaned across the table and patted my hand. 'You don't have to tell him. Not unless he pounces.'

I sighed. 'You're right.'

I wasn't sure what I wanted. That he never made a move, and I didn't have to tell him. Or that he pounced.

There was the additional complication of George. I was

looking forward to seeing him. Half of me wanted to confide in him. The other half was worried what he might say.

And so, later that morning, I didn't know if the knot in my stomach was caused by the twist and turn of my emotions, or by the bends on the Haute Corniche where the land plunged dizzily to the sea.

'Magnificent road, isn't it?' Rocky shouted. 'Built by two emperors. Augustus and Napoleon.'

I glanced at him, turning the wheel to take the curves on the narrow, shelf-like road, a smile at the corner of his mouth, as little murmurs of delight reached him from Isabel and the boys in the back seat.

Hotels and houses, all pink and white stucco, half-hidden in the cypress trees, tumbled towards the coast. Green headlands ran out into blue water. Furls of white sails drifted like feathers on the brilliant surface of the sea. Above Monte Carlo we stopped and looked down on the tower blocks of hotels and apartments rearing towards us. Although it seemed that every available inch of land was occupied, from time to time I would glimpse a narrow valley, thick with dense, green vegetation, and think I was seeing what the Romans saw two thousand years ago.

Above Cap Martin, we slipped into a winding descent towards sea level. Rocky swerved to overtake a swarm of cyclists and nosed the Mustang into the queue of cars crawling into Menton. 'Ready for a spot of lunch?'

He decanted us at a pavement café near the end of the promenade and pointed to an empty table under a pink-fringed parasol. 'You bag that. I'll park the car.'

We shared a platter of seafood, sucking the last sweet morsels from the shells, smacking our lips with delight. When the boys began flicking water from the finger bowls at each other, I chased them from the table, which was, of course, what they wanted. They made straight for the beach. I hoped there weren't too many bare-breasted women for them to goggle at.

'Now I get a chance to talk to you properly,' Rocky said. He hoisted the bottle of Bandol from the ice bucket. 'I can't believe two attractive women don't have a couple of men in tow.'

'We could say the same about you,' Isabel said.

He laughed. 'I wouldn't want a man in tow.'

'Have you a woman in tow?' she said.

His laughter died. The plates and glasses rattled as he set the bottle down. 'My wife died.'

I gulped. 'We know. We're so sorry.'

Surprise flickered in his eyes.

'Duffy told us,' Isabel said.

He took a moment to react. 'You've been to the bar?'

'Yesterday afternoon,' I said.

'I didn't think Duffy knew. It's not something I talk about.'

'He said a friend of yours from Chamonix had called into the bar and mentioned it.'

'Did he tell you what happened?'

'He said she died in a fall. Terrible for you,' Isabel said.

'Did he tell you the most terrible thing?' His mouth twisted. 'That I profited by her death?' He turned and signalled to the waiter. A nerve twitched in his cheek. So that's why he didn't mention Northern Ireland, I thought.

Rocky turned back, his throat constricted, a bleak expression on his face. 'She left me well off. I was able to move here. Become a lotus-eater. Enjoy the good life in the sun.' He retrieved his sunglasses from the pocket of his shirt and adjusted them on his face.

The sound of laughter from the next table filled the silence that fell on us. He had disarmed me.

'When my parents were killed,' I said slowly, 'I got everything. Insurance policies, and the house. But I would give everything I own to have them here again.'

I saw my face, all compassion, reflected in his sunglasses. 'When did they die?' he asked.

'Nearly twenty years ago,' I said, 'but sometimes it still feels like yesterday. They were hit by a car. Joyriders.'

'My parents' car was hit by a lorry!' he exclaimed. 'In Kenya.' He shook his head slowly. 'Just as long ago and just as near.'

We stared at each other for a moment. Rocky picked up the wine bottle. 'Enough sad talk,' he said, giving the bottle a professional swirl as he topped up our glasses. 'No more wine for me. I've got to drive you back safely.'

The waiter brought the bill. Rocky refused our attempts to pay our share. 'My treat.' He sat back and smiled again. 'Now you've seen the corniche, what's next on your list?'

'There's so much to do and see,' Isabel said.

He picked up his mobile phone. 'Can I give you a call? Try to arrange something?'

Isabel hadn't brought her mobile on holiday. I gave him my number.

'Great. What are you doing tomorrow?'

'We haven't decided,' I said. 'I think the boys have had enough art for their attention span this week. They'll probably want to stay around the campsite. Isabel and I might drive to the Château de Gourdon.' I looked to Isabel for confirmation.

'I'd like a day just lying around and reading my book,' she said.

'Would you like to go to Gourdon?' Rocky addressed me

directly. 'I could pick you up at the same time as today?'

The invitation wrong-footed me. 'I'm not sure. I need to sort out lunch for the boys. Check when George is arriving.'

'I thought you didn't have a man in tow.'

'He's just an old friend.' As soon as I had spoken, I felt uncomfortable, as though I had disparaged George in some way.

'I can look after the boys,' Isabel said.

'That's settled then,' Rocky said.

'No it's not,' I said. 'Thank you for the offer, but I'm going to stay by the pool and read my book as well.'

He was taken aback for a moment. Then he flashed a smile. 'I hope it's a satisfying read.'

On the drive back, Sam and David quizzed Rocky about French numberplates. They knew each administrative area, or départe-ment, had a two-digit number. They were aiming to spot all of them. From time to time they would call out to Rocky.

'What's 83?'

'Var.'

'What's 06?'

'Alpes-Maritimes.'

I had to admire his tolerance. When we got out of the car at the entrance to Les Arcs, I said, 'I hope you haven't been bothered.'

His breath was soft on my cheek as he leaned towards me. 'I love a challenge.'

He waved away our thanks. 'I'm in the bar most evenings. Drop in again.' He drove off in a swirl of dust.

Isabel nudged me. 'Game on,' she murmured.

The boys were still counting.

'I've written down twenty so far,' Sam said. 'David's got eighteen. We're going to do the whole campsite.'

'I hope you don't grow up to be trainspotters,' I called after them as they ran off.

'Don't worry, Mum,' Sam shouted over his shoulder. 'It's only a phase.'

Two girls, riding one bicycle, cycled languidly past us. They wore pink pedal-pushers and heart-shaped sunglasses, and looked about ten going on sixteen. One of them sat on the seat, pedalling forward. Her friend sat on the handlebars, facing her, legs rotating backwards. Their blonde hair flopped across their faces as they wheeled effortlessly round Sam and David and cycled back towards Isabel and me, chatting to each other, apparently oblivious of Sam and David, who had stopped to look at them.

'I don't think the phase will last long,' Isabel said.

We sauntered back to the caravan. The smell of grilled sardines wafted past our noses. Here and there a cork popped. I was thinking about merguez sausages and mustard and crusty white bread when my eye was caught by a trampled-over sheet of white paper lying at the edge of the path. I stooped to pick it up.

'Looks like a timetable.' I handed the paper to Isabel.

'Local cycling clubs,' she said, after a quick scrutiny. 'Times and routes for training. It was probably dropped by our bicycling neighbours.'

'I'll send Sam over with it later.' I didn't fancy being leered at by hairy men in Lycra shorts. Being fancied by John Rock, I had decided, was something else entirely.

Chapter 26

The following morning we walked to the nearest village – a compact huddle of golden stone, glimmering on a steep mass of rock about a mile from the campsite. The path to it ran for a time along a river, reduced to a trickle by the summer heat, and then wound steeply through pines and cypresses until it met the main road a hundred yards short of the village.

We stepped from the dappled shadow of the pines as a group of cyclists hummed past us on the sweating tarmac. Our eyes followed twenty tanned, muscular legs, rotating like copper pistons as they powered into the village and wheeled towards the ancient stone fountain in the square.

'They shave their legs,' Isabel announced as we trailed into the square behind them.

The cyclists dismounted, unclipped plastic bottles from their belts and filled them from the stream of clear water gushing from the throat of an ancient stone lion and splashing into the stone trough at his feet.

'Makes them go faster. Less wind resistance, I suppose,' Sam said.

'It's to massage their legs more easily,' Isabel said.

I looked at her in amazement.

'My first boyfriend was a cyclist. He was in the Milk Race in nineteen eighty. I had to massage his legs after every stage.' She gave a wicked smile. Sam and David giggled.

'Those cyclists who dropped the timetable have hairy legs,' Sam said.

'That's because they don't have girls to rub them,' David said.

Isabel and I hooted with laughter. We collapsed round a table at the Café des Sports, overlooking the fountain, and ordered Coca-Cola and *citrons pressés*. The air was sweet as honey. The mid-morning hum of conversation was like the buzzing of contented bees.

We watched the cyclists drain the last drops from their water bottles and refill them.

'The Tour de France riders get a ninety minute massage every night,' Isabel said.

'I don't want to hear that!' The screech echoed round the square. Conversation stopped. All eyes turned to stare at the redhead, hands clamped to her ears, backing away from a stocky male companion. The man lurched forward, grabbed one of the redhead's arms and tried to detach it from her ear. She kicked him on the shin. He hopped back, unbalanced, face blazing with rage. She took a swipe at him, missed, and strode off, silver bracelets bouncing on her arm. He began to hop after her, but halted after a few paces to rub his injured limb. His back stiffened as he became aware of the audience on the café terrace. The redhead disappeared into the shadow of an archway at the far side of the square.

The conversational buzz began again, but Sam, David and Isabel stared silently at the man limping across the square until he too vanished in the shade. Sam gripped my arm. 'You know who they are?'

I thought I had seen them before, but I couldn't place them. 'A footballer and his wife?' I hazarded.

Sam rolled his eyes. 'Mum only watches the news,' he said to David.

'I've no idea who they are either,' Isabel said.

'That was only Desmond and Yvonne from *Drumkeerin*,' David said, with awe.

'The television series? I hear people talking about it at work but I've never seen it.'

'It goes out on Sunday night,' Sam said. 'They have a hotel in the west of Ireland. People come and stay with them and they tell them their problems and Desmond and Yvonne sort it all out.'

I know when I'm supposed to act stupid. 'They do this for real?'

'It's a drama series. They're actors, Mum. Everybody knows them. Only I've forgotten their names.'

David said, 'Amy O'Keefe and Jimmy Johnson.'

I was too startled to speak.

'They must be on holiday here,' David said.

I wondered if they knew their old friend John Rock lived in the area. Isabel put my next thought into words.

'Maybe they're staying with . . .'

'Isabel!' I kicked her ankle under the table.

'The whole cast of the show,' she finished. 'Maybe they're filming an episode here.'

The boys were still sending text messages to their friends as we left the square.

'I wish I could text like that,' Isabel said. 'Gives new and opposite meaning to the phrase "all thumbs".'

'It has made their day,' I said.

'I felt a little frisson myself. A brush with celebrity,' Isabel paused, 'with an extra thrill.'

'Sorry for kicking you,' I said. 'Sam doesn't know I've met Rocky before. Or Amy and Jimmy. I can't believe they're here as well.' I could feel the knot in my stomach. 'This thing just gets more complicated. I wish I'd never met him,' I cried.

Isabel looked thoughtful. 'Didn't you say Jimmy Johnson had been engaged to Dolores? Could he have done it?'

I couldn't remember if Robbie had checked the time Jimmy Johnson left the restaurant on the day Dolores died.

'I don't know,' I said, thinking I might get in touch with Robbie after the holiday.

Isabel persisted. 'That was an ugly scene just now. Do you think you should tell someone?'

I tried to sound casual. 'It's waited ten years. It can wait a week.'

But my brain was racing as I picked my way back down the path through the trees to the river. What, after all, did my previous suspicion of John Rock amount to? An insurance policy and a narrow time band of opportunity? No. More than that, I told myself. He was having an affair. He smoked. He drove a red car. But there were a lot of red cars in the case. Jimmy Johnson had a red car. He smoked. He could have been having an affair with Dolores.

I thought about the bad-tempered jostling between Amy and Jimmy in the square. Supposing Jimmy had been with Dolores on the cliff top at Fair Head?

The path flattened and emerged into the full glare of the sun. The shrivelled river seemed to writhe in the heat. I looked up at the cloudless blue sky and wondered what had made Robbie and me so certain John Rock had been with his wife when she fell to her death?

I had left my mobile on charge in the caravan. There were two text messages. The first read, *C U abt 6pm. Want me to do supper? G xxx*

Yes pls, I texted back.

'George will get here about six,' I called out to Isabel. 'He's going to cook.'

I scrolled down to the second message.

Still wnt t go Gourdon? C U noon tmrrow? Answer pls. Rocky.

'What's up?' Isabel said.

I showed her the message. 'I'm not sure I should go. I feel bad about abandoning George.'

Isabel gave me a sidelong glance. 'Do you think George is keen on you?'

'Not at all,' I said. 'I just think it's a bit rude if I go off somewhere when he's just arrived.'

'When we're old,' Isabel said thoughtfully, 'do you think we'll regret the things we did, or the things we didn't do?'

She read the answer in my face. 'Text Rocky back,' she said. 'I'll look after George.'

Chapter 27

We spent the rest of the day sunbathing by the pool. When we returned to the caravan, just before six o'clock, George was sitting at the table outside. He was wearing a pale blue and white rugby shirt and jeans. I realised I had never seen him in summer clothes. They suited him. There were two white plastic shopping bags on the table.

He stood up and gave me his once-familiar, slow smile. I stopped, shy and unsure what to do or say, but conscious of a great rush of pleasure. Ten years suddenly seemed like a day.

'How long have you been waiting?'

He laughed. 'Long enough.' He tilted his head and surveyed me. 'You look different,' he said. 'Wonderful, but different.'

'Amazing what a week in the sun can do,' I said. 'And a new haircut.'

'Come here, wee girl, and say hello.'

I stepped forward, both hands outstretched. He tugged me towards him and kissed me on both cheeks. 'When in France, eh?'

I introduced Isabel.

'Do I get to kiss you on both cheeks as well?'

She laughed. 'Maybe one cheek, since we've only just met.'

They're going to get on, I thought, pleased with myself.

George nodded at the plastic bags. 'I bought fish in the market. I thought we could barbecue them.' He reached into one of the bags and brought out two bunches of violets. 'I bought these as well. One for each of you,' he said.

Isabel clapped her hands in delight.

'What a lovely present,' I said, burying my nose in the velvety, almost black petals and inhaling their sweet, mossy scent. 'Thank you, George.'

He busied himself with the barbecue. The boys came back in time to watch him make two slits with a knife in the silver skin of a sea bream, before putting it on the barbecue.

'I wish I could have brought the dollaghan I caught this morning.'

'What's a dollaghan?' David asked.

'It's like a sea trout, except it runs to a freshwater lough instead of the sea. I caught five of them this morning in the Ballinderry river, on their way to Lough Neagh.'

'You must have got up early,' said Isabel, looking at him in wonder.

'The early worm catches the fish,' he said.

The boys wanted to learn how to fish. 'Can we learn here, George?'

He stood back as the white hot coals spat blue smoke into the air. 'I'll find out.'

Isabel called out from the caravan, 'I'll do the salad!'

I had told the boys that George worked with Customs and Excise to break drug smuggling rackets. When we sat down to eat, they began to interrogate him.

'How do you catch drug smugglers?' Sam wanted to know.

'We do a lot of surveillance,' George said.

'Do you need a disguise?'

'You need patience,' George said. 'You need to be able to sit for hours on end just waiting.'

'Waiting for what?'

'Waiting for something to happen.'

'Like what?'

'Maybe a car or a person arriving at a suspect's house.'

'What would you do then?' David asked.

'Take a note of the number, and maybe photograph the car or the person.'

'What if it's night time?'

'We've got special equipment.'

'What kind of special equipment?'

'Night vision binoculars. Infrared cameras. And you learn how to take notes in the dark.'

'Drug smugglers, fast cars, fishing. It's like Christmas in July for them,' I said to George as we put things away in the kitchen.

'Fast cars?'

'We met someone who owns a music bar in Nice. He has a red Ford Mustang. He drove us along the corniche in it yesterday.'

'Very nice,' George said. 'Where does this go?' He held up a bread knife.

'In that box.' I pointed to a blue plastic box marked PAIN.

Isabel put her head round the door. 'I got another bottle of white wine from the shop.'

The air was fresher when we sat down again in the gathering dusk. The cypresses stood out like spear-carriers. The gas lamp hissed softly. I lit a citronella candle to keep the mosquitoes at bay. The sharp, lemony smell made us wrinkle our noses.

Isabel filled our glasses. 'You two have a lot of catching up to do.'

'Plenty of time,' George said, pulling a pack of cigarettes from his shirt pocket. 'Do you smoke, Isabel? I know Claire doesn't.'

She shook her head. 'But I like the smell of French cigarettes, and the mosquitoes don't.'

'I'm down to one a day, after dinner.'

'You were saying that ten years ago,' I said.

He looked sheepish. 'Wishful thinking. It was more like five a day then.' He lit his cigarette and settled back in the chair. 'Did I tell you Robbie Dunbar has joined a unit reviewing old murder cases?'

'That's a lot of cases,' I said.

Isabel opened her mouth to speak. I thought she was about to mention Rocky. I kicked her under the table again.

'How do they decide which cases to look at?' She flashed me a look of indignation.

'They'll give priority to police murders,' George said, 'where they've kept the evidence, and there's a chance of getting DNA from something.'

I relaxed.

'They used to need big amounts of body fluids to get enough DNA for identification,' George continued. 'With this new technique, they only need a trace of blood or sweat or saliva on a piece of clothing, or a scrap of paper.'

'Cigarette butt?' Isabel asked casually.

'Only if it's been kept properly, and not degraded or contaminated.'

'What does that mean?'

'Not handled with bare hands, not coughed over. Air-dried, and stored in a new paper bag, not plastic. No staples.'

Isabel sat back. 'Amazing.' She gave me a satisfied smile.

I could take my time contacting Robbie about Jimmy Johnson, I decided. It was unlikely the cigarette butts had been stored in the way George had described, if they had been kept at all.

'Have you seen Robbie recently?' I asked.

'I hadn't seen him in years, until I ran into him at the airport last week. We had a quick chat. He'd just dropped off his wife.'

'I knew he was engaged. Who did he marry?'

'Some teacher. She's a quiz fanatic too. He told me she keeps him under control.' He laughed. 'He took his time settling down.'

'It can take a long time to find the right person,' Isabel said quietly.

George leaned his head back and blew a smoke ring at the stars. 'Right enough.'

We sat in companionable silence for a moment.

George said, still looking at the stars, 'I assume Claire told you about me and Maggie, my ex-wife.'

'She told me you were divorced.'

'Claire's discreet,' George said. He straightened up and gave me a quick smile. 'But you might as well know. It's all over the papers. My wife ran away with another woman.'

Isabel said in her careful, psychologist's voice, 'Were you surprised?'

'Not really.' He blew another smoke ring. 'Relieved, probably. I knew for a long time things weren't right. We were staying together for Judith, our daughter. I found out about Heather three years ago. When Judith went to London, Maggie went over more and more often to see her. Heather got a job in London. Maggie joined her. End of story.'

'And Judith is fine?' I said

'So she says.' He paused.

'What about you?'

George studied the tip of his cigarette. 'When you've picked up body parts in the street and seen people with their heads blown off, two women making love to each other doesn't seem so bad.' His breath escaped in a great sigh.

'Do you have a woman in your life at the moment?'

'I'm not a monk,' he said. 'Never have been.'

'I didn't imagine so,' I said. 'Anybody special?'

He smiled at me. 'I'm not saying anything till I talk to a solicitor.'

A sudden metallic thump startled us. George got up and walked to where our pool of light ended and the path began. He peered into the darkness.

'Looks like some eejit with no light on his bicycle has just run into the side of a mobile home. I don't think anybody's hurt.' He dropped his cigarette on the path and ground it under his heel. 'I'd better get back to the hotel. What are you planning to do tomorrow?'

'Nothing much,' Isabel said. 'I fancy a game of boules in the evening, when it's cooler.'

'The boys have a thing about French car registrations.' I laughed. 'They're collecting numberplates at the campsite.'

I stood up and began clearing the table.

'What about you, Claire?'

I shook out the red-checked tablecloth. 'I'm going to the Château de Gourdon.'

'I could drive you,' George said.

I was embarrassed. 'Sorry, George. The man we met on Wednesday. The one who drove us along the corniche. He's driving me.'

Isabel said, 'Come down here, George. Lie around the pool. Play boules with us.'

'Have supper with us,' I said. 'I'll be back by then.'

There was a pause. 'Maybe,' George said.

A burst of amplified, incomprehensible speech, followed by applause, signalled the end of the disco. George lifted his hand and let it fall again. 'See you tomorrow some time.'

'I'll go with you to the gate and meet the boys coming back,' I said quickly.

We walked down the track to the main avenue.

'Are you really going to teach the boys to fish?'

'Sure,' George said.

We drew level with the mobile home occupied by the balding cyclists. A buckled front wheel lay in the rectangle of yellow light falling from the open door. Inside, I could see one of the men extracting a spanner from a tool bag.

'That lot spend most of their time fiddling with bikes,' I said.

'While you're fiddling with fast cars?'

I was glad he couldn't see me blush.

'I didn't realise you were seeing someone,' he said.

'I'm only going sightseeing.'

'Is this man important?' he asked in a quiet voice.

'I don't know.' My mouth dried. 'It's early days.'

'Isabel is nice.'

'I thought you two would get on,' I said with a hint of pride.

'Still the same Claire,' he said. 'Setting the world to rights.'

He leaned forward and gave me a quick kiss on the cheek. I turned my other cheek for the second kiss, but he had already spun on his heel and was heading towards the gate. I watched him vanish into the dark beyond the rainbow arch. He didn't look back.

Chapter 28

The road to Gourdon zigzagged up the side of a ravine. Rocky took it in great swooping movements, slowing up at the bends, accelerating through them. Ahead and above, the bleached stone walls and turrets of the château stood out against the blue vault of the sky. We drove through a tunnel in the rock, swept up the last straight stretch of road, veered right into a car park and berthed in the shadow of the ramparts.

'Lunch first,' Rocky said. 'I've booked a table.'

That hand under my elbow again, steering me through the hot and swarming streets below the château. The air was heavy with the lavender sold at every teeming shop.

Rocky brought me to a small square, like a terrace surrounded by a low stone wall, and guided me towards a viewing telescope on a round, wrought-iron platform. I stepped up to it. The land fell away below my feet. The sky reared above me.

'I'll point everything out to you.' Rocky's arms encircled my shoulders. His linen trousers brushed against the backs of my bare legs. His chin hovered above my right shoulder. 'We're on an outcrop of rock in the Gorges du Loup, the valley of the wolf.'

The land unfolded beneath us like a green rug rolled out towards the coast. The sea in the distance shone like silver plate.

'That's Cap d'Antibes straight ahead. The Bay of Cannes to the right. Nice is to the left. See those white shapes, like pyramids? Those are the apartments at the Marina Baie des Anges.'

Cars crawled like insects along white strips of road criss-crossing the broad valley below.

'Seven hundred and sixty metres. Two thousand feet down. Makes you think, doesn't it?'

His words ricocheted in my head, dislodging the memory of a body on black rocks, and a pounding sea. A shiver ran through me, and I felt dizzy. I put out a hand to steady myself. Rocky tightened his grip on my shoulders.

'Are you OK?'

I focused on the soft blue smudge of the horizon. 'Fine, thank you. It's a fantastic view.'

He stepped off the viewing platform, and took my hand to help me down. He didn't let go of it as we walked across the square and down a flight of broad stone steps to the restaurant.

Our table was on a balcony jutting out above the valley. I tried not to think about two thousand feet of empty space below me, about a body tumbling through that space.

'You wonder how I can bear places like this?' Rocky smiled crookedly. 'If I let myself think about it, I would never walk up another alp, or visit another *village perché*.' His smile straightened, became bold. 'Or take a beautiful woman to admire a beautiful view.'

'It's spectacular,' I agreed in a faint voice. 'Thank you.'

'It's a pleasure.' He picked up his knife and fork. 'No sad talk,' he added. 'We're here to enjoy ourselves.'

I concentrated on my salad of broad beans and courgettes.

'So what kind of soliciting do you do?' Rocky asked.

'Small stuff. Conveyancing, petty crime. A lot of twocking.'

'Twocking?'

'Car theft, otherwise known as twoc. Taking without consent.'

He leaned towards me and said, 'I promise I won't take anything without consent.'

In the silence that fell between us, I sensed the start of a whispering conversation between cells and nerve ends separated by a table. Eventually Rocky said, 'Why did you get divorced?'

'My husband preferred blondes.' I felt the blood rise up my neck. A picture of Jacqueline Duchêne flashed into my mind, followed by a picture of Maxine. I batted them away.

'Anybody since?'

'Why do you want to know?'

'I'm interested,' he said.

'Nobody special,' I said, holding his gaze.

Our knees were almost touching under the table. The whispering nerves began to shout.

'I have tickets for a concert tomorrow night,' he said. 'Part of the jazz festival. An old friend and his wife are driving down from Chamonix. There's a spare ticket. Would you like to join us? We could have dinner afterwards.'

'That would be great.'

'I'll pick you up from the campsite at six o'clock.' He pushed his plate away. 'Mind if I smoke?'

I looked around the restaurant. Wisps of blue smoke curled into the air from almost every table. 'Everybody else seems to,' I said.

'Despite the warnings.' He tapped the thick black-on-white lettering that took up half the packet. *Fumer peut diminuer l'affleux sanguin et provoque l'impuissance.*

I summoned all my French to translate. 'Smoking can reduce blood pressure and cause . . .'

'Impotence,' said Rocky. His smile teased me. 'I haven't noticed any lowering of my blood pressure.' He paused. 'Quite the opposite, I'd say.' Another pause. He blew a cloud of smoke at the sky. 'What do you say I get the bill and we go to the villa for coffee? Leave the tour of the château for another day?'

I had read about the château in the guidebook. It was famous for its armoury.

'If you've seen one musket,' I said, trying to be nonchalant, 'you've seen them all.'

I was glad we didn't talk on the drive to the villa. I needed time to get used to the feeling of excitement flooding through me. I rested my neck on the warm leather and offered my face to the sun. A little current of power ran through me each time I sensed Rocky glance in my direction. I tried to remember when I last felt so alive. Not since I first met Joel, I decided.

The phrase 'one degree under' floated into my head. I felt I had been one degree under since my divorce. I enjoyed my work; Sam was, mostly, a joy; I had good friends, I reflected. But a part of me had been dying from neglect because of something lacking in my life. It wasn't sex, although I missed that neon-lit circus of thrills. What I had been wanting, I realised, was a degree of romance. No. More than that. The mesmerising possibility of love. I wanted to love, and be loved in return. Somewhere inside me, a tiny voice was whispering, tantalising me, 'Is this the one?'

There was a yellow Renault parked outside the villa. Rocky swore under his breath. He banged his hand on the dashboard. 'Damn Maxine.'

I straightened up.

'Wait here.' Rocky got out of the car, fished in his pocket for keys as he strode to the door. It opened before he got there. Maxine stood in the doorway. Even ten yards away, I could see the delight in her eyes.

'Rocky,' she cried. 'All is forgiven.'

A lanky figure materialised beside her. I almost sprang out of my seat in surprise. It was Duffy. He put his arm round Maxine's shoulders. 'She's taking me back,' he announced with a wide grin. 'We were just . . .' He looked sheepish. 'We heard the car. I wasn't expecting you. Sorry.'

Maxine waved shyly in my direction. I saw she was only about nineteen or twenty. I waved back.

'Hi there,' Duffy called up to me. 'Nice to see you again.'

Rocky looked over his shoulder at me and shrugged. I shrugged back.

'I'm moving all my stuff out,' Duffy said.

Rocky sighed. 'Take your time. I'll open the bar.'

'Thanks, Rocky. I'll get down as soon as I can. I let the group in to rehearse this morning. They've left their stuff. See you later.'

Duffy and Maxine backed into the house. The door swung shut.

Rocky slid into the driver's seat, thrust the engine into gear and reversed up the driveway. 'Let's go to the bar.'

He drove fast, changing gear roughly, as though taking his irritation out on the car. He scowled at a bunch of cyclists, blasted the horn to overtake a bus with millimetres to spare. We fairly hurtled into Nice, slowing only to thread through the narrow streets of the old town, by which time his frustration had faded. When he switched off the engine in an alleyway behind the bar, his face wore its usual lazy smile.

'Duffy was living with Maxine. She caught him chatting up a couple of Polish girls. She threw him out. I offered to put him up until he found somewhere else.'

'It's nice they've made up,' I said, feeling suddenly awkward.

A white van pulled up behind us.

'Deliveries,' Rocky said. 'Go round to the front. I'll open up.'

The lights were on when I stepped through the door. They were dull, compared to the glare outside, and drained the room of atmosphere. Rocky was stacking cartons of cigarettes on a shelf behind the bar.

'Won't be a minute,' he called out. 'Have a look around.'

I wandered towards the stage area at the back. A double bass leaned against the wall beside a drum kit. A clarinet rested on its stand. Next to it, on a soft, yellow cloth on a chair, lay a golden trumpet. I closed my eyes. The sound came a fraction before the picture. Trumpets. White space. Alan McCrea, in the mortuary, looking at me over his glasses. 'You find it difficult to dissociate emotion from sex, Claire?'

I stared at the trumpet. I picked it up. The lights went out. I jumped. A spotlight came on over the stage.

Rocky's voice, full of suppressed laughter, called from the darkness. 'You're on the spot. Want to show me how you blow? Show off your technique?'

'We call it playing.' I raised the trumpet to my lips. 'But it's like blowing a raspberry.'

When I am playing the cornet or the trumpet, I think of nothing but the music. It fills every available space in my brain. I wasn't aware of Rocky moving into the circle of light. I was wholly concentrated on 'Amazing Grace' until I had relinquished the last note.

When I lowered the trumpet my lips were buzzing. I was

breathing heavily. Rocky was clapping, and shaking his head in disbelief.

'Where did you learn to play the trumpet?'

'Cornet. I learned to play the cornet. The technique is the same. The trumpet sounds brighter. That's all.'

'I don't know many women who play either of them,' he said.

'I grew up in The Salvation Army.'

He looked even more astounded. Then he laughed. 'I can imagine you in uniform. Black stockings. Bonnet.'

I hoped he wouldn't say, 'I'd love to see you in your uniform.' I had met that response before. Some men had a thing about uniforms. When I told them I'd been in the police as well, they could barely contain themselves.

'Miss Prim,' he said. 'So that explains it.'

I coloured. 'Do you play an instrument?'

'African drums.' He rolled a goblet-shaped drum into the spotlight. It was about three feet tall and a foot across. He picked up a stick from the top of the piano and sat down on the chair.

'I don't know how our two instruments will work together,' he said. 'But let's give it a try.'

'I only know classic tunes and hymns.'

'You need to loosen up.' He beat out a double roll on the drum. 'You start. I'll find your rhythm.'

I lifted the trumpet to my lips. Rocky beat out a triple roll. I blew the opening bars of 'When The Saints Go Marching In', taking the opening phrase slowly, sweetly. The beat of the drum quickened. I responded. My heel began tapping the floor. I took a deeper breath and began to play again, swaying, feeling the intervals between the notes, starting to squeeze extra notes into the spaces. The drum beat even faster. I caressed the notes. I bent them. I pushed them away. They swirled and eddied around me.

I moved through the music like a fish in a fast-moving stream, leaping, turning in the air, diving under the water and coming up again to the light. The drum roared like a river in full spate. And stopped.

I had been holding a note. It quivered, and died in the air, as my breath left me in surprise. A steady clapping had begun.

I looked at Rocky. He had one hand in the air, the other laid flat on the drum, and he was staring into the shadows.

The clapping slowed, and stopped. A tall woman with narrow shoulders and short, dark hair stepped into the spotlight. Rocky started to his feet.

'Hello, John,' the woman said. 'It's Bernadette. Long time no see.'

Chapter 29

Rocky continued to stare at her. His jaw was working but he didn't speak.

'It is you, John? Isn't it?'

I wouldn't have recognised Bernadette Dargan if she hadn't said her name. She was plumper, her face had filled out, and she had a confident air. She turned to me with a pleasant smile. 'Sorry to interrupt your session. Are you playing here tonight?'

I shook my head. It was clear she had not recognised me either.

'John's my brother-in-law. Or should I say former brother-in-law? He was married to my sister. She died.'

I glanced at Rocky. He looked dazed.

'He told me about it,' I said. 'How dreadful for you both.'

Rocky's jaw relaxed. He cleared his throat. I remembered he had once gone out with Bernadette, or had been engaged to her.

'Life goes on,' Bernadette said. 'Isn't that right, John?'

Rocky seemed to jerk into action. In three swift movements he switched off the spotlight, switched on the lights behind the bar, and grasped Bernadette's hands.

'You haven't changed a bit. Your hair is shorter. But that's all.' He kissed her on both cheeks and stepped back. 'Let me introduce you to Claire.'

Bernadette shook my hand. 'Hello, Claire. Nice to meet you.'

I stammered a conventional reply, adding, 'I'm sorry about your sister.'

'It's ten years since she died,' Bernadette said, 'but I still think about her.'

'The people we love are always with us,' I said in a rush. 'It doesn't matter how long ago they died.'

There was a silence.

'I'm sorry we lost touch,' Rocky said.

'It happens,' Bernadette said, in a light tone. 'So, how have you been these last' – she tilted her head – 'eight? nine? years, since we heard from you?' She paused. 'Did you marry again?'

'Dolores was a hard act to follow,' Rocky said. 'But,' and he shot a sideways smile at me, 'who knows what's waiting round the corner?'

My colour rose. Rocky said quickly, 'What about you, Bernadette?'

She shrugged, and held up ringless hands.

'Still teaching?'

'Still teaching. Same subject. Same school. Some things don't change.'

'How's your mother?'

'Still complaining about being run off her feet behind the bar.' She smiled. 'You'd know all about that, now you've got a bar yourself.' She paused and looked around. 'When did you give up academia?'

'Not long after I left Coleraine,' he said. 'A friend gave me the chance to buy into a little music bar in a ski resort. It was too good an opportunity to turn down.' He gave a slight start. 'That reminds me, I have to organise staff for next week.' He slipped behind the counter. 'First,' he took a bottle of champagne from a glass-fronted fridge, 'let's celebrate!' He set three champagne flutes on the bar. 'How did you track me down?'

'Amy O'Keefe,' said Bernadette. 'You remember Amy? Friend of Dolores? She married Jimmy Johnson. You'll remember him, of course. They've rented a place down here for the summer. Amy spotted the bar a couple of weeks ago and had a look in. She thought she recognised you.'

Rocky concentrated on pouring the champagne. 'I don't remember her speaking to me,' he said.

'You were busy, and Amy wasn't sure. I'm staying with them for a few days. I thought I'd come in at a quiet time and see for myself. So here I am. Amy and Jimmy will be here in a minute.'

Rocky slid a flute of champagne across the bar towards her. 'It's wonderful to see you.'

I had retreated, leaving them to talk. Rocky beckoned to me. Handed me my glass.

'Don't feel you have to go, Claire,' Bernadette said. 'I just popped in to say hello, and catch up.' She raised her glass. 'What should the toast be?'

The door swung open bringing a blast of hot air and the rumour of traffic from the street. I turned to see Amy O'Keefe planted in the doorway, hands on hips. 'Can I join the party?'

She swayed up to the bar. 'I hope you're going to pour champagne for me, John Rock. Whether you remember me or not.'

He leaned across the bar to kiss her proffered cheek. 'Who could forget you, Amy?' He looked at her admiringly. Her features were the same, but she had acquired the glow that comes with money and success. Her hair shone like a red-gold helmet and her skin was the colour of honey.

'Jimmy's putting the shopping in the car,' she said.

Rocky put two more glasses on the counter. Amy turned to me, her face bright with curiosity. 'I'm Amy O'Keefe.'

I stuck out my hand. 'Claire Watson.'

Jimmy Johnson wrestled half a dozen stiff plastic carrier bags through the door. 'Hello, everybody.' He dropped the bags on a table and disentangled his hands from the silky rope handles. 'As you can see, Amy's been shopping.' He swiped a hand across his brow.

'You've earned a glass of chilled champagne,' Rocky called out to him. 'Come and say hello, Jimmy.'

Bernadette picked up her handbag from the counter and walked towards the door marked *'Toilettes, Dames'*.

Amy took my arm. 'Come on and sit down. My feet are killing me.'

Rocky took another bottle of champagne from the fridge. 'Would you like to open this, Jimmy? I have a couple of telephone calls to make.'

I seemed to have become part of the company. Amy leaned towards me. 'John was married to Bernadette's sister, Dolores. She died in a terrible accident. She fell off a cliff.'

'He told me,' I said.

'Are you his girlfriend?' She gave me a playful nudge with her shoulder. 'He's entitled. It was ten years ago.'

'I'm sure he's had lots of girlfriends since then,' I said, thinking I could cross Maxine off the list.

'I always thought he was dead sexy,' Amy murmured in my ear.

'If he hadn't been married to my best friend, I might have had a fling with him myself.' She took a long swallow of champagne. 'He used to go out with Bernadette, you know.'

Bernadette reappeared and sat down beside me. 'Where did you meet John?'

'I'm here on holiday. I bumped into him when I was out walking.' I strangled a nervous laugh. 'Or rather, he bumped into me, or rather his car did.'

'Were you hurt?' Bernadette's voice and expression were so full of concern I almost blurted out that I had met her before.

'I had two cut knees and a few scratches,' I said, 'mostly because I jumped into the ditch.'

I heard a champagne cork pop. Amy cupped her hand to her ear. 'Is there a wee bit of a Northern Ireland accent there?'

'You have a good ear,' I said.

'I'm an actress. Where are you from in Northern Ireland?'

'Belfast, I suppose. But I lived in Coleraine and worked in Ballymoney for a while.' I glanced around. Rocky was behind the bar, holding the telephone to his ear. He hadn't heard me.

'My sister lived in Portstewart,' Bernadette said.

Put any number of Irish people in a group and we immediately look for connections between us. My stomach tightened.

Jimmy was refilling our glasses. 'You might have seen Dolores on stage. She used her maiden name. Dolores Dargan.'

I saw Rocky put the phone down.

'I'll propose a toast,' Jimmy said.

Amy was peering at me. 'Have I met you somewhere before? Northern Ireland's a small place.'

My mouth dried.

Jimmy said, 'Absent friends?'

Amy wriggled in her seat. 'Hold on! My phone's vibrating.'

She extracted a mobile from the pocket of her pink jeans and fastened it to her ear. 'Hello?' She mouthed a name to Jimmy. 'Fantastic. You're a star.' Her face bunched into a grin. 'Brilliant!' She flapped a hand excitedly at us. 'How much?' Her grin widened. 'We can celebrate at the party.'

We were all agog.

'My agent,' she said. 'He's got me a wee part in a film down here. *To Catch a Thief*. I auditioned for it last month. I'm the first person you see. I scream and scream. I love it!'

'A remake?' said Rocky. 'It was made in the nineteen fifties with Katharine Hepburn.'

'Grace Kelly,' Bernadette said, automatically correcting him, 'nineteen fifty-five.'

Amy nudged me again. 'Bernadette sets all the questions for quiz night at Dargan's.'

'Well done, Amy,' Jimmy said. I thought there was a hint of envy in his smile.

'We're having a party on Wednesday night, to celebrate our tenth wedding anniversary.' Amy beamed up at Rocky. 'Do you want to come? You and Claire?' She turned her smile on me. 'It's fancy dress.'

'Congratulations,' I said. The party sounded impossibly glamorous, and my regret was genuine when I added, 'Thank you for including me, but I have friends with me. I don't think I should leave them.'

'Sure bring them as well,' Amy cried.

I hesitated. Isabel would love it. There would be safety in numbers and strangers to talk to, I reasoned. I could avoid difficult conversations. George might even be persuaded to come as well.

'Oh, go on,' Amy said. 'Do you watch *Drumkeerin*?'

'My son never misses it,' I said.

Amy looked gratified. She pulled two publicity photographs from her handbag. 'What's your son's name?'

'Sam,' I said. 'His cousin David is a fan as well.'

Amy autographed the photographs and handed them to me. 'There you are then. For Sam and David.' The ruby and diamond ring on her finger caught a sunbeam and threw it at the wall in dazzling splinters, like a million shards of stained glass. 'There's a fancy dress shop on rue du Congres,' she said.

I felt as though I too was an actor, and the entire cast of a still-unfolding drama was gathering around me.

I wondered how much it would cost to hire a costume for the evening and how difficult it would be to persuade George into fancy dress.

Now they were deciding where to meet for dinner.

'Are you going to join us, Claire?'

'Sorry,' I said. 'I have to get back to the campsite.'

The clock behind the bar showed nearly half past six. There was no sign of Duffy.

Amy proffered her mobile. 'Call your friends and tell them you're having dinner with us.'

I imagined the bright chatter over dinner and the resumed hunt for acquaintances in common, and so I was glad to be able to say, with complete honesty, 'I promised my son I would be back, and we have a friend coming to eat with us.'

Rocky raised an enquiring eyebrow.

'Of course you have to get back then,' Bernadette said.

'I can't drive you back just yet, Claire,' Rocky said. He set his glass down on the table and checked his watch. 'Can you wait a few minutes?'

I was suddenly anxious to get away. 'I'll get a taxi,' I said, getting to my feet.

'The barman will be here any minute,' Rocky said.

'Sure we can drop you off,' Amy said to me.

'I can look after the bar,' Bernadette said. 'I'm used to helping out at home.' She took a postcard from her handbag and handed it to Rocky. 'Before you go, would you scribble a few words for Mammy? Here's a pen.'

Rocky sat down and wrote a couple of sentences on the postcard.

'I always put postcards in envelopes,' Bernadette said. 'They get there quicker. It's awful when you get home before them.' She pushed an envelope towards him. 'I've got a stamp here somewhere.' She delved in her handbag again.

'I've a stamp,' I said. I was glad to help.

Bernadette beamed. 'Thank you. I can't tell you how much the card will mean to Mammy.'

Rocky's pink tongue curled along the flap of the envelope. He winked at me.

'I hope the card gets home before you,' I said to Bernadette.

A broader version of Duffy, sporting a baseball cap back to front and a brilliant, toothy smile, ambled into the bar.

'Dr Rock? I'm Duffy's friend, Joe. He told me you needed a barman tonight.'

As we walked to the car, Rocky said, looking uncomfortable, 'I was almost engaged to Bernadette when I met Dolores. When she died, Bernadette thought . . .' He bit his lip. 'Let's just say it's one of the reasons I didn't try too hard to keep in touch.' He stopped and took my hand. 'There's something else I have to tell you. One of the calls I made earlier was to my friends from Chamonix.' His gaze slid away from me. 'They're bringing another friend to the jazz festival.'

'You mean the spare ticket is no longer spare?' I said brightly.

'I phoned to see if I could get another ticket, but . . .' He made a face. 'Sold out. I can't abandon my guests. I feel awful about it.'

Jacqueline, I thought. They're bringing Jacqueline.

'I'm sorry. I can see you're disappointed.' He tucked a finger under my chin. 'We'll have a good time at the party.'

'If I go,' I said, with a little flounce in my voice.

He opened the car door for me. 'It'll be great fun.'

'What about your friends?'

'They're going back on Wednesday morning.' He paused. 'I'll have the house to myself again.'

'I'm leaving on Saturday,' I said.

'All the more reason you should come to the party.'

'I can't go without Isabel and George.'

He whacked the door shut. 'You're not joined at the hip.'

'I can't abandon my guests.'

He swept an ironic bow.

I hunted for something neutral to say. 'So you have a new barman?'

'I've given Duffy time off to sort himself out.' He arranged himself in the driver's seat. 'No point in having him turn up late, with half a mind on the job. Better to get himself settled back with Maxine.'

'That was nice of you,' I said.

'The hardest part of running a bar is finding reliable staff. Duffy's good. I want to keep him sweet until he has to go back to California.'

I thought about Maxine and how happy she had looked. 'Maybe Duffy won't go back,' I said.

Rocky reversed the car out of the alleyway. 'I always have to look for staff at the end of the summer. It's a pain. Sometimes I think about selling up and going to South Africa.'

I looked at him in surprise.

'Don't you ever think about making a fresh start somewhere else?' The Mustang leapt towards the sunlight at the end of the shadowy street.

Chapter 30

When we got to Les Arcs, Rocky said, 'When am I going to meet this man friend of yours?'

'He's probably here now.'

He slipped his fingers through mine 'Good. You can introduce me.'

We set off down the main avenue.

'How did you meet him?'

'Through work.'

'He's a lawyer?'

'A detective.' I said.

Rocky slowed his walk.

'I don't much care for detectives,' he said, in a cool tone.

'Why not?' I tried to keep a squeak out of my voice.

He didn't look at me. 'Two detectives came to interview me when Dolores died. Sergeant Plod, and a sour-faced woman constable. They looked like two drowned rats. I felt they were accusing me. It was pretty traumatic. I was glad I could prove I was with a friend.'

Now was the moment to tell him. I took a deep breath. Before

I could speak, I heard Sven's booming laugh, followed by a squeal. 'Mum!'

Sam came bounding towards us. 'Hi, Rocky. We're playing boules.' He took my free hand and tugged us towards the boules court under the parasol pines.

Sven and Ingrid were standing beside a bench at the far side of the dusty rectangle. David and Isabel had their backs to us, eyeing George as he stooped to throw what looked like a silver cannonball.

Thud. Click. The silver ball knocked another one out of the way and rolled to a stop about two inches from what looked like a golf ball. I guessed the idea was to get close to it. I slipped my fingers from Rocky's grasp, and began clapping. They all turned to look. I made the introductions, adding, 'Rocky has a music bar in Nice.'

'We must visit it some time,' Sven said, pumping Rocky's hand.

Rocky had put his sunglasses on, so I couldn't get the true measure of the smile he flashed at George when they shook hands. George was polite, but didn't smile.

'I need to ask a favour,' I said to Ingrid. 'Could you keep an eye on Sam and David on Wednesday night? We've been invited to a party.' I explained how the invitation had come about, and whom it was from.

Sam said, 'Cool, Mum.'

Ingrid cried, 'How exciting.'

Sven said, 'Of course we will look to Sam and David when you are at the party.' He looked at his watch. 'But now, I regret we must get our skates on as you say. We are going to a restaurant in the village for dinner.'

'We didn't finish our game,' Sam complained, when they had gone.

'Your mum and I can take their places,' Rocky said, smiling at me. 'I like boules.' He picked up one of the metal balls and tested its weight.

'You'll have to tell me what to do,' I said.

'The white ball is the jack. Nearest the jack scores a point.'

'George is nearest the jack,' David said. 'He knocked Sven out of the way.'

'Who's winning?'

'We're all square,' George said. His voice sounded odd, and he was smiling the way Sam did when he disapproved of a man I wanted him to like. I was disappointed. I had wanted Rocky and George to like each other, but they were beginning to prowl around each other like big cats.

'Twelve points each,' Sam said, jumping up and down. 'Thirteen points wins the match. You and Rocky are on my team, Mum.'

'You first,' Isabel said, 'then me, David, Sam, George, and Rocky. In that order.'

I picked up the metal boule, and lobbed it down the pitch. It landed about six feet beyond the jack, and wobbled to a stop.

'Never mind, Mum,' Sam said.

Isabel's boule landed near mine. She grinned at me.

David had acquired the knack of throwing backhanded, palm down. His throw landed about six inches in front of the white ball. I applauded. 'Played!'

David glowed.

Sam bowled like a cricketer. His boule landed an inch to the right of David's. They were now equidistant from the jack.

'Well done, Sam!' I cried.

He beat his fists on his chest.

George threw from the shoulder, like a shot putter. The boule transcribed an arc and landed about four feet short of the jack.

Isabel murmured, 'Played, partner.'

George smiled at her.

Rocky swung the boule, palm down, back and forward a few times. He blew me a kiss with his free hand, stepped forward gracefully, and threw. Thud. His throw split Sam and David's boules. Click. Click. They spun off to each side. Rocky's boule rolled forward and hit the jack.

'Well played,' David called out in a small, defeated voice.

Sam was biting his lip. I gave him a hug. 'You played a great shot too, Sam.'

'Game to us, I think,' Rocky said, with a satisfied nod to Sam and Isabel. He put his arm round me. 'I like to win, I'm afraid.' He kissed me just below my ear, in a way that sent an electric current to my toes, whispered 'See you at the party', waved farewell to the others, and sauntered off.

The little quiver of excitement subsided, but I knew my face had reddened. I looked around. George was helping Sam and David to pick up the boules, and wasn't looking in my direction. Isabel was regarding me with a knowing smile.

'Where did you get the boules?' I said.

'George and I bought them at the market in the village this morning.'

'You went to the market?'

'We got sausages for the barbecue, some cheese, tomatoes, peaches and bread. And we had a nice chat.' She patted my arm and added in a low voice, 'Don't worry. We didn't talk about Rocky.'

It was nearly dark when I lit the gas lamp and the candle, and we sat down to eat. Isabel put a bowl of salad on the table, and passed round a plate of sausages. 'Tuck in!'

I waited until we had finished a dish of strawberries with ice cream, and settled back in our chairs with small, contented noises, before telling them the party on Wednesday night would be fancy dress.

George groaned.

Isabel gave a little jump of delight. 'I haven't been to a fancy dress party in ages! Please say you'll come, George. It'll be great fun.'

'I'd go if I was asked,' David said. 'I'd love to meet Amy O'Keefe. Nobody at school would believe me.'

I produced the publicity photographs from my handbag. 'They'll believe you now,' I said.

'How does Rocky know Amy O'Keefe?' Sam asked.

'He was married to a friend of hers.'

'Are they divorced?'

'She died,' I said.

There was the usual, reflective pause that follows the mention of a death.

'It was generous of Amy O'Keefe to include us all in the invitation,' Isabel said brightly.

George frowned. 'I know that name.' He craned his neck to look at the photograph in Sam's hand.

'You must have seen her on television,' Sam said. '*Drumkeerin*. It's on Sunday night.'

'I don't watch much television,' George said. He stared into the candle flame. 'I might have seen her on stage,' he said slowly, 'in Belfast, in *Othello*.'

'You've a good memory, George,' I said.

I thought I saw a faint expression, like a shadow, flicker across his face. 'Some people you never forget,' he said. He looked up and added, 'Red hair?' His hands made a silhouette in the air. 'Shapely?'

Sam and David giggled.

'So you'll come to the party?' Isabel said.

George sighed. 'Aye, all right then.'

We all clapped. I felt suddenly glad that Rocky had withdrawn his invitation to the jazz concert. I wouldn't be neglecting my old friend a second time.

After George left us to go back to his hotel, I went to the boys' tent to say goodnight. They weren't there. I walked up to the main avenue, and lingered near the reception hut, watching little groups of boys and girls drift past me, arms linked, faces bleached by the blue lights of the disco.

Here and there, a boy and girl held hands, or smooched along, still entwined. None of them looked older than fifteen, sixteen at most. After sixteen, they didn't want to go on holiday with their parents, I thought.

I remembered my reluctance to go with Mum and Dad to Mallorca, the summer I was seventeen. Aunt Madge had scolded me. 'You'll be at university next year. Working in the holidays. Going off with new friends. Give them one last summer with you.' I had trailed behind Mum and Dad, gracelessly, not wanting to be with them, wanting to be with the teenagers at the hotel disco.

'Go to the disco. We want you to enjoy yourself,' Mum had said.

'I can't go on my own,' I had said, mulishly.

It occurred to me that when my mother died, she had been my age. Thirty-nine. I wondered when Sam would stop wanting to come on holiday with me. Soon, probably, I thought, and was caught off guard by a glimpse of loneliness, the sense of time accelerating, of the years flashing by like months, then weeks, then days. What was it Isabel had said? '*Gather ye rosebuds while ye may*?' I had learned the poem at school. Now I softly recited it to myself.

'Gather ye rosebuds while ye may
Old time is still a-flying;
And the same flower that smiles today
Tomorrow will be dying.'

I thought of Rocky, and at that moment my mobile phone beeped. I slipped it from my pocket and cupped my hand around the screen to read the text message.

Thnkg abt U.R U thnkg abt me? R

My spirits lifted. The screen flashed brighter. The disco lights had gone out. I looked around. The last, chattering cluster had disappeared. There was no sign of Sam or David. I assumed they had left the disco early.

As I passed the shower block, on the way to their tent, I heard rustling in the hedge that separated it from the nearest emplacement. I stopped and looked around. A dog? There was no sign of an owner. I walked up to the hedge. The leaves glistened bronze under the lights that lined the path. Something moved behind them.

'Who's there?'

There was a gasp and a giggle.

'Come out,' I said.

David brushed through a gap in the hedge. Sam followed him. Their faces were streaked with dirt. Sam was holding a plastic carrier bag.

'What on earth are you doing? You're filthy.'

'It's camouflage,' Sam said. 'We're practising surveillance.'

I tried to sound severe. 'You can't go around spying on people. What's in the bag? Give it to me.'

I looked inside and saw crumpled cigarette packets, and bits of paper.

'Go and wash your faces. Go to bed.'

I slipped through the cypress trees and returned to the caravan. I hoped they couldn't hear me laughing.

Just before I went to sleep, my mobile phone beeped again. *Mssng U. Rxxxx*

It was just after midnight. I texted back. *Me 2x*

Chapter 31

George walked down from the village to the campsite after breakfast, carrying a bag of groceries. He began unloading them on the kitchen table in the caravan.

'My turn to cook this evening.' He waved away our objections. 'I've been domesticated.' He checked the contents of our food cupboard, and put a package in the fridge.

We had hoped he would come into Nice with us, to hire fancy dress for the party.

'I'll just stay by the pool, and read my book,' he said. 'Don't look so distrustful, Claire. I'll improvise something.' He tapped the side of his nose. 'Less is more.'

'George might have the right idea,' Isabel said, an hour later, as we faced rack upon rack of costumes, covering most of the available floor space in a shop the size of a bus depot.

Dummies in fancy dress were dotted about. I saw shepherdesses, firemen, nurses, gendarmes, nuns, bishops, a Marie Antoinette, an Elvis Presley, and most of the animals of the African rainforest. I peered into glass cabinets displaying wigs, deep drawers full of hats, and boxes bursting with boots and shoes.

Isabel fingered a velour leopard skin, and shuddered, 'too hot'. She rejected the silk crinolines, 'too big'. She weighed a powdered wig in her hands, 'too heavy'. She picked out a lion tamer's costume, and held it against her, considering the sleeveless red silk waistcoat with silver tassles, and the short, white, pleated silk skirt.

'This is the one for me,' she said. 'Can you find me a pair of silver boots, please? European size thirty-eight.' She continued flicking along the rack, eventually selecting a wide black skirt with pink polka dots and a boat-necked pink top for me.

'The nineteen fifties, rock and roll look. Perfect. You've got flat shoes.'

The sunlight dazzled us when we stepped into the street with our big brown carrier bags. We didn't see Rocky at the pavement café about fifty yards away until we were nearly upon him. He was facing in our direction, talking animatedly to a blonde who had her back to us. I noticed a brown carrier bag underneath the table, and wondered if she had helped him choose his disguise for the party.

If Rocky saw us, he gave no sign. He went on talking and smiling to his companion as we approached. Isabel lifted her free arm as though to wave. I grabbed it and wheeled her round.

'I think that's Jacqueline,' I hissed in her ear, pulling her into a side street. I saw a palm tree, framed with blue sky, at the end of the street, knew it signalled the Promenade des Anglais, and tacked through the traffic towards it.

We found a café near the Hotel Negresco and ordered two *salades niçoises*.

'Arm and a leg here,' I said, 'but the view is nicer than back there.' I told Isabel about the invitation to the concert that Rocky had extended and withdrawn.

'I'm sure it's because Jacqueline decided to come as well,' I said, 'and he didn't want her to meet me.'

'He still doesn't know you met her, and him, before?'

'No.' I put my hand up. 'And yes, you're right, I must tell him.'

'How keen are you?' Isabel asked.

'I haven't been so physically attracted to a man since I first met Joel,' I said. 'I've tried to work out how I feel, but it's all mixed up with desire. I can't separate the two. I think we're genetically programmed to like, and fall in love with, the men we fancy. It's as though we have to create an emotional bond to justify our instincts.'

Isabel sighed in agreement. 'I know. Somewhere at the back of my mind I'm always asking myself, prince or frog?'

'Rocky's a bit of a boy,' I said. 'He likes driving fast and he likes to win.'

'Even against twelve-year-olds,' Isabel said drily.

'I know. He's a typical male. But he's fun. He makes every bone in my body feel alive, and my brain goes round in circles, and I think I'm falling in love with him, and then I wonder if that's only because I fancy him.'

'Life's simpler for men,' Isabel said. 'They can have sex with women they neither like nor respect.'

'Only some men.'

She gave me a dark look. 'You'd be surprised.'

'What about your detective?'

'His image is fading,' she said gloomily. 'I put his name into a search engine yesterday. Nothing. I was hoping for a newspaper story. Maybe even a photograph.'

I offered her my mobile. 'Call him.'

She shook her head. 'I need to think about it.' She brightened. 'Anyway, we're having a wonderful time. George is easy company, and we have the party to look forward to.'

'Maybe you'll find a lion to tame,' I said. For some reason, an image of George came into my head. We got up to leave.

'That's terrific,' Isabel said, staring at something behind me. I turned and saw a statue about ten feet tall, with a brown face and brown hands, holding a golden trumpet. His jacket was a mosaic of mirrored glass, and plastic fragments in primary colours. He towered, shimmering, above us, seeming to bend and sway in the heat haze. I read the inscription: Miles Davis, trumpeter.

'I've tried to play jazz,' I said, remembering my efforts in Rocky's bar, 'but I'm no good at it. Not loose enough.'

I went looking for George when we got back. He was dozing on a sunbed beside the pool, deaf to the shrieks and splashes all around. Sam and David seemed to be part of a multi-national game of water polo.

I sat on the vacant sunbed next to George. 'Do you think I need to loosen up, George?'

He took off his sunglasses and looked up at me.

'Who's been saying that to you?'

'A few people have said it. Joel used to say it.'

George swung his feet on to the ground and sat up. 'You're a serious person, Claire.' He met my gaze steadily. 'I like that.'

I thought he was going to say something else when Sam appeared, dripping and panting, at my elbow. 'Have you asked her yet?' he demanded.

'Asked me what?'

'I was going to take Sam and David canoeing and fishing tomorrow,' George said. 'If it's all right with you. There's a lake, Saint-Cassien, less than a hour's drive away.'

'Is this a way of avoiding the party?'

'You have a low opinion of me, Claire.'

'No I don't.'

'I'll be on parade at the appointed time.'

'Lucky you,' I said to Sam.

'You could come too,' said George.

'They'll have more fun without me to cramp their style.'

As I spoke, a flash of pink caught my eye. I saw Sam glance sideways, but he didn't turn his head to meet the gaze of the girl on the handlebars, pedalling backwards along the path beyond the swimming pool, chatting to her friend.

We spent a companionable afternoon lazing by the pool. Sam and David, exhausted by the heat, played games on their mobile phones. Isabel, George and I lay in the purple shade of the pink parasols, getting up occasionally to swim a few lengths before picking up our books again. George seemed absorbed in his book. It had a blonde in black leather, blowing smoke from a gun, on the dust jacket. Isabel was reading the last chapter of *Lorna Doone*.

'Classic romance,' she said, snapping it shut. 'Love at first sight, and happy ever after. John Ridd is only twelve when he first sees Lorna Doone. Imagine.' She paused. 'George, do you believe in love at first sight?'

George didn't look up from his book. 'It happens.'

'Has it ever happened to you?'

'Once.'

'And?'

'I was married. She was married.'

'Did you have an affair?'

'You ask a lot of questions, Isabel,' George said, sounding more amused than offended. He closed his book, got up, and walked to the edge of the pool.

'He's attractive, your detective,' Isabel said, with an appraising stare.

'He's not my detective,' I said, watching George powering through the water. 'I thought you were only interested in French detectives.'

'No harm in a wee bit of distraction,' Isabel said. 'Or a bit of practice.'

She reached across for the hardback George had been reading. 'You can tell a lot about men from the books they read.' She opened the book where a ticket stub marked a page. She caught her breath.

'What is it?'

'I've heard of people hiding complete tosh behind a highbrow cover, but never the other way round.' She looked up. 'Where is he?'

'Miles away.' The pool was the size of a small lake.

Isabel read aloud from the book.

'Time was away and somewhere else,
There were two glasses and two chairs
And two people with the one pulse
(Somebody stopped the moving stairs)
Time was away and somewhere else.

And they were neither up nor down;
The stream's music did not stop
Flowing through heather, limpid brown,
Although they sat in a coffee shop,
And they were neither up nor down.'

She folded back the dustcover and showed me the title on the spine. *Louis MacNeice. Collected Poems.* She turned again to the marked page. 'The poem's called "Meeting Point".' She recited:

'Time was away and she was here
And life no longer what it was,
The bell was silent in the air
And all the room one glow because
Time was away and she was here.'

We both turned to look at George, treading water at the far end of the pool.

'He must be in love,' I said.

Isabel replaced the book. 'Lucky woman.'

'He hasn't mentioned anybody.'

'Maybe they've broken up.'

George got out of the pool and announced he was going to light the barbecue. As soon as he had gone, I rang Helen on my mobile.

'There's been nothing in the papers since Sunday,' she said.

'I wondered if he'd been living with anybody?'

'So that's the way the wind's blowing?' I could hear the smack of satisfaction in her voice. 'Which one of you is interested?'

'Neither of us, Helen.'

She grunted her disbelief. 'I heard he moved in with a friend of Maggie's for a while. I don't know her name. She lives in Castlerock. He didn't mention anybody to you?'

'He dodged the question.'

'I could find out if you really want to know.'

'It's all right,' I said. 'We were just curious.' I didn't want it all round Coleraine that I was interested in George McCracken. I wasn't.

Chapter 32

George was cooking chicken on the barbecue when we strolled back from the pool. The lip-smacking, saliva-inducing smell filled my nostrils and I inhaled greedily.

'Locally grown chicken, marinated in lemon juice, olive oil, garlic and herbs,' George said. 'Sam is sous-chef. David is head waiter. He'll show you to your table.'

David had draped a tea towel over his arm. He pulled out chairs for us. Sam was wearing an apron, and brandishing a set of tongs.

'I picked the herbs,' he said. 'There's a rosemary bush near our tent, and a bay tree beside the shower block.'

'So I noticed last night,' I said, sitting down. 'Sam and David have been trying surveillance on some campers,' I called out to George. 'I told them even the police need permission for that. Isn't that right, George?'

'Absolutely,' George said, managing to keep a straight face.

'What if we suspect a crime?' Sam asked.

'You should tell the police,' George said.

'We don't know any French police.'

'Isabel does,' said George, smiling at her. I was surprised by a prick of jealousy. Isabel had been confiding in George. I felt usurped, and then guilty about being mean-spirited. Isabel and George? Why not? A real detective might distract her from impossible dreams.

Sam and David clamoured to know all about Isabel's French detective. She told them about her encounter with the airport undercover team, adding more detail about the hidden camera, subtracting the romantic subtext.

'Maybe we could tell him about the men with the white van,' Sam said.

'Tell him what?' I said.

'You mean the white van I see every morning on the way to the shop?' said Isabel.

'You see, but don't observe,' Sam said, with a great air of satisfaction.

'It's a different van every day,' David said.

'How do you know?'

'It's got an "I" registration for Italy, but the number plate changes.'

'Full marks for observation,' George said, with a note of surprise.

'I think they're jewel thieves,' Sam said. 'Like that story you showed us in the paper, Isabel. We should tell your detective, honest.'

'Nonsense,' I said, thinking I would have to put a stop to this fantasy. 'They'd never get through the roadblocks. Bound to be stopped.'

'I saw lots of white vans at the market,' Isabel said.

'We've got clues,' Sam said. 'Mum confiscated them.'

George looked thoughtful. 'Where did you find them?'

'They were under the van, near the door,' Sam said. 'Like they'd fallen out.'

'If you've still got them, Claire,' George said, in a casual tone, 'I'll have a look.'

I retrieved the plastic bag from the wastepaper basket in the caravan, and shook two empty, scrunched-up cigarette packets, and what looked like receipts from a shop or restaurant, on to the table.

George picked up one of the packets, and smoothed and flattened it into a semblance of its former shape. It was white and gold, with bold black lettering. We studied the health warning, inside a black-rimmed box. I hoped the boys wouldn't ask me to translate *impuissance*.

'Very French,' George said. He smoothed out the second packet.

The warning in the black box was: *Il fumo uccide.*

'Smoking kills,' translated Isabel. 'That's pretty blunt.'

George turned the pack over. The warning on the back read, *Il fumo invecchia la pelle*.

George and I looked to Isabel.

'Smoking damages your skin,' she said. 'Very Italian.'

George looked at the receipts. 'Restaurant receipts. From Ventimiglia.'

'So the van crosses back into Italy,' I said. 'Nothing illegal about that.'

'They're probably operating a little business,' George said, 'selling cigarettes in the local market.'

'If you ask me,' said Isabel, 'those cyclists at the end of our row look a lot more dodgy. They're always coming and going at odd times.'

'You just think they should shave their legs,' I said lightly. I didn't want Sam getting any new ideas about surveillance.

George smiled at Sam and David. 'You've done the right thing telling us about the white van. Well done. But,' he put on a stern face, 'no more surveillance. Or no fishing and canoeing tomorrow? Understood?'

They nodded meekly. I sighed with relief. 'Promise?'

'Promise,' they solemnly replied.

When the boys had gone to change for the disco, George lit a cigarette. 'These have gone up a lot in the last year,' he said, squinting at it. 'The French government put up the tax.' He blew a smoke ring. 'There's a big price difference between France and Italy now.'

He picked up the flattened packets and slipped them into his pocket. 'Fancy a stroll?'

The occupants of the nearby caravans had retired for the night. Ours was the only circle of light in our little backwater, and when I turned off the gas lamp and blew out the candle, the moon seemed to fly up out of the trees.

Isabel, George and I walked up the track to the pulsing beat of the cicadas, turned on to the main avenue, and followed the well-lit route to the bar. It opened on to the swimming pool, and had a roof of fake grass, to make it look like a Polynesian hut. At the back of the bar, a television screen the size of a snooker table was showing silent aerial pictures of cyclists streaming along a mountain road.

George said quietly, 'Would you recognise the men who drive the white van, Isabel?'

'They're at a table near the screen,' she said. 'They have a couple of beers in front of them, and they look as though they'll be there for a while.'

We walked down the tented avenue and looked at the white van parked beside a larger version of the boys' tent. It was about the size of a minibus and gleamed in the moonlight.

'Will you keep dick while I have a look around?' George said in a soft voice.

An image of Dick Jordan flew into my mind and I almost laughed out loud at the thought of what he might say if he saw what we were doing, the absurdity of it. I wondered if we had all had a little too much to drink.

'Like old times, Claire,' George threw over his shoulder in a whisper, as he prowled around the back of the tent. 'There's a motorbike here,' he added. He struck a match.

In almost the same moment, I heard footsteps approaching, and men talking in the too loud voices they used when they were drunk. The match went out. I pulled off an earring, and called out, 'My earring has fallen off. Help me look for it.'

Isabel and I dropped to our knees and began scrabbling around. Two shadows fell on the ground before us. I looked up and saw two moonlit faces wearing foolish, drunken smiles. One of them said something in a language I didn't recognise.

'I've lost my earring,' I said, pulling on my earlobe.

He pulled his earlobe in imitation, and laughed. His companion snapped open a cigarette lighter and held it up like a miniature, flaming torch.

'Got it!' I cried, picking my earring off the ground. We stood up. 'Thank you for your help,' I said, grabbing Isabel's arm. 'Goodnight.'

We walked past the men, towards the shower block. I sensed them looking after us. One of them called out something and the other one laughed, more coarsely this time. I heard the sound of their tent being unzipped, and zipped up again.

George stepped out from behind the hedge. 'Smart work,' he said. 'What language was that?'

'Not Italian,' Isabel said. 'Some Slavic or Balkan language. Serbo-Croat? Albanian?'

George whistled softly. 'The motorbike had an Albanian numberplate,' he said.

We cut back through the trees to our mobile home. I switched on the light. We sat down at the kitchen table.

'I could see through the windscreen into the back of the van,' George said. 'It's full of cigarette cartons.'

'You think they're smuggling cigarettes?' I said.

'Aren't they just like English people going to Calais to load up with cheap booze and cigarettes? You don't mean serious smugglers, do you?' Isabel said.

'Maybe. It depends on the quantities,' George said.

'They mightn't be anything at all,' I said. 'They might just like hiring white vans. Or they might be buying cigarettes in Italy and selling them in France perfectly legally. Just making a living.'

'They're probably refugees, just trying to make a living,' George agreed. 'Small fry, anyway. I might file a report with our people. They can pass it on.'

He got up to leave. Before I could suggest walking to the rainbow arch with him, my mobile rang. I had left it on the table outside. I hesitated.

'Answer it,' George said. 'You never know who it might be.'

It was Rocky.

'I thought I saw you in Nice today, but you slipped away before I could introduce you,' he said.

'Did she help you choose a costume for the party?'

'Are you jealous?' He sounded amused.

'Don't be ridiculous.'

'I came outside to phone you, to say goodnight,' he said. 'Make arrangements to pick you up tomorrow night.'

I imagined him on the terrace of his villa, under the stars, smoking, looking through the French windows at two blonde women and a man in a brightly lit room. I could see George and Isabel chatting inside the caravan.

'I have to go. I'm with my friends.'

'You'd better get back to them,' Rocky said. 'Pick you up about half past eight? We can all go in my car.'

The door of the caravan banged. George gave me a brisk wave, and headed up the track.

'I'll see you tomorrow,' Rocky said. I heard a shout in the background. 'Must go.'

'George,' I called out. He stopped. Turned round. 'Rocky will take us all to the party in his car,' I said.

'I wouldn't want to cramp your style,' George said, in a tight voice. 'Isabel and I will take a taxi.'

'That was amazing,' Isabel said, bright-eyed, when I went back inside. 'All that stuff about cigarettes. Watching George snoop around, and you and me playacting.'

'It was fun,' I said.

'Do you miss it? The police and all that?'

'Sometimes,' I said. 'I miss the camaraderie. The excitement. The sense of belonging. It's hard to describe. It's like being in a big, extended family. You feel more loyal to your colleagues than anyone else. You'd do anything for them. They're your best friends. When one of you is hurt, you all feel it. I had great crack. Especially with George and Robbie. I couldn't settle into another police force after that. There was a closeness. Maybe it was because Northern Ireland is such a small place.'

'Would you go back?'

'To the police?'

'To Northern Ireland?'

'Maybe. I don't know. When I hear someone with a Northern Irish accent, I always ask where they're from, and we have a chat. But Sam has grown up in England. He'd miss his friends. I'd miss you.' I smiled at her.

'I'd miss you too,' she said.

I told her what Rocky had said about Sergeant Plod and the sour-faced constable. 'I was mortified. But I feel relieved. It will be easier to tell him, now that he's brought the subject up.'

'You feel you can come clean? That's good,' she said.

'I'm not looking forward to it.'

She looked at me closely. 'What else is wrong?'

'George doesn't want to go to the party in Rocky's car. He said he didn't want to cramp my style.'

'Why do you mind him saying that? It's nice of him.'

'He didn't say it in a nice way,' I said.

Isabel looked thoughtful. 'I wish you'd tell George who Rocky is. He's curious about him. I had to keep changing the subject.'

'They're never going to like each other.' The thought depressed me.

'You'll feel better when you tell him.'

'I'll tell him tomorrow,' I said. I wasn't looking forward to that conversation either.

That night, I lay in bed remembering how I had cried in George's arms, sat in his kitchen, and been comforted by him. He was one of my most trusted friends. Why had he been so sarcastic?

A memory hopped into my mind. Sitting with George and Robbie in the canteen, a few weeks after I joined North Region CID. Robbie got up to intercept a young, uniformed constable he wanted to ask out.

'She makes me want to be bad,' he said, grinning. 'Sorry, Claire.' He hurried after his quarry.

If Robbie had learned to watch what he said in my company, I had learned to laugh at him. I moaned to George, in mock disappointment, 'Why don't I make Robbie want to be bad?'

George said, 'You're much more scary, Claire. You make men want to be good.'

Chapter 33

George was wearing a black rugby shirt, white shorts and a pair of boots. He had hung a whistle round his neck, and painted REFEREE in white letters across his chest. 'The taxi is waiting at the entrance. Will I do?'

I had to laugh. 'You look great.'

'You look lovely. You both look lovely.'

'I feel ridiculous walking through the campsite dressed like this,' Isabel said, adjusting her epaulettes.

My costume was less eye-catching, but I, too, felt self-conscious in a polka dot skirt and white ankle socks. We drove to the car park at reception.

Rocky roared up in the red Mustang. He was disguised as a cat burglar in a black and white horizontally striped shirt, black trousers and sneakers, and a black eye-mask. He whistled appreciatively at me. 'Love the silver boots!' he said to Isabel. He nodded at George. 'You can follow me. I have the directions.'

The light was fading from the sky when we pulled up at the gates of a walled *domaine* in the hills above Grasse. Rocky spoke our names into the intercom. The gates swung open. We entered the courtyard of an eighteenth-century *manoir* of perfect proportions. Its pale stone walls glowed in the dusk and lights shone from its long windows. It seemed to float lightly above the ground.

We crossed the cobbled yard in the mauve light of sunset, and joined an informal queue swirling up the wide stone steps and along a candlelit entrance hall, to where Amy and Jimmy stood welcoming guests.

Amy was dressed in a nineteen twenties flapper dress, encrusted with gold sequins. She fingered a gold necklace, like a collar, studded with diamonds.

'My anniversary present from Jimmy,' she said. 'Show them what I gave you, Jimmy.'

Jimmy withdrew a bare brown arm from his white toga, and displayed a gold watch. 'Patek Philippe,' he said, admiring it. 'I've always wanted one.'

They smiled fondly at each other. 'Enjoy yourselves,' they chorused.

We flowed through a series of interconnected rooms, each with a French window opening on to a terrace. In the shifting swarm of guests, I spotted two men in powdered wigs and frock coats, a monk, three nuns in black veils, white wimples and miniskirts, and a man in a near-full-length cardboard box, with tiny windows painted on it, and a toy gorilla stuck to the top.

Waiters weaved like bullfighters through the crush, holding trays of canapés above their heads. I caught reflections of white linen, champagne bottles in buckets, lobsters on cracked ice, plates piled high with vol-au-vents, silver bowls of strawberries and raspberries.

We drifted on to the terrace like boats on a stream. The air smelled of lavender and roses. White fairy lights outlined the windows, the balustrades and the paths through the formal garden below. Beyond the box hedges and the statues, a swimming pool, lit underwater, flared luminescent, silvery blue. Beyond the pool lay a dark, velvet lawn, dotted with candlelit tables.

The sky faded to black. The lights burned brighter. I felt I was on the deck of an ocean liner sailing into the night. Somewhere a band struck up. A speaker crackled above our heads and music burst out, like a tidal wave drowning all the talk and the laughter. Amy ducked and dived through the crowd like a golden fish.

Rocky introduced us to a hawk-faced woman in a black dress and a witch's pointed hat, and her partner in an embroidered waistcoat and a powdered wig. I couldn't hear a word they said.

We made our way down the steps to the garden and laid claim to a table at the back of the lawn, from where we made trips into the house for food and drink.

'I still can't believe I'm here,' Isabel shouted in my ear.

'Me neither,' I yelled back.

I looked around the table. Rocky, on my left, had put on his eye-mask. He sprawled in his chair, lazily watching the gyrations on the terrace. Isabel and George put their fingers in their ears and grinned at me.

There was no sign of Bernadette. Once, I saw a swan-necked Dresden shepherdess flit past, and thought for a moment it was her. She turned to wave at someone on the terrace and I saw it was someone else entirely.

The rock music stopped. Amy and Jimmy swayed to the sound of Frank Sinatra singing 'Moon River'.

Rocky put his hand on my arm. 'Let's dance. I've been dying to get my arms round you all night.'

I rested my head on his shoulder, and let him steer me through the shuffling throng. Amy, dancing with the Empire State Building and King Kong, gave me a wave. I saw George and Isabel sitting on the balustrade, heads together, Isabel talking rapidly. More confidences, I thought.

The music stopped. We all returned to our seats. Amy and Jimmy toured the garden, stopping at each table in turn to chat. When they sat down with us, they tried to find an acquaintance in common with George. He frowned, considering the names thrown out to him, before shaking his head.

'I'm sure I've seen you somewhere before,' Amy said. 'I've a great memory for faces.'

She turned to me.

Isabel called out, 'I have a cousin who's an actor. I wonder if you know him?'

I gave her a grateful smile. Amy was happily diverted. It turned out she had spent a season at the Theatre Royal in Glasgow, and had a store of scandalous and funny stories to tell.

The crowd thinned. 'There's a group going on to a party in Saint-Tropez,' Amy said. 'I'll just say goodbye to them.' She darted away.

Jimmy's eyes followed her as she flitted between tables, stopping here and there to kiss a proffered cheek. Now she was clinging to the Empire State Building. Jimmy drummed his fingers on the table. His features worked to fight off a scowl.

We had been drinking champagne for the best part of two hours. Everything seemed exaggerated in a slightly hallucinatory way. A Pierrot with a white face and a red spot on each cheek swayed past on the arm of a monk. The talk swirling round us was too fast and too loud. George and Isabel were wearing glassy smiles. I had drunk three or four flutes of champagne, and felt pleasantly woozy. Rocky, I had noticed, drank hardly at all.

Jimmy got up, grabbed the bottle on the table, and went round topping up our glasses. He slopped the last of the champagne into my glass, straightened the olive wreath on his head, and recited, with a slight slur:

> *'What men call gallantry, and gods adultery,*
> *Is much more common where the climate's sultry.'*

He moved unsteadily towards Isabel. 'What's sauce for the goose,' he said, 'C'mon, let's dance.'

George got to his feet. Isabel said quickly, 'What was that you just quoted?'

Amy was a flash of gold coming across the lawn towards us. She stopped when she saw Jimmy on his feet, swaying, waving the empty champagne bottle.

'Byron, *Don Juan*,' Jimmy said. He pointed at Rocky. 'Watch him. He's a Don Juan. He stole my fiancée.'

'That was a long time ago, Jimmy,' Amy said, stepping forward and touching him on the arm. 'Come on. That's enough.'

Jimmy fixed her with a stare. *'Aye. That was in another country, and besides, the wench is dead.'*

There was an awkward silence. The music started again. Jimmy collapsed into his seat, muttering, 'Sorry, no offence.' His face was as white as his toga.

Amy said, 'I'll get you some coffee, Jimmy.'

Isabel pushed her chair back. 'I'll go.'

'I'll help you,' said George.

'I thought we'd need a referee,' Jimmy said.

'Excuse us,' Rocky said abruptly. He drew me to my feet. 'Let's take a stroll around the garden.'

I looked back. Amy was sitting on Jimmy's knee. Her arms were round his neck.

'That was awful for you, I'm sorry,' I said.

'Jimmy's a fool. Amy's a flirt. I don't want to see much of them. I don't want them coming to the bar,' Rocky said.

'You mightn't be able to avoid them.'

'Oh, yes I will.'

We walked along a path beside the wall. Rocky led me through an archway into a small, lantern-lit courtyard. We sat on a bench beneath a life-sized stone Cupid. Music and laughter drifted in the air above us. Rocky pulled off his mask. His eyes were bright with excitement.

'I've decided to sell up and move on,' he said. 'I'm tired of rules and regulations. I want to speak English again.' He took both my hands. 'Have you ever thought of starting a new life somewhere else?'

'I did that when I moved to England.'

'I mean somewhere far away. Australia, New Zealand, South Africa.'

'I like where I live.'

'Maybe I should think about moving to England.' He paused for a moment. 'How much do you think I would have to pay for a bar in Henley?'

I had the sudden sensation of my life running away from me. I put my hand up. 'Stop. Listen. I've something to tell you.' I was babbling. 'I've been meaning to tell you. I've met you before. In Northern Ireland.'

Rocky looked puzzled.

'I was the sour-faced constable.'

'What?'

'I was one of the detectives who came to see you, to tell you we'd found your wife's body.'

His face froze. His eyes narrowed, then hardened. He pulled his hands away. 'What are you doing here?'

'I'm on holiday,' I said. 'I'm not in the police any more. I told you. I'm a solicitor.' The words were pouring out of me. 'I was in the police. Before I became a solicitor. A detective constable. I was based in Ballymoney. I interviewed you when your wife died.'

He jumped up. 'Are you still working for the police?'

'No!' I cried. 'I'm on holiday. I didn't realise it was you. Not at first. You look different. I thought your name was a coincidence.'

He took a step backwards. His shoulder hit a lantern hanging from the outstretched arm of Cupid. Our shadows danced crazily on the walls. He made fists of his hands by his side.

'When did you know?'

'In Menton. When you told us your wife had died in a fall. That you'd benefited. I realised it was you.'

'You've known for days,' he said. 'Why didn't you tell me before?'

'I wanted to. There never seemed to be the right moment. You didn't want to talk about it.'

'You thought I had something to do with it,' he said in a hard voice.

'No,' I cried. 'Not now. Maybe back then. But not now.'

The corners of his mouth quivered. I thought for a moment he was going to cry. 'You suspected me.'

'It was my job.'

His mouth was set now in a stubborn, downward curve. 'You had no evidence.'

'We still had to ask questions.'

'Ask me now,' he said, in a goaded tone. 'Go on.' His hand shot out and grabbed my wrist. 'Ask me!'

'I don't need to ask you,' I said.

'Sure?'

'Positive.'

He dropped my wrist. He held my gaze for what seemed like ages. 'I wasn't with her. I swear.'

A sense of relief washed through me. 'I believe you,' I said.

My skin was burning from his grip, and a red mark had formed. I looked at it wonderingly. Rocky took my hand, turned it over, and kissed the inside of my wrist. The music started again. He pulled me to him, almost lifting me off my feet.

I laid my cheek against his, and we began to waltz. We floated up the steps to the terrace. I felt I was dancing on air.

I was humming with content, a few minutes later, when George tapped Rocky on the shoulder. 'Excuse me.'

Rocky ignored him.

'This dance is an Excuse me,' George repeated.

'Excuse me?'

'Delighted,' said George. Before I could take in what was happening, he had twirled me away.

'George,' I protested.

'I have to kidnap you to have a conversation,' he said, executing a slow turn. 'You're spending all your time with him.'

I made a half-dissenting noise.

'You shouldn't forget your old friends. I thought we'd have time to talk. Catch up properly.' He gave me a lopsided smile, and began to croon with Frank Sinatra:

'There may be trouble ahead,
But while there's moonlight and music and love and romance,
Let's face the music and dance.'

It was surprisingly agreeable to have George's arms round me. He gave me a despairing look. 'You think I'm a bit drunk? You're a terrible puritan, Claire. That makes it hard . . .' He stopped. Dancers manoeuvred around us, like ships avoiding a rock.

'I'm not a puritan, George.'

Jimmy appeared at George's shoulder. 'Excuse me.' He detached me from George. 'You seem to have started something,' he said.

All over the terrace, dancers were swapping partners.

'Great idea,' Jimmy said. 'Makes people get to know each other.'

Isabel floated past in the arms of Louis the Fourteenth.

Now Frank Sinatra was singing 'Strangers in the Night'.

'Appropriate,' Jimmy said. He seemed to have sobered up. 'You know, you remind me of somebody. She had dark curly hair too. She was the first woman I fell in love with.' His eyes grew misty.

A French Foreign Legionnaire tapped him on the shoulder. 'You can't monopolise all the good-looking women just because it's your party.' He swung me away with an admiring stare.

I began to process the story of the party for Sam, for Isabel, for Helen, for Enid in the office.

Rocky tapped the Legionnaire on the shoulder and spun me away in his arms. He steered me from the terrace into a candlelit room. 'Come home with me tonight.'

'I can't. Sam won't sleep properly until I'm back.'

'Tomorrow night? Come to the villa. I'll cook dinner for you.'

A voice in my head whispered, '*Gather ye rosebuds . . .*'

A door opened and the lights came on. 'Sorry,' Jimmy said thickly. He was standing in the doorway, his hand still on the light switch. Behind him I could see a monk in headphones, and a group of dancing nuns. 'I came up to make a request for Amy. Do you know where she is?'

'I'm here.' Amy appeared in the French window. I extricated myself from Rocky.

'Excuse me,' I said, brushing past her to sit outside on the balustrade. A whine, a crackle and a blast of music from the loudspeaker above my head made me jump. Mick Jagger began to sing 'I Can't Get No Satisfaction'.

The number of dancers had dwindled to a dozen couples. I couldn't see Isabel or George. Rocky came and sat beside me.

'Sam will be all right,' he said. 'Isabel's there.'

'I promised I would look in when I got back.'

'He'll be asleep.'

'I won't break my word to him.'

'Don't make any promises tomorrow night,' Rocky said, 'except to me.'

I traced an invisible line on the ground with the toe of my shoe. 'Are you seeing anybody else?'

'I see lots of people.'

'I thought maybe a woman friend had come down from Chamonix for the concert.' I traced another line with my toe.

He blew his breath out, and stood up. 'You're jealous.'

'I just like to be clear about things,' I said.

'Be clear about this,' he said, pulling me to my feet. His breath was on my face. I closed my eyes, waiting for his kiss.

Chapter 34

Someone crashed into me, nearly knocking me off my feet. Amy and Jimmy jigged past, in a conga, chanting, 'Duh duh, da da duh, duh duh duh duh, da da duh . . . *I can't get no satisfaction* . . .'

Rocky started to laugh as the line snaked past us across the terrace. A hand came out and jerked me sideways. I grabbed the tailcoat of Louis the Fourteenth, and felt Rocky's hands settle on my waist as we hopped and swayed down the steps into the garden, and snaked around the statues. Half the conga peeled away when we did a circuit of the swimming pool; the remainder weaved in and out through the now half-deserted tables on the lawn, and trailed back up the steps to the terrace again, before breaking up.

We bumped into the hawk-faced witch and her partner, clinging to each other, wearing bright, disordered smiles. There was a fast exchange in French. I caught the word 'casino'. They were bent on detaining Rocky. I slipped away and sat on a stone bench at the back of the terrace.

There was a ripple of gold. Amy sat down beside me.

'Thank you for a wonderful party,' I said.

'We put on a good show, Jimmy and I.' She paused. 'Sorry about the little scene earlier.'

'He's a jealous husband,' I said.

'I wind him up.'

'I haven't seen Bernadette,' I said.

'She had to go back,' Amy said.

'Nothing wrong, I hope?' I liked Bernadette. 'Shame to miss the party.'

'It was just a flying visit. We're going to have a big party in Belfast.' Amy paused. 'Can I ask you a personal question?'

'I might not answer it.'

She flicked her lashes towards Rocky. 'Are you in love with him?'

'It's all moving a bit too fast for me,' I said. 'I might have a better idea how I feel when I get home.' Her openness had charmed me, and champagne had loosened my tongue. 'He doesn't look like Che Guevara any more, does he?'

Amy gave me a sharp look. 'Have we met before?'

I glanced around. Rocky was now talking to a blonde in a gym-slip. He looked over at me and gave a helpless shrug. I felt curiously relaxed. I said to Amy, 'I met you when Dolores Rock died. I used to be in the RUC. I interviewed you and Jimmy at the theatre.'

'Omigod,' Amy said. She looked from Rocky, to me, and back to Rocky again. 'Does he know?'

'I told him earlier tonight.'

'I'll bet he got a bit of a gunk to say the least,' Amy said. She shook her head in wonder. 'Did you meet Bernadette before? When . . . you know . . .' Her voice faltered.

'I only met her once. I wouldn't have recognised her when she came to Rocky's bar if she hadn't said her name.'

'We've all changed in ten years,' Amy said.

'You haven't.'

Amy laughed. 'Actresses aren't supposed to age.' She peered at me. 'I remember you now. You came with Robbie Dunbar.'

I wasn't surprised she had remembered Robbie. 'You made a big impression on him,' I said. 'He talked about asking you out.'

'It's a funny old world,' Amy said. 'Now he's . . .' She stopped.

'Now he's what?'

'That's what I'm wondering. Now he's what?'

'Still in the police. He's in a new unit, reviewing cold cases.'

'You couldn't make it up,' she said. She stood up. 'I need to clear my head. I'm going for a swim. There's a crowd gone down to the pool. Want to join us?'

There was a sound like a small cannon being fired. A rocket whined into the night and erupted in a galaxy of gold and silver stars that burst again and again, and fell to earth like tiny, twinkling parachutes. A cheer went up, and a Strauss waltz burst from the loudspeakers.

'I'll just stay here and watch the fireworks,' I said.

There was an end-of-the-party feel to the evening, after the fireworks. I heard occasional bursts of laughter from little knots of guests on the terrace, and squeals from the direction of the swimming pool. The house was quiet, except for the dull clatter of plates being stacked by the waiters on the long tables that had supported the food. I found Isabel sitting in an empty room between a vast display of cream and pink roses and a white baby grand piano. She patted the sofa beside her. I sank on to the pink brocade.

'I told him,' I said.

She put her arm round me and squeezed my shoulders. 'Well done. Is he all right about it?'

I smiled. 'He wants to see me tomorrow night. I hate abandoning George again, but I feel I owe it to Rocky. He's been so nice about everything.'

'George and I can be gooseberries together,' Isabel said. 'Have you enjoyed the party?'

'I've enjoyed watching it flow past me. If you sit here long enough, you see everybody. A lot of guests have gone down to the pool. I think they're skinny-dipping.'

A nun came into the room, pushing Jimmy towards the piano. 'The music's stopped. Give us a tune,' she urged.

Jimmy slumped on to the piano stool. His fingers strayed over the keys. He picked out a few notes with his right hand.

'He's a great pianist,' the nun announced.

Jimmy's face seemed to focus itself. He straightened up and vamped a few chords, with his foot on the pedal to dampen the sound. Isabel got up and wandered over to the piano. Jimmy played 'Danny Boy'. Gradually, a little group gathered round him.

An impromptu concert began. The Empire State Building and King Kong broke into 'My Way'. Jimmy sang 'When I'm Sixty-Four'. The Dresden shepherdess followed with '*Je Ne Regrette Rien*'.

The nun flopped down on the sofa beside me. Jimmy was nodding and talking to George. He played a series of rising, rippling chords. George began to sing in a light baritone.

'When I was a young man courting the girls,
I played me a waiting game.'

I had never heard George sing. I sat upright in surprise.

'Oh, it's a long, long while from May to December
But the days grow short when you reach September.
When the autumn weather turns the leaves to flame . . .'

A picture came into my mind. George, sitting at my desk, in a pool of sunshine, drinking tea from my mug.

> *'One hasn't got time for the waiting game.*
> *Oh, the days dwindle down to a precious few,*
> *September, November!*
> *And these few precious days I'll spend with you,*
> *These precious days I'll spend with you.'*

The last reverberations of the piano died away. The nun murmured, 'He's dead handsome. Is he with your friend?' She nudged me. 'He's looking over here. I wonder which one of us he fancies?'

Jimmy closed the piano. 'Fancy a swim, anybody?'

'Only if I can keep my shorts on,' George said. He caught my eye and smiled.

And at that exact moment, we heard a heart-stopping scream. An alarm bell went off like a drill. We tumbled out of the room. Electric light flooded the hall. Amy was stumbling down the stairs in a white towelling robe, shaking her head wildly. Even above the din of the alarm we could hear her wail, 'Somebody's stolen my necklace. I took it off to swim,' as she ran blindly past us, into Jimmy's outstretched arms.

Jimmy led the sobbing Amy back upstairs. Guests flowed from every part of the house and grounds into the hall and grouped into little clusters, unable to speak and be heard above the din of the alarm, miming their shock and uncertainty about what to do.

The alarm died after about five minutes, and a general hubbub filled the hall. George mounted the stairs and blew his whistle. The blast, and George's air of command, brought silence. He addressed us in passable French. I got the gist. He repeated himself in English.

'No one can prevent you leaving, but it makes sense and would help if we wait until the police arrive. They will probably let us go quickly. Whoever did this will be long gone. There is no need for alarm.'

He looked over at me and made a writing sign. I saw a notepad on a table beside the telephone, and gave him the thumbs up.

One or two guests made as though to leave, then shrugged, and subsided on to chairs. I moved from guest to guest, asking them to write their names and contact numbers on the notepad. Nobody refused.

I saw Jimmy come down the stairs and slap George on the shoulder. George pointed at me. Jimmy mouthed his thanks. I made my way over to him.

'They broke into the safe in our bedroom. It's not just the gold necklace. It's all Amy's jewellery. Her engagement ring. Her pearls.'

Then the French police were in the hallway. I gave them the list of names, addresses and telephone numbers. As George had forecast, we were all allowed to go.

There was a faint whitening above the horizon, the stars were shrinking in the sky, and a high lamb's tail of cloud was smeared with pink as we trailed across the courtyard. Rocky was yawning. I was suddenly exhausted.

'I'll go back in the taxi with Isabel and George,' I said to Rocky. 'Save you an extra journey.'

'Are you sure?'

'Positive.'

George held the taxi door open, waiting for me, ostentatiously not looking as Rocky kissed me goodnight.

Chapter 35

The first police roadblock was on the outskirts of Grasse. We were beckoned past, half asleep. Isabel's head was on George's shoulder. He lolled back, looking peaceful. I rolled down the window to let in the cool morning air, and a tentative trill of birdsong.

The sun was pencilling gold along the horizon when we ran into the second roadblock, at the bottom of a hill near Les Arcs. This time, a gendarme opened the door, snorted with laughter, and called his colleagues to look at us, slumped together in a huddle of fancy dress. We were waved through on the tail of a column of cyclists, doggedly pedalling up the hill in the first light.

Sam didn't waken when I unzipped the tent to look in, as I had promised. I staggered to my cabin, pulled down the blind against the sun, lay down on the bed, and fell asleep.

The smell of coffee, and an orchestra of cicadas, wakened me just before midday. I emerged, blinking and stretching in the sunlight, and found Sam and David drinking in the details of the party and the robbery, recounted by Isabel. A copy of *Nice Matin* was spread over the table.

'The police think the thieves got in through a skylight,' Isabel was saying. 'They blew the safe. Nobody noticed anything, with the noise and the music, and the fireworks going off.'

'The white van wasn't there when we went to bed last night,' Sam said.

'I thought I said no more surveillance.'

'We couldn't help observing, Mum.'

'Those men are not jewel thieves, Sam,' I said sternly. 'Put that thought out of your head. They've probably checked out.'

In the afternoon, George walked down from the village. 'I slept all morning,' he said. 'I think I had too much to drink.'

'Me too,' I said.

I felt shy in his presence, remembering how he had flirted with me the previous evening, and had seen Rocky kiss me goodnight.

George said, 'There're a few things I'd like you and Isabel to take a look at.'

Something in his tone made me stop sweeping our sun creams and towels into a bag, and sit down beside Isabel. George pulled a fat packet of cigarettes from his shirt pocket and placed it on the table.

'I bought these in the *tabac* in the village,' he said. He fished two empty, flattened cigarette packets from a trouser pocket, and placed them on either side of the full pack. 'These are the ones Sam and David picked up.'

Isabel said, 'Is this some kind of conjuring trick?'

'You could call it that, I suppose.'

'What's wrong, George?'

'Nothing to be worried about,' he said. 'Nothing that would put the boys in any danger.' He sat back in his chair. 'Take a good look. Compare the packets.'

'They look the same to me,' Isabel said. 'Apart from one warning being in Italian, and the other in French.'

George looked at me. 'Claire?'

I picked up the fresh packet, and examined the words printed on it. I set it back down on the table. I picked up the crumpled French packet, and did the same.

'The health warning is in a different typeface,' I said.

George nodded. I studied the Italian packet.

'The warning's different, but the typeface is the same as the packet you bought today.'

'Good girl,' George said.

'I had a good teacher.'

Isabel looked mystified.

'The Italian packet is genuine, maybe smuggled,' I said. 'The French packet is a fake. Our friends are not just smuggling cigarettes, they're selling counterfeit ones as well.'

'Full marks,' George said.

Isabel stared wildly at us.

'Big criminal business, fake cigarettes. Made in factories in China, and Greece. Smuggled through the Balkans,' George said. 'A lot of drug smugglers have switched to cigarettes. Real and counterfeit.'

'Sam and David,' I said. 'Where are they?'

'Probably at the pool,' Isabel said.

I moved to get up. George put his hand on my arm. 'They're not in danger, Claire. These men won't be armed, or violent. There's big money in cigarettes, but the penalties aren't harsh. Not compared to drug smuggling. Using guns or violence would double or triple the sentence if they get caught. If these men thought someone was on to them, they'd just make a run for it. I still think they're well down the distribution chain.'

'I don't care how far down they are,' I cried. 'If they're working for organised criminals, I don't want them thinking Sam and David are on to them.'

'The boys aren't in danger, Claire. I promise you.'

'You have to do something. What are you going to do?'

'Make a report to our own team.'

'When?'

'I'll phone right now. I'll email as well, for the record. They'll be under proper surveillance soon. In the meantime,' he looked me calmly in the eye, 'I think we should say nothing to Sam and David.'

Logic told me George was right, but the heart is not a logical muscle. 'They can't stay in the tent on their own. They'll have to move in with us,' I said.

Isabel could hardly keep up with me as I ran to the pool. It was all shrieks, laughter and normality, but I still felt weak with relief when I spotted Sam and David, side by side on a sunbed, heads down, playing games on their mobile phones.

'I want to ask you a favour,' I said to Sam. 'Isabel and I heard funny noises last night.'

'What kind of funny noises?'

'Creaking noises, that kind of thing,' I said vaguely. 'We got a bit nervous about prowlers. Would you and David mind staying in the mobile home?'

'You shouldn't be nervous. We're not far away,' Sam said.

'We'd feel a bit more protected,' Isabel said.

'The sofa converts into a bed. You could put your sleeping bags on it.'

Sam gave a lofty sigh. He looked at David. David said, 'I don't mind.'

'I'd feel a whole lot better,' I said.

'OK, Mum,' Sam said.

Isabel and I bagged a couple of sunbeds. I started to show her how to text on my mobile phone.

'Select MESSAGES, then TEXT, then WRITE NEW.'

I keyed in a message to Rocky. *Mst stay at csite tnite. Will fone t xplain*. I showed it to Isabel.

She raised an eyebrow.

'Never mind what it says. The point is, I can send this and he can read it, and reply, without disturbing everybody around him. Don't you hate those loud conversations on mobile phones on trains?'

Sam mooched over. 'You're hopeless at texting, Mum. I'll teach Isabel.'

'Where's David?' I pressed SEND.

'Talking to a couple of girls,' Sam said, in a gruff, dismissive voice. 'Where's your phone?' he asked Isabel.

'I didn't bring it on holiday,' she said.

'What's the point of having it if you don't use it?'

'I only use it to stay in touch when I'm out of the office,' Isabel said.

I fell asleep listening to their murmurings, interspersed with beeps, and was wakened by an enormous splash. Two men had dived into the pool, within a few feet of me, and were pounding through the water like seals. Sam had disappeared. Isabel was pressing phone keys with grim intentness. She looked up at me. Her face relaxed into a smile.

'I think the boys have got more interested in girls than white vans,' she said.

I followed her gaze to where David was steadying himself on a bicycle, one foot on the ground, while a blonde girl in heart-shaped sunglasses arranged herself on the handlebars. Sam was a few feet away from them. His hands were in his pockets. He was looking down at the ground, ignoring the second blonde girl standing beside him, and tracing lines in the dust with his foot. I sat up with a pang of sympathy.

'Sam can't work out what's going on,' I said. 'David's three months older. It's a big difference at that age.'

'He'll catch up soon enough.'

'Look at their body language,' I said. 'The girls are all relaxed, and flicking back their hair. The boys are all red-faced and awkward. They don't stand a chance.'

'Girls have the upper hand at that age,' Isabel said. 'The problem is, we lose it later on.'

'Those two have been circling Sam and David for days. Like Apaches round a wagon train.'

'I should take the initiative,' Isabel said, staring at the phone.

'Do you know his number?'

'Off by heart.'

'Send him a text,' I said. 'It's unthreatening. He's not obliged to reply.'

'What if he doesn't?'

'Less embarrassing than if you spoke to him,' I said.

'What will I say?'

'Try *Hello*.'

'Actually,' she said, with a desperate smile, 'I've written a message and saved it.' She passed Sam's phone to me. 'Have a look. It took me ages.'

Hello. Staying at a campsite near Nice. Having a lovely time. Hope you are well.

'I'm not surprised you took ages. You've spelled everything out properly.'

I held the phone up and pressed the camera button on the

side. Isabel's image appeared on the screen, grainy and impressionistic, like a tiny painting. I pressed CAPTURE. Swish. Click. Her image was swallowed into the phone.

'You can send him your photograph,' I said.

She made a grab for the phone. 'No!'

I dodged her, laughing. 'It's all right. I don't know how to send it. I think it's saved. Are you going to send the text?'

'I'm thinking about it,' she said.

'I sent the message to Rocky, telling him I won't leave the boys tonight.'

'If you want to see him, we could all go to Doctor Rock,' she said. 'The boys would love it. You could talk to Rocky. We could enjoy the music.'

George came smiling towards us. 'I spoke to one of my colleagues. Message received and understood.' He paused. 'Can I treat everybody to a meal in the village tonight?'

The blood rushed to my face. 'We were thinking of going to Rocky's music bar.'

'Count me out,' George said.

His tone was cool and offhand. My ribs tightened. I was seized with a sense that I had done something wrong. George was wearing an expression I hadn't seen before and couldn't read. I was silent with dismay.

'You'll need to eat first,' George said, in the same cool tone. 'The music doesn't usually begin until after nine o'clock in these places.' He pulled his shirt over his head, kicked off his sandals, and dropped his shirt on top of them. 'Do whatever you like.' He walked to the edge of the pool and dived in.

'We could eat in the village and then you and the boys could go to Doctor Rock,' Isabel said.

'Don't you want to come?'

'I'll do whatever you want me to do,' Isabel said.

George climbed out of the pool and stood with his hands on his hips, looking down at me.

'What does this Rocky character do all day?' he said.

I remembered, guiltily, that I had performed casual introductions at best, and had not yet told George about my previous connection to Rocky.

'He owns a bar, remember?' I said. 'He probably works late and gets up late.'

'And just hangs around the rest of the time, I suppose.'

'A lotus-eater,' Isabel said breezily.

George muttered something. It sounded like 'lounge lizard'.

'I'd rather eat in Nice,' I snapped.

'What about you, Isabel? Would you like to have dinner in the village with me?'

Isabel looked uncomfortable. 'I haven't given much thought to what I want to do this evening.'

George slipped his feet into his sandals. He avoided looking at me. 'Call me on my mobile when you make up your mind,' he said. He picked up his shirt and strode off.

Isabel gnashed her teeth and glared at me. 'Never put me in that position again,' she said.

'You told me you didn't mind what you did. It's hard to please everybody.'

'Please yourself,' she said. 'At least where your male friends are concerned.' She turned her back on me and opened her book.

Out of the blurry corner of my eye, I saw two men climb out of the pool and saunter towards the vacant sunbeds on the other side of me. I recognised the two cyclists from the mobile home near us. I turned away from Isabel and pretended to study the phone as they settled themselves. The man nearer me took off his sunglasses, raked both Isabel and me with his eyes and bared his teeth in a mirthless grin. His bald head shone like a copper dome on the tiny screen in front of me. On an impulse, I pressed CAPTURE.

I rolled over, and saw Isabel reaching out her hand. 'I'm sorry,' she whispered. 'We're all a bit tense and hungover today.'

'It's my fault,' I said, gripping her fingers. 'I feel all churned up. Please, tell me what you want to do this evening.'

'I honestly don't mind. You decide.'

'I can hardly blame George being fed up,' I said miserably. 'I invite him out here. He's looking forward to catching up, chats about old times, gossip about old friends, and I virtually ignore him. At least he doesn't know I'm ignoring him for a man I once suspected of being a wife killer.'

'You haven't told him?'

'Not yet,' I said, feeling guilty.

My mobile phone trilled. Rocky's number flashed up on the screen.

'I hope it's a good excuse,' he said.

I made a little sign to Isabel, got up, and sought out a corner of the bar where I wouldn't be overheard.

'We need to see each other,' Rocky said. 'I'm cooking you dinner. No arguments.'

I explained my reluctance to leave Sam and David alone at night.

'A couple of cigarette smugglers are hardly much of a threat,' Rocky said. 'Your friend George should be able to see them off.'

'I'm a mother.'

There was a silence. 'There's no answer to that,' he said.

I noticed the cyclists transfer their interest to a blonde who sashayed past them.

'We could come to Doctor Rock,' I said.

'Who's we?'

'Sam and David, obviously, Isabel, maybe.'

'Half a loaf,' Rocky huffed. 'I was looking forward to a candlelit dinner for two. I was going to cook for you.'

The cyclists got up and followed the blonde. I was glad to see them go.

'It's easier if we eat here first,' I said. 'Sorry.'

'I'll have to come to Henley and cook your dinner.' For a second I thought he had been going to say 'goose'. I almost laughed out loud. There was a fluttering in my ribcage. I had a sensation of things moving too fast for me again.

'See you about nine o'clock,' I said.

I sent a text to George. *Wd love to eat w U. 7OK? Friends?*

When the answer flashed back, *Yes & Yes*, tears pricked my eyes.

'I don't know what's wrong with me,' I said to Isabel. 'I'm weepy, and cross as a bag of cats.'

'You're worried about Sam and David. You don't know how you feel about Rocky. You're guilty about neglecting George.'

The heart is an inarticulate muscle too. I burst into tears.

Chapter 36

Isabel stood up and put her arms round me. 'You're a goose, Claire,' she said affectionately. 'Sometimes we abuse our friendship. We do it because we know we can get away with it. Remember that time we were going to Ireland? And I said I couldn't go at the last minute because I'd just met Terry and he'd asked me to Amsterdam for the weekend? And you were furious? But you forgave me.'

'And I stood you up to go motor racing with Jamie? I don't even like motor racing.'

Sam came running over. 'What's wrong, Mum?'

'I've got something in my eye,' I said. 'A bit of dust. I'll be all right in a minute.' I put on my sunglasses.

Sam picked up his mobile phone and stabbed at the keys.

'I was playing with the camera, wondering how to send a picture,' I said, with a sniff.

'You have a text to send. Were you going to attach the picture?'

'No idea how,' I said.

'It's easy,' Sam said. Too late, I saw his thumbs working the keys. 'There. It's sent,' he said, beaming at me.

It took a moment for me to realise what he had done.

Isabel said, slowly, 'Have you just sent a text?'

Sam nodded. 'The one in unsent items.'

'Did you attach a picture?' I said.

'Yeah. I'm amazed you wanted to send that ugly mug to anybody.'

'Don't be rude, Sam,' I said. 'Apologise to Isabel.'

His smile faded. 'What have I done wrong?'

'Omigod,' Isabel said, 'you sent my photo.'

'It wasn't your photo,' Sam said. 'It was the hairy-legged cyclist.'

'Omigod,' Isabel said again.

'The person getting it will think it a bit strange,' I said.

Sam bit his lip. 'Didn't you want to send it?'

'That was fine, Sam,' Isabel said. 'Thank you.' Her tone was calm, but her eyes were wildly signalling dismay to me. 'Can I just check what I said?'

Sam's thumbs flew over the phone. He passed it to Isabel. She scanned the screen.

'I forgot to put my name,' she said. 'He won't know who it's from.' Relief and regret fought each other in her face.

Sam said, 'He'll think it's from the baldy man. Wrong number.'

'You can send another text from my phone,' I said.

'It's fate,' Isabel said lightly. 'Wasn't meant to be.' She smiled bravely and picked up her book.

'It's OK, Sam,' I said. 'No harm done.' I paused. 'How would you like to go to Rocky's music bar tonight?'

Sam's face reddened. 'I dunno,' he mumbled.

David dodged and skipped towards us like a boxer. He gave Sam a playful dunt on the shoulder. 'What do you call a girl between two goal posts?'

Sam went bright scarlet.

'Annette!' chortled David.

They ran off.

'I don't think you've got any takers for a trip to Doctor Rock,' Isabel said.

I didn't know whether to be relieved or disappointed. At that moment, I didn't want to think about Rocky, or how I felt about him, or might feel about him in the future. I hated George being cross with me.

'I don't know how to behave on a date,' I said. 'Does anybody call them that any more?'

'It's like riding a bicycle,' Isabel said. 'Not that I've put the theory to the test.'

'Half of me wants Rocky to pounce. The other half wants to run a mile,' I said. 'I haven't been this mixed up since I was a teenager.'

'We're all teenagers inside,' Isabel said in a resigned voice. 'My head is thirty-nine, my lungs are thirty-nine, my liver feels about ninety. My heart is fourteen.'

'You can still send a text to your detective. Or just phone him.'

'I'm ridiculous.'

'My father fell in love with a total stranger,' I said. 'I wouldn't be here if he'd walked on by, and not done anything about it.'

'It's easier for a man,' she said.

'This man doesn't have your phone number,' I said.

Dinner, at a restaurant on the corner of the village square, was an edgy affair. George and I manoeuvred around each other like crabs. I didn't mention my date with Rocky later that evening. He didn't mention his plans for the following day. He talked mostly to the boys, about fishing in Lough Neagh, and County Fermanagh. I wondered if he would walk down to the campsite in the morning, as usual. From time to time, I sensed him looking at me, and glanced in his direction, a fraction too late to meet his eyes.

Isabel was tired. She and I talked, in a desultory way, about what we could do on Saturday, before we caught our flight home. Mostly, we watched the teenagers skateboarding in the square, the couples strolling past, the cats sleeping in the last rays of the sun. My spirits were low. I hoped some live music would raise them. It usually did.

At half past eight I said, 'I'd better go, if I'm going to get there and back before I fall asleep.' I hunted in my handbag for the car keys and my mobile. 'I can't find my phone.'

'Take mine, Mum,' Sam said. 'David's got his.'

'Have a good time,' Isabel said. 'Say hello for us.'

George made a fuss of lighting a cigarette. He looked up briefly. 'Enjoy the music,' he said.

All I craved, as I crossed the square to the car, was time and space to think. I tried to shut my senses to the laughter, and the smell of garlic and tomatoes, and the splashing of the fountain; tried to imagine myself on the rocks at Portstewart, under a northern sky, playing my cornet, emptying my brain of everything except the ability to hear the bright notes being carried away on the wind.

The heavy traffic, all the way into Nice, was oddly calming. It made me concentrate. I began to relax. I parked beside the Mustang and stood for a moment outside Doctor Rock before dropping my shoulders, taking a deep breath, and walking in.

It was half full, and dimly lit. The fluty tinkle of a vibraphone mingled with the clink of glasses and the rumble of conversation. The stage was black. Duffy was behind the bar. Rocky was putting a bowl of olives on a table. He was at my side in a second.

'Where are the others?'

'They decided not to come,' I said. 'They're still tired from last night. Me too. I need a coffee to stay awake.'

'Coffee and fresh air?' He signalled to Duffy. 'I thought I wouldn't be on hand tonight,' he said, with a hint of reproach. 'So I've got another barman coming in to help Duffy.'

'Sorry.'

'I came in specially for you.'

'You make me feel guilty,' I said.

'Good.'

He put his hand on the small of my back and guided me into the street. He put his arm round me, and I put my arm round him, and we strolled, through streets and squares thronged with couples, entwined and smiling, like us, occasionally stopping to be entertained by Peruvians playing Andean flutes, or a group of North African dancers turning somersaults.

The Promenade des Anglais was a twinkling traffic jam. Five lanes of cars, white headlights dazzling, red taillights flashing, strung along the bay from end to end, like a diamond and ruby necklace on the throat of the sea. Hotels, casinos, cafés blazed with lights, and made the night sky seem darker by comparison.

'It's been worth it, driving in to see this,' I said.

He laughed. 'That puts me in my place.'

We sat at a café on the beach. It had a just-before-closing air about it. Not many tables were occupied. Rocky bought me an espresso. 'That will keep you awake,' he said.

'I can't stay too long,' I said. 'I want to get back before midnight.'

'Cinderella,' he mocked. 'I'll have to bring your glass slipper to Henley.'

'Are you serious?'

'About you?'

'About coming to Henley,' I said.

'Don't you want me to come?'

'Are you free to come?'

'What do you mean?'

In for a penny, in for a pound, I told myself. 'I wondered if you were still seeing Jacqueline Duchêne.'

He choked on his coffee.

'I'm sorry,' I said. 'I knew you and she . . .' I hesitated, 'used to see each other, ten years ago, when I . . .'

He sat back, thumping himself on the chest.

'I remembered she lived in Chamonix,' I said. 'I thought maybe she was the extra person who had come down for the concert. I thought maybe you were still seeing her.'

He shook his head. He was still trying to get his breath back.

'Are you all right?'

He nodded. His breathing steadied and subsided.

'I saw you with a blonde woman, at a café, near the fancy dress shop. I thought it was Jacqueline.'

'You were jealous,' he said, wiping his eye. He had recovered his tone of slight amusement.

'You had an affair with her,' I said. 'I just wondered if she was still around.'

'You can stop wondering,' he said. There was a pause. 'That's why you were investigating me back then. Because you thought I was having an affair.'

'It was more the insurance policy,' I said bluntly. 'The affair as well.'

I thought for a moment he was going to deny it. Then he shrugged, lit a cigarette, and sat back. 'That's history,' he said. 'You have history too.'

'We had to investigate,' I said.

'You had no evidence.'

'You had a red car. Witnesses saw a red car at Murlough Bay. You smoked. There were cigarette butts at the scene.'

'They could have been anybody's,' he said.

'Four cigarette butts. French. Two with lipstick. Two without. I still think somebody was on the cliffs with your wife,' I said.

'But you couldn't tell who it was?'

'Only that they smoked Gauloises. Not that common in Northern Ireland.'

'Would you like a cognac?' he said suddenly.

'Just another coffee, please,' I said.

He signalled to the waiter. 'What about DNA?'

'It was only just beginning. We couldn't get DNA from tiny samples, the way they can now.'

Smoke curled from his mouth and nose. 'So we'll never know what happened.' His tone was sombre.

'Never give up hope,' I said. 'Science has moved on. It might be possible to get DNA from the cigarette butts now.'

Rocky started. 'Are you sure?'

'Yes. Providing they've been kept properly. There's a new unit that examines old cases. But there are hundreds of unsolved murders in the queue. I'm sorry. I don't mean your wife wasn't important.'

He sighed. 'I know that.'

The waiter brought the coffee and cognac. Rocky bent his head over the goblet and inhaled.

'You could ask for the case to be reopened,' I said.

'What's the point?' He took a slug of cognac.

'Don't you want to find out who was on the cliffs with her?'

'Not much chance of that now.' He set the glass back down on the table. 'Your colleagues didn't seem interested,' he said. 'It was hardly surprising.'

'What do you mean?'

'Dolores was having an affair with a policeman,' he said.

Chapter 37

It was my turn to choke on my coffee. I stood up. My heart was racing and I couldn't breathe. Rocky threw away his cigarette and thumped me on the back. He put his arm round me until I got my breath back. I sat down again and stared up at him, unable to speak.

'I assumed you knew,' he said.

My mouth was dry. I managed to say, 'How do you know he was a policeman?'

'Dolores told me. She enjoyed telling me about her affairs. Of course, she wouldn't tell me his name.' He snapped open his lighter and put another cigarette in his mouth.

'Whom did you tell in the police?' I asked, thinking it couldn't have been Robbie, or Dick Jordan.

'Sergeant Plod and a big man with a beaky nose. When I made my statement.'

I remembered sitting at Robbie's desk, reading the statement. Had I read it all? Surely Robbie would have mentioned something so startling. My heart began pounding again.

'You don't believe me,' Rocky said. 'You think the RUC was

whiter than white. I only had to read the newspapers to know that wasn't true. Cover-ups. Inquiries.'

I remembered how, during my first few months in CID, George would occasionally say, 'Watch out. He's one of the funny handshake and rolled up trouser leg brigade.' Or, 'I don't like the company that boy keeps when he's off duty.' In this way, he had quietly marked my card about fellow officers. 'There are bad apples in every barrel,' he told me, 'but this is a fine police force. Just keep a straight bat. You'll find out most of us do the same.'

I would have sworn that Robbie kept a straight bat. That Dick Jordan played by the rules. I would have staked my life on their integrity.

'I told Sergeant Plod and Inspector Beak that Dolores was having an affair with a policeman,' Rocky said. 'They only wanted to know about my movements on the day she died.'

A sour taste spread in my mouth. I wanted to cry and beat my fists against a wall. I felt betrayed.

The waiter began banging chairs and tables about, making it clear he wanted to close up. He cleared the cups and glass from the table, and made a remark in French to Rocky.

'He says you look as if you needed the cognac,' Rocky said. 'You're as white as a sheet.'

'My head is spinning without cognac,' I said.

Rocky grasped my arm. 'Look,' he said. 'I don't care about all this any more. I don't want to do anything about it. As far as I'm concerned, Dolores is dead. Nothing will bring her back.'

'Don't you care about justice?'

'Leave it,' he said, in a harsh tone. 'I want no raking over the past.' He took my hand, held it to his cheek and said in a gentler tone, 'I want to think about the future.' He turned my hand over and kissed the palm. 'Come on.' He led me back to the promenade.

The lights that had seemed so bright and sparkling now seemed brash and gaudy to me. The chatter of the crowds had no music in it. I was dulled by shock. I only half heard Rocky talk again about a new start in Australia, or South Africa, or the south of England. I moved mechanically, all the way back to the bar. The woody wail of a clarinet drifted through the open door, into the street.

'I won't come in,' I said.

'I've shocked you,' he said. 'But you must have known there are bad cops as well as good cops.'

'I didn't expect some of them to be my friends,' I said.

'The world is not all sweetness and light.'

The clarinet solo ended. Duffy and Maxine emerged into the street.

'Hi, there,' Duffy said. 'Maxine dropped in. I was just saying goodnight to her.'

'Goodnight, Maxine,' Rocky said.

Maxine smiled at me and wiggled her fingers. I gave her a tired wave in reply.

'Who's looking after the bar?' Rocky said. He seemed irritated that Duffy had come outside.

'Joe's there,' Duffy said.

I got into the car. 'Have dinner with me tomorrow,' Rocky said. 'I'll telephone you.' He tapped lightly on the roof of the car. 'Cinderella is about to leave in her pumpkin.'

'And wolves still wait for Little Red Riding Hood.'

'I only like the ones with happy endings,' he said. 'Home, Cinderella. And don't spare the mice.'

I was idling at traffic lights, on the Promenade des Anglais, trying to concentrate on getting into the correct lane, when I heard the plinking of a Caribbean steel band. It took me a moment to remember I had Sam's phone with me, and by the time I found somewhere to pull in and take the call, the steel band had stopped. The screen told me the call had been from a French number. I assumed it was a message from the French mobile phone company and deleted it.

A text flashed on to the screen. *Prière téléphoner*. It was the same number. I pressed CALL.

A male voice answered in French.

'Hello,' I said. 'Who is this?'

'I should ask you the same question, madame.' His English was clipped and precise. 'You sent me a text this afternoon. And an interesting photograph of a man.'

'You're Isabel's friend,' I said, with a jump. 'The photograph was a mistake.'

He made an unmistakably French exclamation. 'Who are you, madame?'

'I'm sorry. We didn't mean to send it. My son made a mistake.'

'Please tell me who you are.'

'Who are you?' I shouted. I wondered if I was imagining this conversation.

'I am Inspecteur André Viollaz of the Police Judiciaire,' he said, pronouncing each word carefully. 'Where exactly did you take the photograph? This is most urgent. We have traced the nearest base station. We need an exact address.'

'At a campsite. Les Arcs.'

I could hear him relaying my directions in French. 'Are you there now?'

'No. I'm in a car. I'm stopped at the entrance to Nice airport.'

'What is the make and registration of your car?'

'A white Renault Mégane.' I pulled the key from the ignition and recited the number.

'Where is Isabel?'

'At the campsite. With my son. What is this? What's going on? Are you the detective Isabel met at Orly?' I was shaking now.

'Please listen carefully, madame.' He broke off to speak in French again. 'I need Isabel's mobile number.'

'She doesn't have a mobile.'

'Does your son have a mobile?'

'I'm speaking on it,' I said.

Another flood of French. Too fast for me to make out any words at all.

'Tell me what's happening,' I cried.

'The man in the photograph is a known criminal. A thief.'

Suddenly everything made sense. 'The jewel robberies,' I said. My voice rose in panic. 'The cyclists. They're in a mobile home near us.'

'What?'

'My son. David. Isabel.' I was gabbling. 'They're using bicycles. I had no idea.'

'Please be calm, madame. Under what name are you registered at this camping?'

'Watson,' I said. 'Whisky, Alpha, Tango, Sierra, Oscar, November.'

He laughed. 'Well done.'

'My nephew has a mobile. He's with Isabel.' I gave him David's number.

I heard sirens. A police car stopped beside me, lights flashing. I looked in the mirror. A sleek, black car pulled in behind me.

'The police are here,' I said.

'I will talk to them.'

Two men got out of the black car. One was speaking into the lapel of his denim jacket. His black hair was as glossy as vinyl, and he had a tiny goatee beard. He opened the car door and held out his hand. I put the mobile into it. He passed it to his colleague, and held out his hand again to help me from the car.

His colleague gave me back the phone. I put it to my ear.

'Please do not be alarmed. Everything is under control. A detective will drive you quickly back to the campsite. His name is Victor. His colleague will bring your car. I will speak to you again. At your service, Mme Watson.'

The detective in the denim jacket ushered me into the front passenger seat of the black car. He gave me a brief smile. '*Bonsoir, madame.*'

'*Bonsoir, Victor.*'

He clamped a portable siren to the roof, waited until I had fastened my seat belt, and took off like a rocket. The traffic parted for us like the Red Sea for Moses. We accelerated away from the sprawl of the coast. Victor switched off the siren. He drove expertly, and silently. From time to time he shot me a reassuring glance. We flew through the village, and plunged down the hill towards Les Arcs. At the bottom of the hill, he braked, and stopped. The rainbow arch was just out of sight, round a bend. Victor spoke into his lapel again.

'Bravo!' He gave me a triumphant smile. We took off again and sailed round the bend, into a floodlit, unforgettable scene. Two police cars, roof lights flashing, were blocking the entrance to the campsite. About a dozen gendarmes were flitting around in front of them. In the middle of the gendarmes, centre stage, were Sam and David, in T-shirts and pyjama bottoms, jumping up and down on the spot like fans at a football match. They were flushed with excitement.

Victor pulled up near the police cars. Sam and David saw me, and started running. I fumbled with my seat belt. Sam had the door open before I could get out and he was hugging me, and saying, 'It was fantastic, Mum. You should have been here.'

I said my thanks to Victor and struggled out of the car. There seemed to be more gendarmes guarding a black van, parked at the side of the road.

'They're in there, Mum,' Sam said. 'The police found Amy's necklace in the handlebars.'

Behind the police cars, at reception, a small crowd was gathering to see what was going on. Beside them, a white van was parked, askew, its doors hanging open. Inside I could see stacked cartons of cigarettes.

'They got the white van too!' I said.

'When the police came, the white van men thought it was for them,' Sam said. 'They tried to drive out of the campsite. Then they jumped out and tried to run away but they were caught. They're in the black van as well!'

Isabel was talking animatedly to George. She gave me an ecstatic wave. I waved back. Victor presented me with the keys of the hire car, and pointed to where it was parked.

'Bed, you two,' I said to Sam and David. 'I'm going to bed as well. Let's say goodnight to Isabel and George.'

'You boys were right about the cyclists,' George said. 'Showed us detectives a thing or two. Well done, David. Well done, Sam.'

Isabel gave Sam a hug. 'It's because you sent that photograph,' she said.

The police cars and the black van were revving up. The arc lights were switched off. The audience began to disperse. A tide of weariness engulfed me. I'd had enough drama for ten holidays.

'I spoke to André,' Isabel said. 'He asked me to come to Paris tomorrow to see him.'

'That's wonderful,' I said.

'I said if I was going, I'd call him back. I wanted to talk to you first.'

I pressed LAST CALL and handed her Sam's mobile.

'Don't go,' George said.

We both stared at him. He had a curious expression on his face.

'If the man's serious, he'll come to you,' George said. 'It's a statement of intent.'

Isabel handed me back the mobile.

'I hope you're right,' I said to George.

'Don't you know I'm right?' He made an impatient gesture.

Before I could answer, he walked away, calling over his shoulder at us, 'Goodnight.'

Chapter 38

In all my life, I do not think I ever slept as deeply, or as dreamlessly, as that night. I awoke, in hot daylight, to the sound of Sam's voice saying, 'Mum, Mum!', the comforting smell of freshly made coffee, and the familiar rattle of Sven and Ingrid rearranging the golf clubs in their car. They were always gone before nine o'clock. At least I hadn't slept the morning away, I thought.

My body felt like a sack of wet cement. I heaved myself up on to one elbow. Sam put a mug of coffee into my other hand, and sat on the bed beside me.

'This is the best holiday ever,' he said. His eyes were shining. 'I'll remember it all my life.'

I made myself sit up properly, inhaled, took a mouthful of coffee, and felt my body begin to lighten, and my head begin to clear. I stretched out my hand and ruffled Sam's hair. 'Thank you. This is lovely.'

'I didn't hear any noises last night,' he said. 'No creaking. Did you hear any noises?'

'We must have been hearing the cyclists creeping about. They're gone now.'

'So you'll be all right on your own tonight? We can go back to the tent?'

'We'll be fine, Sam.' I took another slug of coffee. 'What do you want to do today?'

He reddened. 'Annette and Louise. These two girls. They've got bikes. We might go up to the village with them. If that's OK. Only we've got no bikes.'

'When your grandfather was a boy, living in the country,' I said, 'they used to share bicycles when they went to the town. One person would start walking and the other would ride the bicycle for a mile, then leave it in the ditch, and start walking. The person coming behind would get on the bicycle and overtake him, and then he would leave it in the ditch, and so on.'

'If you did that today, your bicycle would be stolen,' Sam said.

I laughed. 'You can hire bicycles if you want. I'm glad you're having a good holiday.'

'Are you having a good time, Mum?'

'I'm having a good time.' I took his hand. 'Will you mind if I'm not here to eat with you tonight? You can eat in the restaurant. Or Isabel might cook for you.'

'Are you going out with someone?'

'Rocky has invited me for dinner.'

'Do you prefer him to George?' He looked down at the floor. 'I can tell they both like you.'

'And I like both of them,' I said.

Sam was still looking at the floor. 'I like Annette,' he said. 'She has a nice smile. I think she likes me. But she likes a Dutch boy too. Richard. He's fourteen. He's bigger than me and he's been lots of places and he drinks beer.' The last two sentences came out in a rush.

'Girls aren't always impressed by things like that,' I said. 'She hasn't asked Richard to cycle to the village with her.'

Sam lifted his head. He looked baffled. 'Mum, what do girls like?'

'Girls mostly like boys who listen to them,' I said, letting go his hand and reaching for my purse. 'They like boys who buy them ice cream as well.'

I could hear him hooting with joy through my open window as he scampered back to the tent.

George telephoned. 'That was some crack last night, eh?'

He sounded like his old self. Not cross with me. If anything, he was bit hesitant. 'Will I come down for breakfast?'

'Of course,' I said. My little cabin suddenly seemed brighter, as though a cloud had drifted away.

Isabel put her head round the door. 'We've a guest coming for breakfast.' She was radiant with excitement. 'André flew down from Paris this morning. He'll be here in half an hour. He's going to take me to lunch. Isn't that amazing?'

'I believe it's called a statement of intent,' I said, smiling.

'He's divorced. I didn't ask. He told me on the phone.' She paused. 'How was last night? With Rocky, I mean?'

I had never seen Isabel look happier.

'I'm seeing him tonight,' I said.

There would be time enough, I thought, to tell Isabel my troubles. Besides, I now felt I could talk everything over with George.

Rocky telephoned. 'I've just heard the news on Radio Monte Carlo. Are you all right?'

'It happened just after I left you,' I said.

'So the thieves have been caught? You have no excuse tonight. You have to have dinner with me at the villa.' I imagined his lips twitching in a smile. 'You can enact the whole thing for me.' There was a definite tease in his voice. 'I'll pretend to be a villain, and you can arrest me.' He laughed. 'I'm going to shop for something delicious in the market and spend all afternoon cooking. I'll pick you up at half past seven.'

When I came out of the shower, Isabel was arranging chocolate croissants in a basket lined with a pale blue paper napkin. She had two pink spots on her cheeks and she was humming. Through the window, I could see a lightly built man with fair hair and a neat moustache, drinking coffee at the breakfast table. He had a broad, intelligent smile. He looked pleased with himself. And something else. Suitable. He looked suitable, I decided.

'He wants to take me to the Negresco,' Isabel said. 'It's got two Michelin stars. We can take the fancy dress back.'

'Is he staying tonight?'

She made a face. 'He has to fly back after lunch.' She brightened. 'But he wants us to meet again soon. Paris or Reading.'

'I'd pick Paris,' I said.

I agreed to take the car into Nice and meet Isabel at Doctor Rock in the afternoon, so André wouldn't have to drive her back to the campsite before going to the airport.

'You caught the thieves,' I said to André when I was introduced. I nodded in the direction of the mobile home at the end of the row, still marked off with white tape and guarded by a gendarme. 'Well done!'

He gave a modest cough. 'My colleagues in Nice made the arrests.'

'You passed the information to them. You recognised the man in the photograph,' Isabel said. 'You put two and two together. You'll probably be promoted.'

He didn't demur. 'You took the photograph, madame,' he said to me. 'You made this possible.' With one sweep of his arm, he managed to take in the entire scene, and Isabel. 'I am enchanted to meet you.'

'I feel I've met you already,' I said.

George arrived, with a clutch of newspapers. 'You made the national press,' he said.

The four of us spent a comfortable hour, going over the events that had led to the arrests now featured in the headlines. *'Arrestation de Cambrioleurs-Cyclistes. Montes-en-l'airs à Camping.'*

George seemed more at ease with me. I longed to confide in him. To talk over what Rocky had said. To tell him I thought either Robbie Dunbar, or Dick Jordan, or both of them, had suppressed information, or altered a statement. To ask him what I should do about it. There was nobody whose advice I trusted more.

'Sam and David have discovered girls,' I told him, when Isabel and André had gone.

'Are you happy or sad about that?'

'Both,' I said. 'Sad to see the beginning of the end of childhood. Happy because girls are a good influence.'

I began clearing the table. George stood up to help me. We carried the cups and plates into the caravan and put them in the sink. The air was soft and muggy, and there was a faint whiff of boys' feet. I ran the tap, and squeezed washing-up liquid into the water.

'I hope this will freshen the air,' I said. 'I made the boys sleep here last night. I was worried about the white van men.'

'Don't wash up, Claire,' George said.

I turned to look at him. He had an anguished expression on his face. I left the dishes in the sink, dried my hands, and sat across the kitchen table from him.

'How can men get it right? You see us as big, clumsy, smelly, occasionally useful things. We cause problems and clutter up your tidy lives.' He sounded tired and unhappy.

'That's not true, George. You solve my problems. I bring them to you, and you solve them. Do you remember, when Joel left me? I came to you, and cried in your arms, and you gave me advice?'

'I wish you were crying in my arms again,' he said.

My heart stopped.

'My heart is full to bursting, Claire. I can't stay silent a moment longer.' He drew a quick breath. 'I love you, Claire. I've loved you for years. I gave up hope when you went to England with Joel. I couldn't believe my luck when you asked me to come here. I came out intending to tell you how I feel. I hoped you could feel the same way about me. Then I saw you were with this . . .' He shook his head and looked away.

I was surprised because I wasn't surprised. Some part of me, some deep part of me, was telling me I knew all this, had always known it.

After a pause, George said, 'With this . . . bastard.' He sighed. 'Actually, that's not true. I just want him to be a complete bastard. I'm eaten up with jealousy.'

Like a merry-go-round that had stopped, my heart started to beat again in slow waltz time.

George's face was suffused with pain. I could hardly bear to look at him. I remembered us sitting across a table from each other, ten years earlier, his urgent voice telling me, 'When the message is important enough, you'll hear it. You'll know what to say.' My heart began dictating words to me. They seemed completely natural and inevitable. I repeated them. 'I like Rocky. But I'm not in love with him. I know that now.'

I felt as light as air.

George said, 'Tell me. Have I got a chance?'

I couldn't speak. My eyes, my face answered for me.

George's face was transfigured. 'Claire, Claire!' He repeated my name like a prayer. Then he threw back his head and laughed. I began to laugh with him.

He banged the table with his hands. 'I've loved you since the day Dick Jordan brought you into the office and you stood up to me. And I . . . God, how I wanted to . . .' He breathed a long, contented sigh. 'Wanted to do sixteen sinful things before teatime.'

'You never said.'

'You never guessed?'

'Why didn't you say something?'

'I tried. You said you were going to England with Joel. I thought you'd patched things up. I haven't been able to look at yellow chrysanthemums since.'

Then we were laughing again, and somehow George was on my side of the table and I was in his arms, and we were crying and laughing at the same time.

'I've been so mixed up all week,' I said. 'Rocky was so charming to me. And I wasn't telling him things I should have told him. And I felt bad about that. Then you came. And I wanted to tell you about him. There never seemed to be a right time. Now he's told me something I have to talk to you about. Before anything else. I have to get this out of the way. Can I tell you, George? I need to tell you.'

'You can tell me anything,' he said, holding me closer, covering my face with kisses. 'Anything at all.'

'Rocky used to work in Coleraine, at the university,' I said. 'He was married. His wife died in a fall at Fair Head. I investigated the case. You might even remember it. At the time, I thought he'd done it. But there was no evidence. And then I met him out here last week. And I liked him, and he liked me.'

I was so anxious to confide in George, I didn't notice that his expression was changing as I spoke. His grip loosened.

'I didn't register his surname,' he said. 'What's his name?'

'Rock. Dr John Rock. He's got a PhD.'

'What was his wife's name?'

'Dolores. She was an actress. Dolores Dargan.'

'Sweet Jesus,' George said.

'What is it?'

'I knew her,' he said. His face was white under its tan. 'Her car was stolen.'

'Mickey Greer,' I said. 'Of course. You put me on to Mickey Greer.'

There was a buzzing in my ears. My heart began to thump erratically. I tore myself from his embrace. The merry-go-round went crashing out of control. Words, fragments of conversation, flew at me. Tomcat. Cigarettes. Red car. Maggie's car.

I thought I was going to faint. 'It was you.' My words came out in a whisper.

I found my breath. I yelled. 'You had an affair with her, didn't you, George?'

I snatched my handbag from the table. Backed away from him.

'It was a long time ago,' George said. His eyes were full of fear.

I tumbled down the steps of the caravan and stumbled to the car. He was behind me, shouting, 'Am I not allowed to do anything wrong?'

I was trembling so much, I couldn't get the key in the lock.

'It's ten years ago,' he bellowed. 'I didn't have a marriage. I'm only human. God forgives sin. Why can't you?'

I finally got the door open, squeezed behind the wheel, and

locked the door. I turned the key in the ignition but the car wouldn't start.

George was crying and banging on the window. He must have been heard all over the campsite. 'Haven't you ever done anything wrong?' he roared. 'Even the Holy Ghost isn't pure enough for you.'

I opened the window and shouted at him. 'What happened? Did she fall? Did you have a fight? Did you get Robbie and Dick to cover up for you?'

He froze. I turned the key again. The engine burst into life. I swerved on to the track and accelerated away. In the mirror, I saw George hammering his fists on the wall of the caravan, like a Lambeg drum. My only thought was to get as far away from him as possible.

Isabel was with André. Besides, she didn't have a mobile. I stopped the car in the village square and telephoned Helen. No reply. Rocky didn't answer his mobile either. His voice, with its familiar, laughing undertone, invited me to leave a message. I didn't. I couldn't speak. I could taste my tears.

After a while – I have no idea how long – George drove past me and parked in front of the hotel. If he saw me, he gave no sign. A short time later, he came out, threw his suitcase into the back seat, and drove off.

I went into the hotel, and asked for him at the reception desk. He had just checked out, I was told. Some emergency. He was flying home early. He had left no messages.

I sent Sam a text on his mobile. *Gng to Nice. Back 6pm. B good.*

Chapter 39

I drove like an automaton. My hands and feet worked as though they belonged to someone else. In my mind, scenes unfolded like a concertina of photographs from a holiday resort. Snap. George telling me about his promotion, and how he needed the money for Judith's ballet school, and the new house. Snap. George, with Maggie's red car. Snap. Boot prints on the path from the cliff top to the shore. Standard RUC issue. Snap. George smoking a cigarette in his kitchen. Snap. Lough na Crannog. 'Willie Campbell says you can fish there.' Robbie's casual summary of Rocky's statement. 'He said his wife had enjoyed romantic friendships too.' Snap. Dick Jordan, tossing the file aside. 'Case closed.' Snap. My trust snapped.

I was sweating and shaking when I pushed open the heavy door of The Salvation Army building. It swung closed behind me, reducing the noise in the street to a low drone. The lobby was cool and quiet. In an office to my right, I heard the high-pitched hum and creak of a printer. The door was open. I knocked lightly, and stepped into the room. A soft-featured man with brown curly hair was collating sheets of paper spread out on a table. The corners of his mouth turned up slightly, giving him a permanently cheerful expression. I saw from the shoulder flash on his short-sleeved white shirt that he was a captain.

'Bonjour, madame.'

I returned his greeting and began a faltering explanation of my visit. He switched to fluent English.

'An English Salvationist? Welcome! I am Serge Dupont. How can I render you assistance?'

He held out his hand in greeting, scrutinising my face at the same time. I had dried my tears, and put on my sunglasses, but he must have seen something in my demeanour, for he said, 'Please sit down. May I offer you a cup of tea?'

The mention of tea made tears spring to my eyes again.

'Would you like to talk, madame?'

'What I'd like to do, if it's possible, is listen to a band practice. It will help me think.'

He showed no surprise. He moved about the office, switching on an electric kettle, taking a cup and saucer from a cupboard, a tea bag from a box, opening a small fridge. 'Lemon? Sugar?'

My hand shook as I sipped the tea. It was weak, sweet and comforting.

'My parents were Salvationists,' I said. 'I played the cornet at Sunday services and concerts.'

'I will conduct our weekly practice later this afternoon,' he said. 'About five o'clock.'

I looked at him over the rim of the cup. 'I don't suppose,' I said, 'you have a cornet I could play?'

'At our practice?' Now he looked bewildered.

'Actually, now.' I took off my sunglasses, and looked him levelly in the eye, in the hope, I suppose, that he would see I was sad, not mad. I saw his expression change from wariness to concern.

'When you have drunk your tea,' he said, 'I will see what I can do.'

He led me to the main hall. It had high windows and was filled with golden sunlight. Banners hung on the walls between the windows. Chairs and music stands were arranged in ranks on the platform. Below the platform was the Mercy Seat, a wide curve of polished, dark wood, marked off by twisted cords of red hemp hanging from brass hooks. I recognised the familiar accoutrements from my childhood and teenage years.

We went up the steps to the platform. I looked at the sheet of music on the nearest stand. The tune looked familiar. It was the Old Hundredth. Number two in the Tune Book, I remembered. I hummed the first few bars.

'It's a French tune,' said Captain Dupont. He lifted a silver cornet from its box and handed it to me. 'I will leave you alone for a time, madame. If you want to talk, I am in the office.'

'All people that on earth do dwell, sing to the Lord with cheerful voice . . .' I was conscious of the irony in the words as my fingers began to press the valves. The notes resounded in the space around me. Gradually, all thought left my head, and my mind became a glorious blank.

I played through the tune three times. When I had finished, I laid the cornet gently in its box. A wave of tiredness swept over me. I sat down. I thought about the words of the hymn I had played. *'His truth at all times firmly stood . . .'* I had a duty to the truth. I had to write to the Chief Constable and tell him what I had found out. I had to write to George and implore him to tell me the truth.

I knew what I had to do. I knew my heart was broken.

I stopped on the way out to shake hands with Captain Dupont. I thanked him for his help.

'Our help is in Jesus,' he said gravely.

The street was quieter when I emerged into the heat of the afternoon. The shops were closed. Most people were at the beach, or enjoying a siesta. I felt hungry. I realised I hadn't eaten anything since breakfast. I sat down at a pavement café and ordered a sandwich and a Coca-Cola.

I saw and heard, not the passers-by, nor the pigeons pecking at crumbs on the pavement, but raucous gulls circling over black rocks where a twisted body lay.

I tried to imagine the scene on the cliffs above. George throwing away a cigarette. Some kind of argument starting up. Dolores backing away, losing her footing, falling. The bread stuck in my throat. It was hard to swallow.

I imagined George plunging down the path. Checking Dolores was dead. His hand on her neck. Running back to the car. Deciding to pretend he wasn't there. Keeping silent because he was afraid of losing his job.

He must have told Dick Jordan, and, at some point, Robbie. That hurt. Robbie had been my friend. We had worked well together. Yet he had not confided in me.

I finished my sandwich and dusted the crumbs from my hand, feeling I was somewhere else watching myself go through a set of mechanical gestures.

I wondered if Isabel had finished her lunch with André. There was no one alive I wanted to speak to more. I didn't want to go to Doctor Rock. I was sorry I had arranged to meet Isabel there, but it was a place we both knew. It would be quiet, I told myself. We would have peace to talk. Rocky wouldn't be there because he was at home, cooking a dinner I wouldn't want to eat. I didn't want to see Rocky. I had to decide whether or not to tell him about George.

I didn't want to think about George.

He was all I could think about.

Chapter 40

Doctor Rock was quiet. Duffy nodded a greeting as I came in. He was chatting to a man on a bar stool at the counter. At a table near the window, a young couple had laid a map on a stripe of sunshine. They were arguing quietly about a route. I ensconced myself in the corner at the other end of the room.

Isabel arrived a few minutes after me. I leaned my head on her shoulder, and tried to keep my voice low, as the whole sorry story spilled out of me. How Rocky had told me Dolores had been having an affair with a policeman. How I now knew that policeman was George.

'He might have had an affair with her. That doesn't mean he was on the cliff with her,' Isabel said.

'He smokes, he was driving a red Toyota that day. He was in the area, I know.'

'Did you ask him?'

'I was afraid to ask him. I was afraid of the answer.'

Isabel held my hands and made soothing noises.

'I accused him,' I said. 'He didn't deny it.'

'I'll get you something to drink,' Isabel said. 'Then I'll drive you back to Les Arcs.'

She went to the bar. The young couple folded their map, and got up to leave. They tried not to stare at me. I supposed I looked wild-eyed and pale.

I heard the bump of two glasses on the table, and a pat on the back made me jump.

'Hello, Claire,' said Sven. 'Can Ingrid and I join you?' They took the two free chairs at the table, and sipped their beers with a satisfied air.

Isabel came back to the table with a cognac and a Coca-Cola. 'Sven! Ingrid! Why aren't you swinging a club?'

'We played this morning,' Ingrid said. 'We had lunch in the Cours Saleya.'

'We had such a jolly time here last night, we thought we would stop for a beer before we went back,' Sven said. 'Are you having a nice day?'

I made some glib reply.

'So. What a drama. Real live robbers.' He chuckled. 'The criminal under our nose. Yes?'

'You look tired, Claire,' Ingrid said. 'Have you been shopping?'

I made a jumble of gestures, and muttered something about not seeing anything I wanted to buy. I sniffed the cognac. The fumes caught in the back of my throat.

'You came here last night?' Isabel said.

'There was a Swedish boy playing the clarinet. Wonderful. We spoke for some time to Duffy.'

'A nice American boy,' Ingrid said. 'We told him we had met his boss. He told us about the great sadness in Rocky's life.' She patted my hand. 'So nice for him to meet someone after so much tragedy.'

I remember thinking, in the depths of my misery, that it was time Duffy and Rocky stopped talking as though Dolores had died last week. I suppose I was angry that I didn't love Rocky. That I had made an unconscious investment in the wrong man, and there would be no return.

'His heart begins to mend at last,' Sven said, with a roguish smile.

'He's had plenty of time,' I said.

Ingrid was visibly shocked. 'How can you say that? A year is no time at all for grief.'

Sven said, 'Nearly two years, Ingrid. But even so.'

I was embarrassed, and aware that I had sounded blasé and ungracious. I rushed to explain myself. 'His wife died ten years ago. I'm certain of that.'

Ingrid looked puzzled. 'I thought Duffy said she died last year. In a fall.'

'Yes,' I said. 'She fell from a cliff.'

Ingrid nodded. 'Yes.'

'In Northern Ireland.'

'I thought Duffy said Chamonix.'

I looked at Isabel. She shrugged. 'There must have been some misunderstanding.'

'I remember my conversation with Duffy,' I said. 'A friend of Rocky's came into the bar. Jacqueline Duchêne. She told him about it. Yes,' I said. 'That's where the confusion comes from. She lives in Chamonix. They both lived in Northern Ireland before that.' I sounded muddled and uncertain to my own ears. My mouth dried up. I wet my lips, and took a sip of cognac. 'I'm sure that's right.'

Sven said lightly, 'Of course.' He drained his glass. 'We should go back now. Ready, Ingrid?'

When they had gone, Duffy came over to collect the empty beer glasses.

'Duffy,' I said. 'You remember you told us about Rocky's wife dying in a fall? When was that exactly?'

'Some time last week,' Duffy said.

I kept my voice under control. 'I mean, when did she die?'

'About a year ago? Maybe year and a half?'

'That can't be right.' A ball of feathers seemed to be stuck in my throat. 'I know she died ten years ago.'

Duffy scratched his head. 'Didn't you tell me you knew her?'

'Only in a manner of speaking.' I was becoming agitated. 'I knew who she was. I know how she died.'

He looked mystified. 'The person I spoke to must have made a mistake,' he said.

'Jacqueline Duchêne,' I persisted. 'You told me you spoke to Jacqueline Duchêne.'

'I spoke to a man,' Duffy said. 'A friend of Rocky's. From Chamonix.'

Isabel set her glass down on the table and stared at him.

'He told me Rocky's wife died in a fall. She was climbing near Chamonix,' Duffy said. 'Rocky was with her.'

My heart began to pound. I grabbed Isabel's hand. 'You definitely mentioned Jacqueline,' I said.

'That was Rocky's wife's name,' Duffy said.

I couldn't move or speak. I tried to swallow the feathers in my throat. The blood roared in my ears. Isabel's face swam around me. I heard her tinny, far-away cry. 'Duffy!' Then a hand was on the back of my neck, forcing my head down. I was panting and shuddering.

'Sunstroke,' I heard Duffy say, as I pushed against his hand, and surfaced, like a drowning person, gasping and gulping for air.

I struggled to my feet. The man at the bar slid off his stool and sidled out of the door, gawping at me as he went. I turned away and leaned my forehead against the wall. The brick felt rough against my skin, but it was cool. My brain was still trying to make sense of everything.

Isabel put her hands on my shoulders and guided me back to my seat. She sat down beside me. Duffy set a glass of water in front of me.

'You OK now?'

'Fine.' I managed a weak smile of thanks.

'What's going on?' Duffy said.

I look back and see the three of us like a freeze-frame. Duffy staring at Isabel and me. Isobel and I staring at each other.

I broke the silence. 'Duffy, you know the man from Chamonix, Rocky's friend, the one you said told you about his wife? Can you remember exactly,' I said with emphasis, 'what he told you?'

Duffy put his palms on the table. After a few moments he said, 'He was a ski instructor. From Chamonix. He said Rocky and his wife had been walking near Mont Blanc. She slipped and fell. Rocky couldn't rescue her. She had no chance. He said it was an accident.' He tapped his forehead with his finger. 'I learned a new French proverb. *À quelque chose, malheur est bon.*'

Isabel translated. 'It's an ill wind that blows nobody any good.'

'Her father had been a big player in the car industry,' Duffy said.

A picture of the powerful black Citroën flashed into my mind.

'She left Rocky a pile of money,' Duffy said. 'He has a nice life, a nice house. He goes skiing, he sails, he gambles in the casino.' He paused. 'So what are you guys saying?'

'Rocky's first wife died in a fall. In Northern Ireland,' I said.

'She also left him a lot of money, in a manner of speaking. Her life was insured for a quarter of a million pounds.'

'No shit,' Duffy said, with awe. 'He always seemed like a regular kind of guy.'

'I suppose it's possible someone else was with Dolores when she fell, and Jacqueline's death was an accident,' I said. 'But it is some coincidence.'

Isabel said, 'To lose one wife may be regarded as a misfortune; to lose both looks like . . .'

'Manslaughter,' I said.

As I said it, two men and a woman came in through the open door and followed the shaft of sunshine to the bar. I saw them looking round, blinking, as their eyes became accustomed to the contrasts of light and shade.

'Be with you in a moment!' Duffy sprinted to the counter.

There was a low exchange of words. I heard Duffy say, 'He's not coming in today.' He glanced over at me.

One of the men swung round. I saw his face in the sunlight. It was Robbie Dunbar.

Chapter 41

Robbie blinked and took a step forward.

'Jeez! This must be my day for seeing things,' he said. 'I thought I saw George McCracken at the airport a while ago. Now I think I'm seeing Claire Watson.' He laughed, and shook his head. He looked happy and well fed. Marriage suited him, I thought.

'It's me all right, Robbie,' I said. 'You're not seeing things. You didn't imagine George, either.'

'On holiday together? That was on the cards ten years ago.' He smacked his palms together, and laughed again.

My heart turned over.

Robbie beckoned to his companions. I recognised an older, more confident James McAllister. Robbie dragged him over to where I sat, stupefied.

'You remember James McAllister? He's in CID now. And this is Mme Anaut, from the Prosecutor's office. She's our contact here. Speaks fluent English. A bit better than my French, eh?'

'Hello. Nice to meet you,' said Mme Anaut, a sharp-featured blonde, about my own age. 'My name is Nathalie.' She shook my hand.

I introduced Isabel, who was too amazed to speak.

'I'm here on business, Claire,' Robbie said. 'You'll never believe whose bar you're drinking in. Do you remember the Dolores Rock case?'

'I do.'

'This bar belongs to her husband. We've come to interview him.' He had the air of a card player about to slide an ace on to the table. 'We have new information.'

'You found out about Jacqueline?' I thought I had trumped him.

He was taken aback for a second. 'No,' he said, triumphantly. 'We have John Rock's DNA on two cigarette butts.'

It took at least three seconds for his words to sink in. Then my heart did a couple of cartwheels and a handstand.

'There might be enough now for a prosecution,' Robbie said.

'Oh, there's enough, all right,' I said. 'What was that quotation, Isabel?'

'To lose one wife may be regarded as a misfortune; to lose both looks like . . .'

'Carelessness,' said Robbie automatically. 'And it's parent. To lose one parent. *The Importance of Being Earnest*. What's that got to do with it?'

'John Rock married again,' I said. 'Remember Jacqueline Duchêne? She died in a fall. She left him money.'

'Holy shit!' said Robbie.

I had never silenced Robbie before. James McAllister and Nathalie Anaut were equally transfixed as Isabel and I recounted the story.

'When he told us about his wife, he never mentioned her name,' Isabel said.

'He was talking about Jacqueline,' I said.

Isabel's voice quickened. 'We assumed it was Dolores.'

Three heads swung between Isabel and me, like spectators at a tennis match.

'When Bernadette arrived—'

'—he realised I didn't know he had married again—'

'—that's why he didn't take you to the concert to meet his friends from Chamonix—'

'—and why he gave Duffy time off, in case he told us about Jacqueline . . .'

Then we all began to ask questions at the same time. When the commotion died down, I said, 'I knew you worked for the cold case unit, Robbie. How did this one get to the top of the queue?'

'A determined woman is hard to stop,' he said. 'Especially if she's your wife.' He beamed at me. 'I'm married to Bernadette Dargan.'

'I think we'd better sit down,' I said.

'Married four years next month.' Robbie lowered his brows. 'No thanks to you, Claire. Do you remember after we interviewed her? I was worried it might be too soon after a death in the family to be asking her out and you said it would be all right, just leave it a few weeks?'

I took a few moments to pin down the memory. 'I thought you were talking about Amy!' I cried. 'I'm sorry, Robbie.'

'Bernadette sent me away with a flea in my ear. I cursed you from here to kingdom come,' he said cheerfully. 'Then I met her again at the recording of a quiz show for Radio Ulster and we started going out.'

Nathalie Anaut, still mesmerised, managed to order five coffees using only hand signals.

'Bernadette didn't know about the first death insurance policy until I told her just before the inquest,' Robbie said. 'From that day on, she and her mother were dying to get the case reopened. But they lost contact with John Rock. Then Amy took the house out here and saw him. Bernadette was all for flying out and getting a glass or something with his DNA.'

'Inadmissible,' I said automatically. 'Couldn't be used as evidence. You wouldn't even be allowed to test it.'

'I told her that,' Robbie said. 'I said the only way we could test his DNA would be if we came by it legitimately. If he sent her a letter and licked the envelope, for example. Then we could test it, for intelligence purposes.' He tapped his nose.

'Still not admissible in court,' I said. 'But enough to get permission to fly out here and interview him again. Ask him to provide a sample of DNA voluntarily.'

'Dead on,' Robbie said.

I was filled with admiration for Bernadette. 'Your wife is a wonderful woman,' I said.

'No flies on Bernadette.' Robbie winked.

'We were lucky the cigarette butts had been stored properly,' James McAllister said.

'Not luck,' Robbie said. 'Kenny McKittrick. He was excited, we all were, when he got the match. Of course, yer man could refuse to give us a buccal sample. But that would make him look bad.'

Duffy brought a tray of five coffees to the table.

I pulled Robbie to one side and said, 'George had an affair with Dolores Rock. Did he tell you that, Robbie?'

Robbie looked embarrassed. 'He told Dick Jordan. That's why he didn't work on the case.'

'Was he ever under suspicion?'

Robbie shook his head. 'Dick Jordan checked his alibi. Watertight.' He grinned. 'He was fishing the Margy near Ballycastle with two barristers and a parish priest.'

'Why didn't you tell me?'

'Dick didn't tell me until just before we took the statement from John Rock.'

'You could have told me afterwards.'

Robbie looked even more embarrassed. 'George asked me not to,' he said.

'Why not?'

'Why do you think?' Robbie said.

I lost count of the emotions that ran through me that afternoon. Shock, grief, despair, hope, relief, excitement. Above all, anger. I was sick with anger. At myself, mostly, for jumping to conclusions. For assuming Jacqueline Duchêne had been the friend from Chamonix. For assuming Rocky had been referring to Dolores, that day at Menton. For being so avid for a man's attention, I hadn't noticed how he had kept me away from his friends from Chamonix, from Duffy, from anyone who knew about Jacqueline. I couldn't bear the thought that I had enjoyed his attentions, had flirted with him, had allowed him to destroy my trust in George.

Isabel kept saying to me, 'You couldn't have known. None of us could have known.'

'Lucky you're not rich, Claire,' Robbie said. 'He might have put you down for wife number three.'

I thought about Rocky's interest in house prices. His talk about starting a new life in Henley.

'Better get on with it,' Robbie was saying. 'We'll have to go to his house.'

A cold rage possessed me. 'Would you like me to show you how to get there?' I said.

Chapter 42

It seemed right that Robbie and I, who had begun the investigation ten years earlier, should be standing on the doorstep when Rocky answered my knock.

At first he seemed puzzled to see that I wasn't alone. He turned Robbie's card over in his hand, then stared at James McAllister and Nathalie Anaut getting out of the car behind us. His bright, inquisitive smile began to fade. His face whitened under the tan.

'Inspector Plod would like another word with you,' I said. He moved to slam the door but I was too fast for him. I pushed against it.

Robbie said, 'John Rock, I have to tell you we are in possession of DNA material found at the scene of your wife's death.'

'You set me up,' Rocky said. He was breathing heavily. 'You stole my DNA.' He thumped the door. 'Fuck you.'

I held fast. 'I didn't set you up. I believed you.'

He stopped blocking the door. 'You've got to believe me still.' Now there was a wheedling note in his voice. 'It was an accident. I swear it. She was fooling about. She fell. I was going to tell somebody. Then I thought I wouldn't get the insurance. Dolores would have wanted me to have it.'

I looked past him, through the house, to where the pool shimmered in the early evening sun and hazy smoke drifted from barbecues on the hillside beyond. I had been taken in by a mirage, I thought.

'Jacqueline,' I said. 'Was her death an accident too?'

Behind me, I heard Nathalie Anaut say, 'Can we come in now, Dr Rock?'

I turned and walked up to the road where Isabel was waiting for me in the car. I didn't look back.

When we got back to the caravan, I found that an envelope, addressed to me, had been pushed under the door. I sat down at the table to read the enclosed letter.

It had been dashed off on a single sheet of hotel writing paper.

Claire. I can't bring myself to write Dear. I am so full of hurt and anger. How could you believe such a thing of me? I can't even write it down. I don't and won't repent of my affair with Dolores. She was funny and sharp and not judgemental. She didn't pretend to love me. I was not in love with her. But we were kind to each other for a time. I would not have hurt a hair on her head. I would not hurt a hair on any woman's head. If you don't know that, then you know nothing. You certainly know nothing about me. I used to think that we could be happy together. Now I know that can never be the case. Maybe you will find what you are looking for in this Rocky character. Nobody has hurt me as much as you. Not even Maggie when I found she couldn't love me the way I wanted. There have been lots of women in my life.

Maybe I hurt some of them because I was always waiting for you. Well, I know not to wait any longer. As the song says, 'you just kind of wasted my precious time'.

George.

Isabel put her arms round me, and I cried on her shoulder like a baby.

'Call him,' she said. 'Text him.'

I shook my head. 'I don't know if he will ever speak to me again.'

I didn't tell Sam and David about John Rock. I said George had to fly back early for an important case. I needed them to enjoy their last morning at Les Arcs. I did the packing. I wanted the time to myself. Isabel moved quietly around me, and gave me cups of tea from time to time.

Just before we left the campsite, Sam and David introduced me to Annette and Louise. They shook my hand, smiled shyly, and stood waving as we drove out under the rainbow arch for the last time.

'We're going to text each other,' Sam said.

'I hope it's in French,' I said.

Robbie telephoned me on Sunday night. 'We're bringing John Rock over for questioning. The French are going to re-examine Jacqueline's death as well,' he said. 'Bernadette is delighted. She sends her regards. She'd like to see you when you're next over.'

'Was that Rocky?' Sam asked, when I had hung up.

'No,' I said. 'We won't be seeing Rocky again.'

'He had a nice car,' Sam said, 'but I preferred George. Are you going to see George again, Mum?'

* * *

When I got into the office on Monday morning, Enid said, 'Nice holiday?

'Eventful,' I said.

'Ready for the fray?' Enid handed me a file. 'Here's the twoc with a twist I told you about. It's a good one. A chap puts an ad in the *Reading Evening Post* saying he wants to sell his car. This man rings up, says he hasn't got a car at the moment, can the vendor bring the car to his address—'

I put my hand up. 'Stop. I think I know the rest, Enid. He takes the car on a test drive? Doesn't come back? People at the address don't know a thing about it?'

'I can see you're not taken in easily,' Enid said.

I took the file from her. 'I don't suppose his name is Mickey Greer, by any chance?'

She was still staring after me in amazement when I carried the file into my office and shut the door.

For the next few weeks, I saw and heard reminders of George everywhere. I would see a man with broad shoulders and blond hair, on the edge of my vision. When I turned my head, I would see someone who didn't look at all like George.

Sam was constantly on the phone, relaying the events of the holiday to his friends. He said 'Mum and George' and 'George said' a lot. He wanted to fish. I spent Saturday afternoons at a trout farm, watching him practise casting.

Isabel flew to Paris to see André, and returned glowing. I was happy for her. She, in turn, fretted about me. She kept urging me to get in touch with George. I didn't have the courage. I took a week to write a letter. I tore it up. I couldn't bear the thought of its coming back marked 'Return to sender'.

At the end of September, Robbie emailed to say they were waiting for the French investigation to finish before going for a trial date. John Rock was on bail. His passport had been impounded. Robbie thought there might be trials in both jurisdictions. *We got through to the semi-finals of Top Team on Wednesday night,* he added.

I sat down with Sam to watch Robbie captain a team from the Police Service of Northern Ireland against a team of income tax inspectors.

'I used to work with Robbie,' I said.

The teams were level when the question master said, 'Fingers on the buzzer for the tiebreaker. It's a picture question.'

I looked at the stringed instrument, like a banjo with a long neck and a high bridge. The pale, gourd-shaped case was painted with green and yellow parrots.

'I know what that is. A lady Robbie and I interviewed had one hanging on her wall. I can't think of the name.'

Piiinnnng. 'A kora,' Robbie said.

I pictured Jacqueline in her pink suit pointing at the sea, sheep glowing in the silver dusk, and a black car purring up the glen, past a brown river in full spate.

Sam said, 'Are you crying, Mum?'

'Just something in my eye,' I said.

Helen invited Sam and me to spend half-term in Coleraine. It was the last weekend in October. Sam went ahead of me. I flew over on the Friday. Helen met me at the airport.

'The girls are staying with friends. The boys have gone fishing,' she said.

'I don't suppose Malcolm gets many days off to fish,' I said. 'Nice that he and David can do it together.'

'He's all pleased David has taken it up. He thinks it'll keep him out of mischief.'

'Where have they gone to fish?'

'The Margy,' Helen said. 'Near Ballycastle.'

She began a bulletin of family news. But my mind was tuned to another channel. I was seeing the dark shape of Fair Head looming beyond the beach in Ballycastle where the river Margy met the sea.

Had he killed her? Had he killed Jacqueline? Was it conceivable that both Dolores and Jacqueline had died accidentally? I would never know for sure.

The light was falling fast. We stopped outside Helen's house. 'David forgot his keys,' she was saying, 'so I'll drop you off, and you can let the boys in. I'll get some more potatoes as well.'

I was out of the car with her house keys in my hand and she was driving away from the kerb by the time it occurred to me that Malcolm should have keys.

I stood, puzzled. A car pulled into the driveway behind me. A door slammed. I heard running footsteps. Sam shouted, 'Mum! We're back.'

I turned and opened my arms for him. I gathered David into my hug as well. I felt the slap of a heavy plastic bag around my knees.

'Mum! We caught a salmon! We caught a salmon.'

I laughed at their delight, and waved in the direction of the car. 'Hi, Malcolm!'

The headlights dazzled me. I didn't see who was behind the wheel. George got out. He walked towards us. For a moment I thought he wanted to be included in my embrace.

He stopped about six feet from me. 'Sam thought you wouldn't be here until later,' he said, in a stilted voice.

Sam was jigging from one foot to the other. David was holding the plastic bag open for my inspection. 'Look! It must be six pound weight!'

'I got an earlier plane,' I said unsteadily.

'How are you, Claire?'

'I'm fine,' I said.

Sam said, 'We nearly caught another one.'

'Why didn't you didn't tell me you were going fishing with George?' My voice was sharp with nerves.

Sam looked uncertain. 'Wasn't that all right, Mum?'

'I thought it was your idea,' George said.

I shook my head. I was flushed with embarrassment.

'I should have known you didn't put him up to it,' George said. His face was grey in the dusk. 'Goodnight, Sam, David.' He turned on his heel and went back to the car. He reversed swiftly on to the road. The tyres spun as he screeched off.

My heart was hammering as I shepherded Sam and David into the house. I grasped Sam's shoulders. 'Did you ask George to take you fishing?'

'Uncle Malcolm couldn't take us. So I phoned George,' Sam said, with the simple solipsism of the young.

'What's wrong, Mum? What did I do wrong?'

'Nothing, Sam,' I said gently. 'Nothing at all. I'm the one who needs to say sorry.'

George was standing in front of his garage door, a bunch of keys in one hand and a bottle of whiskey in the other. He looked startled in the security lights that came on when the taxi swung into his driveway.

I got out. Straw legs again, I thought, holding on to the car door.

'Three pounds, missus,' the taxi driver said.

I hunted for my wallet in my coat pockets, dismay and panic rising.

George reached me in three strides. He pushed a five pound note into the driver's hand. He pulled me into his arms. I buried my face in the waxed jacket that smelled of earth and rain, and all I could say was, 'Sorry. Forgive me. I'm sorry.'

Later, a long time later, as we lay in contented silence, I could swear I heard the sound of trumpets.